Kypros Shacolas was born in Cyprus but grew up in London, where he was educated and worked in the fields of shipping and commodity trading. He is well-travelled and enjoys football, good wine, malt whisky and cigars. He is a vegan and an animal rights activist. He is now retired in Cyprus.

In loving memory of my beloved brother Nicolas. You left us very suddenly and far too early. R.I.P.

Kypros Shacolas

WHITEHALL AFTER DARK

AUSTIN MACAULEY PUBLISHERS™

LONDON • CAMBRIDGE • NEW YORK • SHARJAH

A CIP catalogue record for this title is available from the British Library.

ISBN 9781787106444 (Paperback)
ISBN 9781787106451 (Hardback)
ISBN 9781787106468 (E-Book)
www.austinmacauley.com

First Published (2017)
Austin Macauley Publishers Ltd.
25 Canada Square
Canary Wharf
London
E14 5LQ

Chapter 1

West London, England 1983

The fresh northerly breeze and the graphite-looking sky over West London may have deterred the odd tourist and most of the public at large from dressing lightly on what was still, supposed to be, a summer day's morning. The temperature was surprisingly low for the time of year and people going about their business may have been cursing the Great British Summer, or, the lack of it! However, there was a particular group of people that actually welcome near-winter conditions. The football fans. For them it meant that the long football-free summer was at long last, drawing to an end.

It was the last Saturday in August but the first Saturday of the new football season in England. So it was not surprising that a few raucous, rival football supporters were having their eggs and bacon that morning in the small, but popular, café located under the railway bridge in Shepherd's Bush Market. It was irrelevant where their beloved teams were playing. Home or away, it was more or less tradition that the fans were out and about on match-day mornings. Shepherd's Bush in West London is the home of

Queens Park Rangers Football Club, but the wider West and South West London area covering Hammersmith and Fulham also housed Chelsea and Fulham football clubs. But, unlike other places in London and the rest of the country where football hooliganism was rife, the relationship between supporters of these three neighbouring clubs was not all that hostile. The rivalry had miraculously remained a relatively friendly one, something that was hugely appreciated by the local police on match days. However, there was an extra sparkle amongst the buzzing Rangers supporters, the smallest of the three clubs, at the start of that particular season as their team were playing in the First Division, where as their neighbours were confined to the Second Division. They had every right to be boisterous – and boisterous they were.

Saturday was also a popular shopping day and the surrounding open-air market was brimming with people. This particular café on that particular day was therefore the last place in London one would choose to have a quiet, discrete but serious conversation. The noise level was sometimes deafening, the atmosphere filled with smoke mixed with the usual stench associated with greasy food and over-boiled coffee, while the hustling and bustling of shoppers frequently going in and out, tiring and annoying. In fact, it could prove to be quite disconcerting if not enervating. However, that was precisely the reason why the two men sitting at the far end of the premises chose this particular place for their meeting. It was not the first time they would meet here and it would not be the last. They both appeared to be in their early thirties and were casually dressed. However, a closer inspection by a trained eye might have revealed that they did not really fit in with the rest of the crowd. But a trained eye, specializing in observing people would not be found in such a place. The one puffing on a cigar seemed in good shape and was quite good looking with well-groomed jet-black hair and clean-cut face features and bright blue eyes. He had just finished drinking his coffee. The other was a rather pale and slim person with small, prying, grey-blue eyes. He was busy negotiating a cup of tea and a scone. In a plastic ashtray in the middle of their table a cigarette had almost burnt itself to the tip. The pale man stubbed it out and promptly lit another. His fifth in less than thirty minutes.

'These will be the death of me,' he joked before he coughed a little. He was mild mannered and softly spoken.

'This is the advantage of a good Havana cigar, old boy,' said his companion. 'You don't have to inhale them.'

'What is the point of smoking then?' asked the cigarette smoking man.

'We've had this conversation before and we have agreed to disagree.'

'That is a nice way of putting it Bob. Well, are we done here? I am running out of cigarettes.'

'I say we have another cup, if you don't mind, shall we? It may be a while before we meet again.'

'Fine. Another tea then.' The cigarette smoking man looked around him and then added, 'A few more minutes here will not kill us. The place tends to grow on you…'

'Tell me about it,' said Bob. He raised his hand and after some effort, managed to summon a chubby, gum-chewing, middle-aged waitress and ordered tea and coffee. He puffed on his Cuban cigar and then he looked at the man sitting across him.

'Gavin, there are a few things that still bother me. Things I am not comfortable with.'

'It goes with the job. It would bother me if you were comfortable, with all that's been happening and is about to happen,' said Gavin.

'I do not question the information you have just given me and I am not referring to IOPS and MI6. I guess Sir Colin has his own problems to solve.'

'What is it then? F-Branch? The Economic League?'

'No, no,' said Bob with a shake of his head. He removed his gold-rimmed glasses, rubbed his eyes and leaned towards his companion. 'Teasing and testing the enemy's defence response systems has been on going long before you and I walked the planet. But using a civilian airliner with unsuspecting passengers? Jeez!'

'It wouldn't be the first time. It was done a few years ago, as you know, with catastrophic results.'

'Yes, yes I am aware of all that.'

'Why are you surprised then? The Americans have been constantly misinforming their own people as well as exposing their troops to deadly radiation at the advent of humanity's atomic age, weren't they? All in the name of science, progress and national security.'

'But this is different,' said Bob. 'Does the administration know? Does the *President* know?'

'Do our own Prime Ministers know what we are doing most of the time?' asked Gavin. 'They only find out if something goes seriously wrong and by that time what can they do? Accuse their own security forces and intelligence agencies that they acted without authority? If that were the case, we'd have a change of government every other month. Why are you so concerned about all this anyway? It has nothing to do with us. It is an American thing.'

'Oh, I suppose that the MoD will not have one of its satellites looking that way when this happens then?'

'If the opportunity is there, the Ministry of Defence will take it. Why should we miss it?' Gavin managed a smile.

'It is the timing I am worried about. Not knowing *when* this may happen. It would also help if we knew which airline company might be used.'

'It will not be American and it will not be British, that's for sure,' said Gavin.

'Pat, our Irish friend in Saudi is meeting the Crown Prince's emissary and confidant next week. It could jeopardize the deal.'

'Bob, I cannot understand why you are nervous about this. It is not like you. Not like you at all. Spuds is a good field operator and negotiator. He will do his thing for you and George Webb will look after the Prince and his confidant.'

'Do you trust Webb?' asked Bob.

'Do you trust anyone in our business?'

'Being so young I mean. 'We are not exactly geriatrics ourselves, are we? Though, I suppose that for every year in our line of business we age five. Experience, maturity comes with age. Just like a good wine.' Bob puffed his cigar, enhancing the fog effect that was besieging the café's interior.

'I don't know anything about wines. I am tea total, as you know. But, like you, I do know that young George is the arms dealing director of T & S Group but more importantly, he is also an MI5 recruit with the Ministry of Defence. That's why he's where he is and doing what he does, *for* the MoD. As for the timing, as I said before, the best I can do is that this may be attempted over the next few days. We may get to hear about it but then again we may not. It may cause havoc or it may pass unnoticed.'

'Too many maybes, ifs and buts. Nonetheless, they couldn't have picked a more sensitive location, or a worse time-frame for that matter. The Soviets will have a field day with their political rhetoric and propaganda,' said a thoughtful Bob.

Gavin extinguished his cigarette before he spoke, with meaning. 'Not, if world opinion is overwhelmingly against them.'

'What do you mean?' Bob was startled. He raised his left eyebrow as he always did when he wanted to emphasize something. 'You are not saying... God! Are the Americans hoping that the Soviets *shoot* the passenger plane down? I sense... I see shades of seventy-eight here and Kola Peninsula.'

'Well, this time, it could turn into a nice advantage for the free world, wouldn't it? But no such luck I'm afraid! On the other hand, no one in the western world blinked an eyelid or lost any sleep when the Israelis shot the Libyan airliner down over Sinai in seventy-three. But that was a Libyan plane. It is not so easy to predict aftermath reactions.' Gavin fiddled nervously with his empty cigarette packet before he spoke again. 'Look, I guess the worst thing that can happen is that the Russians will attempt to force the plane to land, only if they are fast enough.'

'How long will the plane be violating Soviet air space?'

'I don't have that information and I don't know for sure whether it will actually enter USSR air space or have a close border encounter. Either way I assume it will only be long enough to get a response. Long enough for their defence systems to light up and document what follows.'

'Light up. Just like a Christmas tree! But this, if it goes wrong, it could spark off a *real* international crisis. It would make the Cuban missile crisis look like...' Bob stopped talking as the waitress approached their table and served them their beverages.

'Anything else my darlings?' she asked. 'If not, please pay me as I am taking my break now. I need a ciggy and an aspirin with all this noise in 'ere.' She handed them a hand-written receipt and Bob gave her some money and asked her to keep the change.

'Could you spare a ciggy for me please love? I've run out.' Gavin managed a half-smile at the waitress.

'Sure, why not?' she said as she offered him one. 'I hope you don't mind menthol.'

'Oh, don't worry,' said Bob. 'He'll smoke anything... anything *inhalable* that is!' The waitress smiled and left.

'Talking of Cuba,' said Gavin as he paused to light up the cigarette, grimacing with disapproval as he tasted the menthol flavour, 'be aware that an assassination attempt on Fidel will take place next month, again. Alert our DGI friends in Havana. God knows what will happen to the status quo if one of any of these attempts succeeds.' Gavin passed a piece of paper to Bob. 'I was going to verify the exact date and make the usual drop regarding this, but since we are here...'

Bob put his glasses back on and had a quick look at the note, before he destroyed it. It read: *Raphael Ramirez – source: US Defense Secretary.*

'I'll ask Arantxa to alert Pepe in Havana,' he said.

At that point a rowdy football fan trying to make his way towards the toilet door recklessly bumped into Gavin causing him to spill his tea and drop his cigarette on his lap. The fan did not apologize, in fact he laughed as Gavin, anxiously, tried to remove the burning cigarette from his trousers. Bob was on his feet in a flash and grabbed the young man by the collar of his blue football shirt.

'The least you can do is apologize and offer to buy this gentleman another tea,' he said. Bob was over six feet tall and looked twice the size of the young fan who, nonetheless, turned around and looked Bob squarely in the eyes with an abundance of insolence and audacity that seemed to defy the logic of the moment.

'Fuck off! Let me go, you pervert,' the fan screamed as he tried to free himself. Bob thought that this defiance could only have stemmed from an excessive use of chemical substances. He tightened his grip on him, with both hands.

'Let him go,' said Gavin. 'It is not worth it. We are drawing attention.'

Bob realizing that heads were turning round and the other six or seven football fans in the café were, by now, having his full attention, released the young man who took a step back and eyed the two men.

'What the fuck are ya? Some kind of a queer couple? In love with each other are we?'

Gavin was becoming exasperated and mumbled something to himself. He shook his head disapprovingly, as the fan headed for the gents. He then got up, nodded to Bob and without saying another word walked out of the café into the busy open-air market. The light rain carried by a fresh breeze hit his face as he glanced at the overcast sky. He seemed to welcome it and stood there for a second or two. He felt cleansed. He then turned right and rapidly headed for Goldhawk Road train station.

A few moments later Bob also walked out of the café but turned left, indifferently walking towards Shepherd's Bush train station at the other end of the market. The drizzle was gradually turning to a downpour and within a couple of minutes people were scurrying for cover, while others were hastily opening their umbrellas. He seemed oblivious to what was happening around him and kept walking at a casual pace, as if in a trance, looking neither left nor right. However, he was deep in thought. His thoughts not focused on the incident with the young football fan but on an incident yet to happen, probably somewhere in the far-eastern skies over an area dotted with Soviet military bases. An area that was also extremely rich in unexploited crude oil and natural gas deposits.

Chapter 2

The Kingdom of Saudi Arabia. A land where the treasured values of yesterday are sometimes sacrificed for the realities and necessities of today, the expectations of tomorrow. A land where imported technology, imported influence and ideas are gradually changing a way of life. A land where local culture is coming to terms with the ways and means of another. A land that managed to remain largely untouched by the madness and turmoil that was cursing most of the Middle East. So far.

Jeddah. The Kingdom's main city and port on the Red Sea coastline. A city of the old, a city of the new. A city of business, a city of contrast. A city that had become the main gateway for millions of faceless pilgrims flocking to *Makkah.* The faithful from near and afar arrive at the King Abdul Aziz Airport to be herded through the new, purpose-built, one hundred acre *hajj* terminal on the final leg of their arduous but holy trek to the holy city, patiently preparing, putting on *ihram* garments, waiting to mutter, to whisper, to recite the pilgrim's prayer, the *Talbiyah*; to shout out aloud those treasured and fulfilling words: *Here I am, Oh Allah, Here I am.....!* The hajj period is a trying and hectic one, stretching human endurance to the limits. It is also an ideal time for those wishing to slip into the country unnoticed.

To go on hajj is to meet God. Having drunk the water of the *Zamzam*, which effectively ends the hajj, the *hajjis*, fortified with new vigor from a sense of inner satisfaction are preparing to embark upon the somewhat less strenuous return journey to their homes, their lifelong ambition duly completed. They can now look forward to the *Eid ul-Adha*, the sacrifice celebrations. But not all make it back or want to make it back. Despite increased efforts by the authorities there are those who unfortunately perish, overcome by a combination of heatstroke, exhaustion and malnutrition. There are others who tend to lose themselves, seeking a better life within the Kingdom. Seeking opportunities perhaps denied to them back in their homeland. Some have no homeland, a legacy of the senseless wars that have been tearing the Middle East apart. Finally there are those whose real mission is yet to be accomplished.

Like a golden eagle, the sun had started its imposing descent over the Red Sea, spreading its wings of fire and setting alight what little cloud was scattered across the horizon to the west, before the tranquil waters in the distance, slowly but gracefully, began to engulf the majestic oval fireball. The sea, gently swaying like a copper-coloured veil, occasionally reflected flashes of red as the silent waves caressed the coral reef, momentarily justifying the name given to that long and narrow body of water that separates two continents.

The sunset in all its glory was indeed peacefully beautiful. The few romantic observers who invariably gather on the Al Corniche every afternoon were not disappointed. They saw what they had come to see. A picture of serenity. A serenity that belied the violence that was about to be unleashed on the city. A city that boasted little or no crime at all. A city where the only apparent disturbance or excitement had been the odd lashing for petty theft or for drunkenness, the latter not unusually associated with European expatriates who, though gratefully reaping the financial rewards their host country has to offer, they nonetheless occasionally defy the local law.

There was a curious breeze threading its way through the streets of Jeddah. A breeze that would have normally been welcome during the hot summer months and thankfully received by the pilgrims in the sweltering conditions endured over the holy period. But his was no Zephyr. It was blowing in from the wrong direction, not from the sea to the west but from the east, from the desert. It had all the ominous signs of a developing sandstorm. It was not long before it raised its ugly head, blowing stronger, blurring and clouding the atmosphere, slowly eclipsing the last remaining orange brushstrokes that painted the sky to the west, as the now howling wind carried with it that fine but non-marketable commodity that is so much in abundance on the Arabian Peninsula.

The evening prayer calls normally blazing out of loudspeakers high up on the minarets were subdued, muffled and dissipated by the force of the angry winds. There was evil in the air. The Aeolian bags reaped open, the ferocious and merciless winds unleashed, driven by rapacity for destruction and doom. This was no ordinary sandstorm. Death was lurking.

Isolated and exposed to the elements on the outskirts of the city to the north, the residential compound, where the T&S Construction Company housed its expatriate staff and their families, was taking a savage battering by the sandy gusts. The ever-humid air hovering over the city was transforming the hot dust into tiny droplets of mud, causing it to adhere to all kind of surfaces and limiting visibility out of the large windows of the luxurious villas in the compound. Outdoor chairs and canopies were sent flying, the swirling gusts turning the water murky in the large swimming pool, while the few sunbeds that were blown in it resembled governless ships caught in a hurricane on the high seas.

Inside one of the villas, a frail looking man in his early-fifties with a bushy beard that complimented his ginger hair was talking, with some excitement, on the phone.

'You can hardly see out of the window. I am telling you lass, in all the years I've been here, I've never seen anything like it. You just would not recognize the place; everything's covered in sand. What? Yes, me included. By the time I got indoors I was ten pounds heavier! I spent thirty minutes in the shower getting cleaned up.' He paused for a while, listening, smiling and nodding his head in acknowledgement, his Irish accent stronger than ever. 'I know lass. I stayed much, much longer than I anticipated. Another three days, four at the most and I'm out of here. Kiss Siobhan for me and tell her dad will definitely be there for her eleventh next week. Wouldn't miss her birthday for the world. That's a promise. Tell her how much I miss her, how much I love her. She's everything to me. You tell her that.' He paused. 'Yes, yes will do, the moment I have the flight details. I'll have to stay overnight in London. Office work. Love you too, bye for now. Me too. Say hello to Dublin for me. Bye now.'

He hung up. The phone rang almost immediately.

'Brennan.'

'*Salam alekum.* How are you Paddy?' The voice was familiar.

'*Wa alekum es salam.* Khalid? Is that you?' The Irishman sounded pleased.

'Hello Pat. What on earth have you done to annoy the Almighty? This is quite a sandstorm, even for the Bedouin.'

'Yes it's a bad one. Almost as bad as the day I've been having.'

Patrick Brennan, a senior consultant and Board Member of the multinational T&S International Enterprises Group, the London-based parent company of T&S Construction, tried to peer through the dusty window. 'I've never seen anything like it. I was just telling Fiona the same thing.'

'Fiona's in town?' The caller sounded surprised. He was a Saudi Sheikh and trusted *confidant* to the Saudi Royal Family. He also acted as the main liaison between the Royals and the powerful group.

'I wish! No, no she's back home and can't wait to see me back too. Khalid where are you? I tried to call you earlier on, several times in fact. Your office in Riyadh kept telling me that you were out. Just *out.*'

The Sheikh laughed down the phone. 'I *am* out,' he said. 'I'm in Jeddah. How else would I know about the sandstorm?'

'Jeddah? Oh good. Where?'

'I am staying at the Red Sea Palace, downtown near the old Souq. I left early in the morning by car and stopped in Taif for a while to see my parents. I then drove here, just missed the storm by a whisker.'

'You drove here?' The Irishman was stunned, for he knew Khalid hated the driving across the desert. Besides, he had a helicopter at his disposal.

'Yes. Isn't that cute? Scaling new heights you might say. Why were you calling me by the way?' Khalid's accent was quite enviable, a legacy of his early upbringing in England where he had the opportunity to completely master the English language during his academic years at a London private school and later at the London School of Economics. His father, now retired, was a long-serving Saudi ambassador to London.

Brennan composed himself and picked his words carefully. 'We have a problem with the time schedule and with some of the insulating materials we propose to use. Still top-notch mind you but there's gonna be a significant variation from the specs in the contract.'

'Go on.'

'Also, well,' Brennan hesitated for a moment. 'Actually, I wanted you to sound out the Palace if we can make some major changes without too much fuss over contract stipulations and deadlines.'

'Changes? Regarding…'

'Regarding the materials, granite, instead of marble for example. Our Italian exporters have let us down on the marble supplies and our contacts in Greece tell us that they cannot export the quantities we want, not before March next year. We are talking, six, seven months; far too long.'

'George Webb phoned me last night from some obscure corner of the dark continent, no doubt. The line was pretty bad.'

'George?' Brennan tried his best to sound surprised. 'I didn't know that young George was all that interested in *minor* details such as specs on building materials and the like.'

'Well he did call about the other deal but he also seemed to be well informed on the subject of the building materials. I am therefore aware of the problem and, believe me, it is a problem. The Prince is fixed on marble. Let me see what I can do.' George Webb was a young London based Director with T&S responsible for the Group's operations in the Middle East and West Africa. Despite his youth he somehow succeeded in becoming the Group's arms dealer, with the full approval and support of Her Majesty's Government. A go-between.

'Oh, good. That's a load off my mind. How soon before you let me know?'

Khalid ignored the Irishman's question.

'However,' he said, 'that was not the only reason George phoned me. The other reason has to do with a chap who goes by the name of Robert Ross, Bob to his friends.'

'Ross you said? Who is he?' Brennan sunk himself in a large sofa, composing his thoughts at the same time.

'Good question,' said the Sheikh. 'He will be coming here, with George and the rest of the delegation next week to discuss the military purchase with the Crown Prince and his advisers. Apparently he will be advising a Mr Gavin Addice, a high-ranking officer at the DIS section of the MoD. Addice in turn will be advising the Minister of Defence whether to proceed with the sale or not.'

'DIS?'

'Defence Intelligence Staff.' The Sheikh was generous with his explanations. 'It is an important division within the Ministry of Defence. Anyway, George seems to think that the presence of this Ross fellow here is by direct Downing Street intervention.'

'The PM?'

'According to George, yes. Now, we neither know what he is nor why he has been assigned to overlook and coordinate the deal. What we do know is that he'll be calling the shots.'

'What is the problem, exactly, and why are you telling me all this?' Brennan sounded genuinely puzzled, as he had never handled any of the Group's sensitive arms deals. As a senior civil engineer his consultancy services were limited to civil construction, the building of roads, bridges, airports, ports, hotels, palaces and the like.

'Well my friend, you scratch my back and I'll scratch yours. You are closer to your Chairman than any other board member within T&S. We want this particular deal to go through the U.K. and not through the Americans. The King has his reasons. However, George seems to think that this Ross character may torpedo the deal purely on financial grounds.'

'How can you know this?'

'Privileged information.'

'Fair enough. I'm listening,' said Pat.

'I would like you to use your influence with your Chairman regarding the funding possibilities of the deal. We need the Group's support on this one for *soft* financing.'

'If I read you correctly, you want T&S to *guarantee* payment?'

'We understand each other my friend,' said the Sheikh. 'That is what I meant when I said, you scratch my back and I'll scratch yours. T&S will gain points in the Middle East, of this I can assure you. Also your building problems with the Prince will vanish. I'll see to that. Of course we shall extend the usual *comfort* by awarding T&S the pending port developments. You, Pat, can look forward to a very comfy retirement.'

'Khalid… please, what, what are you saying, no, no thanks… *la shukran.*'

The Sheikh quickly intervened to save Brennan's blushes.

'If need be we can also throw in a major development project for the Dammam region scheduled for 1985. All will be above board, in black and white. But enough said over the phone. I'll send a hotel car to pick you up. Best you don't drive in these conditions.

'OK. I'll be ready in thirty minutes.'

'We can talk while we dine. They serve your favourite drink here.'

'Luck of the Irish! It is going to be a nice day after all. *Shukran Gidann ya Shaikh*.'

A few thankful words in Arabic spoken with a heavy Irish accent. It must have been anything but music to Khalid's ears.

Brennan smiled as he replaced the phone receiver. He then picked up his Peterson pipe, stuffed it with Captain Black tobacco and put a match to it. After a few puffs he sat in an armchair and rested his feet on a small table. His favourite drink, he thought. What he wouldn't give now for a Jameson or a pint of Caffreys. Saudi was a dry country. A *Laurence of Arabia* would have to do, the kiwi-based fruit cocktail the Sheikh was referring to. He then concentrated his thoughts on more serious matters.

The Saudis have been more money conscious than quality conscious in recent times. They had their own reasons for wanting to swiftly close the arms purchase deal. In fact they were so desperate they would offer the stars and the moon in return. Granting development projects and oil exploration rights to the seller was the norm of the day. That was the way business was done. British firms, some of which actually belonged to the MoD were only too happy to oblige. Selling British Military technology and armoury to the Saudis was really big, huge business for British exports. Brennan also knew that a large part of the sale was to find its way to other Arab countries in the region, Iraq in particular, at a very nice profit for the Saudis. Included in the order, as part of the deal there was something else too. Something that would be neither documented on any export licence nor on any invoice but, all the same, would be handsomely paid for. A relatively small quantity of plutonium. A minute quantity but enough, nonetheless, to raise a few eyebrows here and there. Patrick Brennan knew, but so did MI6. All part of the game. However what the MI6 did not know was that small parts of such arms shipments would regularly find their way to Ireland and the IRA via other Arab countries. He glanced at the time. Seven-forty. By now it was dark outside. Dark and dusty.

Forty minutes later Brennan's phone rang again. It was the compound's entrance guard asking for permission to let the hotel limousine into the grounds. He gave it, thinking that security precautions were a wee bit over the top. However, he was leading by example, abiding by the rules.

A short while later his front door bell was ringing. He quickly placed some papers in a plastic folder, picked up his pipe and tobacco and opened the front door. The warm dusty air was not the only thing that hit his face. Milliseconds after he caught a glimpse of a man in a uniform standing on his doorstep, his world exploded into a thousand pieces. A painful white-hot flash homed in on his retinas quickly followed by an abyss of darkness as he slumped to the floor. His small, grey eyes wide open but motionless were separated by a single bloodstained bullet-hole, not much larger than the size of a pea. Brennan, *Spuds* to his friends back in London, was dead.

The killer checked the Irishman for pulse and then quickly bundled the body inside the boot of the hotel limo that was parked a few feet away. He closed the front door of the villa and hurried back to the car. He removed the silencer from the hand pistol he used and placed both pieces under the seat. He drove slowly to the gate with the headlights on. The guard squinted at the bright light but

25

soon recognized the hotel limo and lifted the barrier. The killer was free but his mission only completed in part.

***

Hong Kong 1983

The intrusive, high-pitched ringing of the telephone set sounded louder, much louder and more persistent than usual, thus feeding the subconscious of the half-asleep listener with impressions of a rude and impatient caller. Perhaps this is how it always sounds in the middle of the night, thought the obese man as he attempted, with some discomfort, to turn on his side shaking the large double bed with each shift of his body. He tossed the red satin covers away as his hand felt for the cordless phone on his bedside table, his eyes trying to adjust to the darkness of the room. The rude ear-piercing ringing was not doing his migraine any favors. The handset finally disappeared in a grotesque, swollen paw of a hand.

'Hello?' His voice was hard and angry ensuring that his displeasure of being disturbed in what must have been an ungodly hour was unmistakably registered on the caller. The ringing however persisted, the call not answered. The obese man swore at himself and then at the caller before focusing his attention on the telephone handset, abusing it, as he frantically punched several buttons until he hit the right one and the call was through.

'Hello. Hello? Who the hell is it?' He screamed the words out with an almost perfect London Cockney accent.

'Hello Moby.' There was nothing but silence for a moment or two, only the static of a long distance call coming through. 'Are you there Moby? It is time to cancel the rabbit.' The caller sounded distant and cold. The words spoken without passion, almost mechanically. He said nothing further, knowing that the man at the other end would need a few moments to digest what he had just heard.

'My God, man! Do you know what time it is?' He did not have a clue what the time actually was but there was a softening in his voice, a trace of uncertainty and a rapid sense of realization. With his free hand he felt around for the light switch by his bed, squinting as the bright light filled the room. Any notion he may have had of going back to sleep soon deserted him, his migraine now seemingly unimportant. Only one person in the whole world called him *Moby,* a sick reference to the legendary mammal, Moby Dick and his own, hugely, overweighed body. 'It is time you said? Time? How... when?' He seemed to stutter as if the words spoken from afar were suddenly meaningful. He froze.

'Yes, it is time and I do know what time it is. It is time to earn your keep.'

'When?' asked the obese man, as he tried to sit himself upright on the bed.

'It has to be done Friday, latest.'

'Look here now Cabus, there, there is simply not enough time. This is, this is not good enough. Not enough time. Why didn't you give me more time, it will...'

'Make the time. You've had the rabbit under surveillance for almost a month now. We have intelligence reports that he may be heading for the Middle East. We expect a change of leadership in Jerusalem soon and your pigeon may want to stretch his wings. Shift that large body of yours and go to work. Besides, I am sure that when you read the morning papers you'll also appreciate the urgency of the matter.' The caller sounded impatient and somewhat irritated.

'But…' the obese man was quickly cut short again.

'It is ten-seventeen in the evening of Wednesday, August the 31st where I am standing and it is five-seventeen tomorrow morning Thursday the 1st of September where you, no doubt, are flat on your back on your expensive jumbo-size water-bed. You have less than thirty hours. Chow, it's *your* pigeon. You don't want it to fly the nest now do you? After all, this is what you have been waiting for.'

'I was promised at least four days' notice. Have you any idea how much planning will have to go into this? Can you really…' Chow was trying his best to make his case but was again abruptly interrupted.

'Well, think of Queen and Country and that sort of thing old chap.'

What an irritating bastard he thought. He quickly returned fire. 'Yes, I'd like to know *what* Queen and *what* country, if any, you ever think of. You are a snake Cabus.'

Cabus laughed. 'Come on Moby, a snake? A *snake?* You are calling *me* a snake?

Chow was literally lost for words. Cabus fired another volley of words. 'What you may not know is that I love Chinese food and all the frills that go with it – fortune cookies included, but, I also have access to your file and your file clearly states that you arrived in this hellish world in the Chinese year of the snake! This is the year of the pig. Now, what is it you want it to be?' Suddenly his voice became steely and icy again. 'Noon Friday, latest. And no loose ends.'

The abrupt clicking sound that ended the call sent a chill up Charlie Chow's spine. He was motionless, dumbfounded for a few moments. He tossed away the cordless handset with the unlisted number and managed to push himself upright, forcing his swollen feet into a pair of flat slippers that instantly disappeared into the soft floor carpet under his massive weight. He then engulfed his elephantine body in a black silk kimono, which looked as if it had enough material to turn out a few parachutes. He went to his living room.

Waterbed? I don't have a waterbed he thought. He glanced at his gold Rolex as he walked to the next room. Twenty-three minutes past five. That Belgian bastard! Or was he French? A pig that could not afford a decent watch. He met Cabus twice, three years ago in London, soon after he was recruited to serve within a clandestine section of Her Majesty's Secret Services. However, it soon became apparent that Cabus was to be his main contact, his only contact in fact. His first impression was that he was a slimy little thing and first impressions are seldom wrong. He remembered the remark the slime made during that meeting. 'Moby Dick' he called him. He did have a passion for good food. Anorexic he was definitely not. Cabus on the other hand looked the part. Too thin, too feminine looking for his own good, a man that could not enjoy life. Too tense. A messenger, a mouthpiece. A nothing. There are many ways of shutting up mouthpieces. He mused at the thought as he drew open the window blinds. The view was, as always, breathtaking. Especially at night. He marveled the lit skyline of Hong Kong for a moment or two. The placid waters near both banks of Victoria Harbour reflected the nightlights through veils of early morning mist, enhancing the effect in such a way that a first time visitor looking at it could easily be fooled that the city was lit up for Christmas – presents at the ready. Christmas it was not, it was the beginning of September in 1983 but somebody was about to get a present, guaranteed to stop his ageing process.

'God help us. God help *me*,' said Chow aloud to himself. He sighed deeply. Tiny drops of sweat were beginning to form on his pale forehead. Did he have second thoughts? Had he lost his nerve?

Any last minute doubts as to what he was about to do were dispersed at the flick of a light switch. The room was flooded with soft lights of different color shades and intensities revealing the luxurious interior of Charlie Chow's living room. A number of priceless vases seemed to glow in the reflected light while other works of art and curios together with designer furniture gave the room class and taste – a very expensive taste. A single beam of soft light was centered at the Goya that dominated one of the walls. The cruelty of the war scene depicted in the painting seemed out of place in the serene surroundings. Charlie approached his prized picture wondering whether the painter, or indeed any of Goya's contemporaries, ever really appreciated the economic necessity of war. Simple economics really. Supply and demand!

Looking around him somehow made him feel better, much better. His masters had been good to him, they *are* good to him and they pay him well for his services. He did not care much about his contact, a pitiful subordinate no doubt. But there is one person in particular that does appreciate his services and his loyalty. Especially his loyalty. A waterfront penthouse in the fashionable area of Tsim-Sha-Tsui, the Kowloon side of the colony, does not come cheap. But even this is small change to what was to come, what was promised to him, after he played his part in the events that were to guarantee Hong Kong its independence from Red China. Or so he was led to believe.

Charlie Chow was born on November 14th 1953 in London's East End original Chinatown of immigrant Hong Kong, Chinese parents. It was a few months after the

Queen's Coronation and as November 14th was also Prince Charles's birthday, his parents decided to name him after the Prince of Cornwall and heir to the throne, thus showing their allegiance to the country that adopted them. Twenty-five years later he graduated from the LSE with an Economics Degree. He soon managed to join the British Civil Service as a translator attached to the Foreign Office and two years after that he accepted a post with the British Embassy in Beijing, where he grabbed the opportunity to perfect his Northern Mandarin dialect. There, he was befriended by an embassy liaison officer who finally recruited him for an SIS sub-section. After eleven months in Red China he was moved back to London where he was prepared for his current post in Hong Kong – a cushy and innocuous job with the British-controlled Administration. But that was just a front job.

He made himself a cup of instant coffee, adding plenty of sugar and cream. He took a sip and paused to think for a moment. What did the pig mean by his reference to the morning papers? He turned the television set on. Nothing. He changed channels. Nothing. He tried the radio. Music. He tuned to several local stations. Nothing, nothing of importance. He then patiently scanned the short waves. An English-speaking station was reporting on an international incident involving an airliner. An air crash? A hijacking? He fine-tuned his expensive receiver to cut out static and interference. There it was: '...*civilian aircraft... however, we stress that these last reports suggesting that the airliner was shot down are not, we repeat, are not as yet confirmed.*

Information is still sketchy, but according to earlier reports quoting American and Korean sources, it is believed that the Korean Airlines flight KAL 007, a Boeing 747 with 269 passengers and crew, flying from New York to Seoul via Anchorage and which apparently disappeared *from radar screens at around 1830 GMT – that was about 3 hours ago, on Wednesday 31st August, has been forced to land on Sakhalin Island by Soviet military jets, after the airliner allegedly violated what they described as sensitive Soviet airspace. What is definitely confirmed is that U.S. Congressman and President of the John Birch Society, Lawrence McDonald, boarded the flight to Seoul in order to attend the 30th anniversary of the official entry of the United States in the Korean War. It is believed that efforts are being made through diplomatic channels to free the passengers and crew. That is all we have for now. We shall keep you up to date with developments as we get them.*

Now, we move on to other news coming in from the Middle East. The Red Sea Port City of Jeddah in Saudi Arabia has endured a night of terror and extreme violence with twelve people dead and at least fifty injured in a spate of car-bomb explosions. No organization has, up to this point, claimed responsibility. In what is believed to be a separate incident in Jeddah, a close aide to the King was found dead in his hotel suite. Sheikh Khalid Bin Ibrahim Al-Assaf was shot in the head at close range...'

Charlie Chow switched the radio off. His expression became steely, his eyes wide open. He swallowed the rest of his coffee, wiped his forehead and picked up a phone. He dialed a number in Hong Kong Island.

After a while a man replied. Chow spoke to him in Cantonese. It was a very short call. He looked out of the window. The horizon to the east began to glow. A new day, a new month, a new assignment. He headed for the shower.

Forty-five minutes and two cups of coffee later, he was in a taxi heading for Aberdeen Harbour, on the southern side of Hong Kong Island. He was holding a small plastic shopping bag, not unlike the thousands of bags held by ordinary people on every ordinary day. But, inside this particular bag was a thick manila envelope with thirty thousand American dollars in various denominations.

Chapter 3

'You think Charlie's up to it?' asked the slim, bald headed man after he put the phone down.

'He's doing fine and he has never let us down, so far. Where would you find a Chinaman who is more British than you or I will ever be?' The man responding to the question was dressed in a dark blue pin-stripe suit. He looked relaxed, his groomed jet-black hair, clean-cut face features and bright blue eyes belying his age. He looked no more than thirty at the most when he was, in fact, a good few years older. Leaning back in a comfortable chair, with his feet resting on a large desk he puffed on a *Cohiba Coronas Especiales* cigar with obvious pleasure.

'I am not questioning his loyalty to Britain, or to his pocket for that matter. Permit me to have some doubts regarding his loyalty to this department. I also find his methods distasteful. He seems to enjoy it and making money out of it. He epitomizes gluttony.'

'He is a good friend nonetheless and deserves more credit than we ever give him,' replied the man in the suit. 'There's no turning back now. We are beyond the point of no return on this one.' He paused for a moment, signs of concern replacing his relaxed expression. 'Contact the *ferret* in the Aegean, tonight, and tell him to expect paperwork in the next few days. We may not have enough time. We must act before the Yanks get the order, again. They use the Israelis, we'll use someone else. Time to give British exports and our manufacturing industry a helping hand, my lad.'

'But, on this one, shouldn't we inform *her* first? Get the all clear? Greek-Turkish relations have been somewhat stretched these last few months. We wouldn't want to start a conflict.'

'Best to leave the Prime Minister out of it. As for conflict, wouldn't be that bad!' The man in the suit had a chuckle before he acquired a more serious expression. 'Military conflicts, full-scale wars are always good for business as long as they take place on someone else's backyard. That is how empires and superpowers are built. Why do you think the Yanks, ourselves to a lesser extent, finance and sustain fascist dictatorships around the globe? To fight Communism? Thank God for the Reds. Where would we be without them? We'd have to invent some other foe. No. We quietly support certain regimes, countries rich in natural resources so we can reap the benefits when conditions are ripe and introduce our own meaning of democracy to such countries. Long-term investment you might say.'

'Pseudo-colonies.'

'Whatever! Do contact the ferret. We shall be monitoring the situation.'

'All well and good but where and how would I find the ferret tonight? We can only contact Chris Leonardou on specific times, as you very well know. Besides, it is past midnight in Greece.' The thirty-three year old man with the shaved head, wearing a blue and white tracksuit, seemed anxious as he strolled around the half-lit room, somewhere in a basement in London's Whitehall. 'Shall we wait till morning anyway? Rethink this one?'

The other man shook his head in disagreement. 'We must set things in motion. There is too much happening, all at once. Try. If no luck, contact *Gitanes*. He never sleeps, he'll *ferret* him out. In fact channel the whole thing through our friend. As for *her*, well, I am sure she has other things on her mind right now. She will be pretty well occupied over the next few days. Same goes for her boyfriend across the water.' He smiled. 'Her landslide victory a couple of months ago, well, that makes her untouchable, wouldn't you say? And with high unemployment and what have you, what?'

'Yes, high unemployment but with the opposition in tatters, non-existent and oh yes, long live the Falklands!' The bald man grinned, having made what he thought was a winning point.

His superior ignored the last remark. 'No, it is best that we leave her out of this one. She is many things, but a convincing liar she is not. What she does not know she cannot lie about. Besides, that is why people like us exist. Ask *Gladys* at DIS to clear expenses and back-up operations with the MoD.'

'What about Sir Colin's vultures?' asked the slim man.

'What about them?'

'They've got people in DIS. That's how they keep taps on the Ministry of Defence and MI5 for that matter.'

'That is why I specifically suggested Gladys.'

The slim man, known to Charlie Chow by the name of Cabus, was clearly not at ease. He looked at his boss and said. 'Gladys I trust one hundred percent, but that is as far as it goes.'

'Trust no one, one hundred percent, not even yourself,' said the boss waving his index finger at Cabus.

'MI6, as you know, have stool pigeons everywhere. How long would it be before they add things up? They feed on scraps of information. They check on ops overseas expense accounts and then muscle in on everybody and anybody who they think they might know something.'

'Thank God for democracy! OK. Leave MoD out of it, even though this is done for their benefit. Use our own kitty in Luxembourg and scrap the back-up.' The boss put his feet on the ground and sat up straight. 'I am surprised that after, what, eight, nine, years at the *Hub* you still get the jitters over the spooks. We *are* the God damned SIS and all the sections, sub-sections and branches you care to name. We are like a spirit level, keeping things straight, on an even keel. We are here to ensure that Government works, unhindered from inside interventions and subterfuge. In fact we are the Government, the *Permanent* Government, the last line of defence against corruption and immorality. People come and go—Directors, Police Chiefs, Ministers, Prime Ministers. We stay. What we do is sacred. Fuck!' He loosened his tie. 'Rant over,' he whispered.

Cabus looked at his boss and said calmly. 'No jitters Bob, just concern, being careful. Remember the disinformation used against part of our team last January by IOPS and the reporters they've sent to quiz the Home Secretary regarding our existence and our role in Her Majesty's Secret Services? Specific questions having been asked in Parliament? You know who was behind that little exercise.'

The boss suddenly seemed to take notice, silently signaling his acknowledgment as Cabus carried on. 'That was a close call and we could have been exposed. And of course there was Cooper, just ten days before the 79 elections. Remember how IOPS fingered Cooper by publishing fake nude images of his wife in porn magazines apparently embroiled in lesbian acts with a Soviet agent?

The tabloids had a field day and we lost a first class operative.'

'And the Labour Party lost the elections. Poor old Cooper,' said the boss. 'Information Operations Planning System. There is no hard evidence that this ghost department of MI6 actually planted the story on Cooper's wife. But then again you could say there is no hard evidence that we do what we do. We need to get one of our own inside IOPS. I'll have a word with Gladys on this one. We did meet the other day at our usual cafe but…' He was calmer now. He puffed on his cigar. 'Poor old Cooper,' he whispered. 'You are right. Of course you are right. It is not Sir Colin and the MI6 I am concerned about. The weak link here is MI5, the connection between Curzon Street and the *Economic League*. Drinking vodka at your local boozer is sufficient evidence for them to blacklist you as a communist sympathizer, a subversive element. That is what I am worried about. Categorizing British citizens. Good and bad. We are slowly being *Americanized!* The League has too much influence, financial and otherwise, especially on F-Branch. In fact they own it.'

'Well, that's how *our way of life* is protected. So much for democracy. The poor people cast their votes thinking that it would make a difference, that it does make a difference. Little do they know that it is almost totally irrelevant.' Cabus allowed himself a smile.

'Absolutely. But as you said, that is democracy, *our* way of life and all that jazz,' agreed the boss. 'Politicians do make the decisions but based on intelligence provided by you know who. Cooked intelligence most of the time. However do not forget how *this* operation came about. It was a single politician, alone, who had the vision and the sense, to set us up. Later on the Royals also endorsed the idea, for their own good reasons sure enough, but that was later. Good old HW. KGB my arse. Balderdash!'

'Wilson? KGB?' Cabus was startled.

'Oh yes. As you know, twenty years ago in 1963, Harold Wilson became the left candidate for the Labour Party leadership. He defeated George Brown and was to lead the party in the 1964 General Elections. Remember, this was at the height of the cold war, the Cuban missile crisis still fresh in the memory along with the assassination of JFK and conspiracy theories that the KGB was involved.'

'Yes, but Wilson and KGB? Where's the link?' Cabus fixed his eyes on his boss.

'I am surprised you've missed all this. The notorious Fabian Cabus falling short on his history lessons?'

'I was a young teenager at the time with innocent visions of a big happy free world and free *grass* for all students who had a Beatles haircut! But please, go on,' urged Cabus.

'Helsinki-Finland 1961. A presumed top Soviet agent, KGB, his name escapes me right now, defected to the West, to the Americans.'

'Presumed?'

'Presumed in as much as American Intelligence thought he was a top dog. Golitsyn! That was his name, Anatoliy, err something or other, Golitsyn. Well, amongst the many astonishing claims he had made later on was that Wilson, the elected PM of this country was, in fact, a KGB agent and that he used the Unions as fledging recruitment grounds.'

'Did he provide any evidence?' asked Cabus, waving his hand trying to disperse the dense cigar smoke that was slowly ghosting towards him.

'Poppycock. Most of the Western intelligence services, even in America, believed that Anatoliy was not genuine, that he had been sent to the West to misinform, providing some chicken-feed and even that was cooked. But, you will simply love this. The, then, Deputy Director of counter intelligence at the CIA and other top intelligence officers took Anatoliy at face value. When Wilson was elected in October 1964, by a small majority mind you, which forced him to another General Election seventeen-eighteen months later, where he triumphed, all hell broke loose. Fueled by information coming from the CIA, our own counter intelligence, kept taps on Harold and a handful of agents tried to undermine him, in more ways than one. We, in the firm, know that was the period when F-Branch evolved, developed and thrived. It somehow had to be checked.'

'And we came to be, the Hub was born.' Cabus was shaking his head in acknowledgement.

'We came to be and also sustained by subsequent leaders to ensure that the British Premier, is never compromised or undermined by his own intelligence community, irrespective of the party in power. Smart move really,' said the boss. 'However, going back to HW, a handful of MI5 parasites, controlled drones, kept at it. When Wilson was re-elected in 1974, they tried in various ways to destabilize his government, by encouraging the Ulster general strike for example. But this is no news to you. You had joined by then.'

He closed his eyes and drew a long drag from the half-chewed cigar, clearly relishing the moment. He allowed the dense smoke to circulate in his mouth for a couple of seconds before letting it escape. He looked at the ceiling of the room, adding philosophical value to his words.

'I say, thank God for communism and its revolutionaries. Without the reds we wouldn't exist.

Without Guevara we wouldn't have these little beauties. Thank you Che,' he whispered as he marveled the distinctive chequered black and white part of the label on his cigar. 'You know, it has only been a year or so since Fidel started to market these masterpieces internationally. Even so, it is difficult to find them in Europe unless you fly to Madrid every other week. Limited production you see. That is why we have the best of both worlds. Good cigars and a good, fulfilling job! Our people in the right places. Arantxa in *Euskal Herria*, Pepe in the *Vuelta Abajo*, Charlie in Hong Kong, Gladys, Claude, Spuds, Christos…'

He looked at the cigar he was holding, with respect and affection. Memories were flooding his thoughts. He smiled. 'It's not the money you know Ian. It's the job, being in control, pulling the strings in the right direction. Balancing the equation. Balance! Remember that. Trying your damn best to keep the people who want to control the world on a leash! A very short leash I might add. That is what it's all about.'

'The devil in disguise playing God…'

His superior was not amused.

'If you *believed* in God, you wouldn't be in this game.'

'Yes, that's all it is. A game. A deadly game.' He paused, awaiting a response from his boss. A response that was never made. Ian Coburn, alias Fabian Cabus went to a small refrigerator in a corner of the room and took out a bottle of Belgian beer. 'Want one?'

'I'd rather have half a glass of Chablis if there's any left, thanks Ian,' said the boss. 'And Ian, start drinking wine and eat some meat, a good steak. You look pale my friend.'

Cabus deliberately ignored the last remark. He served him a full glass of the French white wine, sat in a large leather armchair and raised his beer bottle. 'To Cooper and all the good people,' he said.

The boss picked up the wine glass and saluted his companion before he took a sip. 'To Cooper, to Jenny and her toddler, God rest their souls.' He looked at the glass in his hand, quickly changing the subject. 'The best thing to come out of Frogland, what? The wine I mean. Did you know that Chablis is not so well known within France as it is out of France? Outside the Serein valley and its nineteen, twenty odd villages, not many people know about this little treasure. Not yet, anyway.' He laughed and then turned his attention to his prized Havana cigar. 'Well, perhaps Bardot too,' he added.

'*Sureté*. Don't forget that if it wasn't for Surete and Claude in particular you'd be in hell now.'

'Oh, I don't know. Maybe the Elysian Fields. Strange really, I sometimes feel much more comfortable with them than with our own lot, or the cowboys across the water for that matter.'

'I'll drink to that,' said Cabus.

The boss yawned and then looked at his watch. 'It really *has* been a long day and tomorrow will be an even longer one,' he said. 'I'll have to prepare for the Mid-East trip. What happened in Jeddah is definitely a setback but not a disaster. By the way, have you been able to contact our man yet?'

'In all honesty I am beginning to worry. Not all of the bodies have been identified in Jeddah. I am almost certain Mossad are behind the assassination of the King's envoy, but there is no way they could have known about our man.'

'Spuds has always walked on a tightrope,' said the boss. 'Don't worry about Brennan, he's a seasoned operator. He's a survivor and he knows the Arabian Peninsula better than his knows the pubs back in Ireland. I only hope proceedings will be swift over there, I don't want to miss Doncaster.'

'Doncaster?'

'The St Leger.'

'The what?' Cabus was still puzzled.

'It's a famous horse race *Fabian*, up in Doncaster. I have a date with a Princess on that day, the *Sun Princess* as a matter of fact.' Cabus was not following the conversation so his boss talked business again. 'I'll find out from Gladys tomorrow what they are really thinking over at the MoD regarding the deal, post-Khalid. I shall then have a chat with Maggie, the Lady herself and I'll take it from there.'

'The deal itself is really of no concern to us. One way or another it will go through. The dates are,' said Cabus.

The boss smiled. 'The Gods are on the side of the good people. Who would have thought it? *Yom Kippur* and *Eid Ul Adha,* major Jewish and Arab holidays just one day apart this year. 17th and 18th September. Saturday and Sunday. Perfect time for diplomacy and black ops, what?'

'And two nuclear tests showing the world that the two superpowers are alive and kicking and still at each other's throat. Thank you Ron! We couldn't have planned it better ourselves!' Cabus picked up a Financial Times pocket diary with a bordeaux-colour leather cover that was resting on a small table next to him. The initials *I.C.* were printed in gold at the bottom right corner of the front cover. He leafed through the pages. 'In fact the Americans are testing tomorrow in Nevada. September 1st, 1983.'

'Of course they are. Late August, early September has always been and always will be a good period for the Americans to make political statements through a show of strength and black operations. That is how and when their unpopular policies are approved. They justify their course of action over the next year. Straight after the hols you see.

Catch people off guard, or so they think.' The boss took another sip from his drink. 'But I'll bet you on one thing. Unlike summer last year there will not be a million people plus in Central Park tomorrow protesting against Reagan's nuclear policy. Not after what happened over Sakhalin and the Korean airliner. It is a win-win situation for the Yanks.'

'This time around there may be people in Central Park tomorrow *supporting* Reagan's policies.' Cabus was being sarcastic. 'The manipulation of the masses in all its glory! One fabricated event leading to another. A controlled event yielding the desired result.'

'What's the story on the Soviets? When are they testing?'

'The Soviets will surely reply soon, time wise, oh, I'd say pending on how good, or not so good, the Sakhalin incident is going for them. Nasty business that...'

The boss frowned. 'Yes, nasty is the word. Still, I'd like to think that if our *cousins* across the pond, if they ever thought-even for a minute that the airliner would be shot down....' He shook his head from side to side.

'The feedback from our contact was spot on. It is not as if we didn't know and if we knew we have to assume that our government also knew. Or worse, could they have participated?' Cabus posed the question but it was more of a statement than a question.

'Careful now. When we say *government* we must mean the Prime Minister. Well I don't think she knew and neither did the US President. Intelligence divisions? Yes. They sanctioned it. But who was in the know from our side and what have we gained from it, if anything? That is what I intend to find out.'

'Also why it happened and why now,' added Cabus. 'It looks as if the Russians were waiting for it. Tipped off in fact!'

'I don't know if the Soviets knew but it *had* to happen. The Cold War was thawing out. Business was bad! However, we could have stopped it with a word or two at the right time and the right place. Our job is to protect our government, the PM. But then again I can't see how we could have averted it. I suppose the shuttle plus half-a-dozen spy-birds were in place up in space and waiting. Sometimes I...'

The boss did not finish the sentence but did finish his drink, took another puff and tossed what remained of the cigar in a large black ashtray that was resting on his mahogany desk. 'Harold once said that a week is a long time in politics. A day in our business is a fucking eternity.'

'Don't I know it,' added Cabus.

'Oh, I almost forgot. Let Pepe and Domingo know about Raphael Ramirez flying to Havana from Madrid in the next few days.'

'What do you mean? Tell them *what* he is?' Cabus was startled.

'Yes, tell them he is CIA and that he will try to organize yet another assassination attempt on Fidel. He should be thwarted but not arrested and definitely not killed. Send the message to Pinar del Rio via Bilbao and give Arantxa my love, would you?'

'If our lot ever found out that we are actually collaborating with Cuba's DGI they will burn us at the stake in front of a cheering crowd in the middle of Trafalgar Square!'

The boss raised his left eyebrow as he always did when he wanted to emphasize something. 'We are not working *for* DGI or *with* DGI. You should know that Ian. We are working with Pepe and Domingo, full stop. We scratch their back they scratch ours. Besides, don't forget where the information on Ramirez and every Ramirez came from. And why!'

'From the Office of the U.S. Defense Secretary,' whispered Cabus shaking his head with amazement. 'All in the name of profit. Keep up the pretenses, prolong the conflict and therefore the arms race. Boost the industry. I feel like vomiting sometimes.'

'Name of the game my boy. I love the smell of napalm early in the morning. Brilliant!' He paused for a moment, thinking. 'At least we are not as bad as the Yanks. Even I find their little ploy with the RC 135 and their gambit with the civilian airliner hard to stomach. They actually sacrificed civilian passengers. What can I say? Money makes the world go round.'

'I suppose it is comforting to know they exist, don't you agree?' Cabus looked at his boss and his puzzled expression and promptly expanded on his thoughts. 'The Americans I mean. Knowing, at least, that we are not at the top of the scum pile.'

'Or the bottom of it for that matter. Well, we have not nuked anybody yet and I don't think we ever will. The Americans on the other hand, well, if they really have to, they will bomb themselves and blame someone else in order to achieve their objective.'

The boss stood up, tightened his tie, adjusted his gold-rim glasses, picked up his trademark godfather style fedora hat and headed for the door. 'I'm calling it a day. Lock-up when you are done and go home. I'll contact you tomorrow and do get your girls some nice *English* chocolate, lots of it, from Uncle Bob. Kiss them for me, would you?' He paused at the half-opened door and smiled. 'Don't break a heel now. And Fabian, you were never here. You don't exist my friend. Make the calls and *Bob's yer uncle*.'

Robert Ross, better known as *The Rolls* in the trade, winked at Cabus and left.

'No, I am not here,' whispered Cabus as the door was shut behind his master. 'In fact I'm neither here nor there. Invisible. That is what I am, a bloody invisible idiot!' He looked at the closed door and yelled. 'God Save the Queen to you too!'

He drunk the rest of his beer and sunk himself in the large leather armchair, thinking for a few minutes. He looked around the strange, unfriendly, underground room near the Cenotaph in Whitehall. A room that has become his home away from home. Two desks, one much larger than the other, two revolving desk-chairs, two large armchairs, a small table with a lampshade, a larger table with four telephone sets, one attached to the latest group three facsimile machine. Then there was a photocopier, two telex machines, a coffee machine and a small refrigerator. There were three doors. One was the steel-reinforced entrance to the room, the other was a toilet and bathroom and another leading to an adjoining room. His gaze stopped on a painting of the Princess of Wales, the only item decorating any of the walls. He looked at Diana smiling at him, a beaming smile and then looked into her blue eyes. He smiled as his mind raced to his toddlers, his girls; his six-year old twin daughters back home in Antwerp. Chocolate, he thought. He did not approve of giving young kids lots of chocolate, especially *English* chocolate when his own, adopted, country had the reputation of producing some of the best chocolate in the world. Ah, he was just saying that to annoy him he thought. Yet he did respect his boss, admired him in fact, no doubt about that.

For the next twenty minutes he made some notes. He then took a file out of a feminine-looking briefcase and browsed through some pages. Five minutes later he used the telex machine. He sent a coded message to Bilbao, Spain, in the Basque Country. His message would soon be forwarded to Jose 'Pepe' Guerrero in the heart of the Cuban tobacco producing area, the Vuelta Abajo and Pinar Del Rio. Once the telex had gone he picked up the same, secure, phone he was using earlier to call Charlie Chow and dialed a long number. No connection. He tried several times, cursing under his breath. The number was now ringing and kept ringing till it was disconnected. He redialed. Ringing again. Damn! No reply. He then tried another long number. He was luckier this time. A woman answered the call.

'*Parakalo? Parakalo?*' She was barely audible, her young voice drowned with the sounds of bouzouki music and people apparently having a good time.

'*Kalispera, ton psara parakalo.*' Cabus had a good working knowledge of the Greek language, but his accent was a complete giveaway. He had asked to speak to the fisherman. The young woman said nothing more. Cabus waited patiently, the phone pressed to his ear, listening to excited voices mingled with Greek music and the occasional smashing of plates. Almost a minute later a man's hoarse voice came through the other end.

'*Nai? Empros*?'

'I want to speak to the fisherman please.'

'Only if you know what the catch was today,' said the heavily accented hoarse voice.

'A handful of red mullet and one lobster,' replied Cabus, almost mechanically, having obviously been through this charade numerous times before. However, he did appreciate the need for the fisherman's protection.

'Hey Cabus my friend, how are you?' asked the fisherman.

'I am good. What's all the noise about?'

The fisherman, also affectionately known to his friends as *Gitanes*, raised his voice. 'Oh, it's nothing really. End of the holiday season may be. End of the month, I don't know. People get paid so they are out and about having a good time. One moment, I turn the music down. ***Efi, hamilose ligo tin mousiki*.**' He screamed the words out and a few seconds later the loud music subsided.

'Was that *Efi*, your daughter who answered the phone?'

'Yes,' said the fisherman proudly. 'That is my Ifighenia. She has, how you say, flowered, bloomed, into a good-looking young princess. She will be eight in two months and looking more like her mother God bless her.'

'My, my, eight already. Kiss her for me will you?

'With pleasure. How are your twin girls?'

'Pure gold. They are coming along fine.' Cabus quickly changed the subject. 'How's the business?'

'You know running the taverna in the fishing village of *Kotsinas* during the summer months is more of a hobby. It is very close to the island's air base so I keep up with the gossip. You know I don't complain. Thanks to you, I invested well. The two cargo ships are working, again thanks to you. You are a good friend Cabus. A decent person.'

'You are welcome and I do appreciate your assistance in various matters.'

'I think my family, well what's left of it, Efi that is, well, I would like to think she's safe for life, secured.' He swallowed hard, the hoarse voice breaking. 'I am almost forty and believe me she, yes, she is the *only* reason in the world that I... that... I...'

Cabus cut in quickly. 'I know, I know my friend.'

The fisherman snapped out of the emotion that was filling the air. 'OK. What is it Cabus? I'm surprised you are still up this time. Us Greeks we start to drink, after

49

midnight, till morning. Not beer, but the real stuff. *Ouzo, tsipouro, retsina.* You should visit sometime so I can show you *mouhlas* how to drink, dance and enjoy life. Live a little. Work, work and no play, not good my friend' After the barrage of excited words a moment's silence. 'Well? Cat eat your tongue? I am here.'

'*Mouhlas?*'

'Yes, how you say? Fungus. Wet in the head. Too much rain and not enough sun.' The fisherman laughed aloud.

'I seem to recall that you did not mind the rain so much and as to the beer, well, you must have raised the De Koninck Brewery share a few points once you started swallowing dozens of *bollekes* in the *brown pubs* every night!'

'Yes those were the days. Rain in Antwerpen, a bolleke and mussels!' The fisherman sighed. 'Well, what is it? You didn't call to give a lecture on my drinking or to remind me of my youth.'

Cabus composed himself and looked at his notes. 'We currently have a *friend* on your back yard on Limnos Island that is dug in deep. Uniformed. Wings in fact. I couldn't locate him directly and it is probably unwise to do so. There will be a live courier arriving for you with the early morning Olympic flight from Athens on Sunday the 4th. He will come at your taverna asking for a room and a boat to rent. He will be carrying an envelope with the instructions. Have you got that?'

'Understood.' The fisherman paused for a moment and then lowered his voice. 'Cabus, please, do me a favor. Make it a large envelope and throw in it a couple of cartons of Gitanes. It is difficult to find French smokes on the island of Limnos.'

'Will do. Oh, and another thing. Do not believe everything you may read in the papers tomorrow.'

'I never read the papers. You know that.'

'Well, you may do this time.' Cabus said goodbye before the fisherman could respond and replaced the receiver. He allowed himself a smile as fond memories of his pub drinking days with the fisherman in Antwerp came rushing back to him. The rattling noise of an incoming telex message interrupted his thoughts. Arantxa Abasolo, talented Basque woman from Bilbao was confirming that the message had been passed on to Cuba.

Cabus picked up his papers, placed them in his briefcase and headed for the adjoining room – a bedroom without any windows. He stripped naked and sat in front of the dressing table with a large mirror. He turned the mirror lights on. His boss was right. He was a lot paler than he was three months ago. He cursed and opened the top draw. He took out a make-up box and a black wig.

Chapter 4

'*Iphigenia, Iphigenia*, Trident calling, *Iphigenia,* come in please.' Justin released the radio transmission button and listened. His eyes were full of anxiety, expecting the unexpected. No reply. He repeated the call. No reply. He was calling the cargo ship *Iphigenia* on the radio with no success. He had been engaged in this futile routine for the best part of three hours, calling regularly, every ten, fifteen minutes or so.

Standing in the small radio room he looked around him without really looking at anything. He was becoming frustrated. He sighed and tried again. Nothing. Nothing from the ship coming through, but the barrage of other radio traffic on the busy VHF contact channel 16 was, as always, ever present and vibrant. Numerous voices more than often overlapping each other, sometimes barely audible, unable to surface above the crackle and static which most radio operators love to hate over the years, despite the fact that they become invariably concerned, suspecting a malfunction in their transmitting apparatus on those rare occasions when favorable atmospheric conditions enhance reception by reducing interference to the minimum.

Justin Oladapo was not just a radio operator. He knew he was being groomed for better things within the large shipping agency where he worked, in Apapa-Lagos, Nigeria. He had shown intelligence and maturity that belied his young age and a genuine appetite for work not usually associated with the majority of the local workforce in the agency. He was the first to arrive at the office that morning despite the transportation difficulties caused by heavy rainfall the night before. He had been 'assigned' the motor vessel *Iphigenia* from start to finish, to make arrangements for the ship's quick docking, discharging and sail. This was *the* test case for him, his big opportunity. He had been waiting for months for his chance to prove to his superiors that after fifteen months of doing insignificant work with insignificant pay, he was now ready and capable of joining some of his older and more experienced colleagues in attending to a ship's needs while in port. A shipping agency Supervisor! He relished the thought. The *Iphigenia* was *his* ship, his passport to a better job and better pay. He was not going to fuck-up and nothing would stand in his way. He was more than confident that he would do a good job. But where on earth was she?

The ship, a 16,000 deadweight bulk carrier loaded with American corn, was supposed to have arrived at the anchorage, *the roads,* just outside the port of Lagos eight to nine hours earlier in the small hours of the morning. 02.30 a.m., Thursday 1st September 1983. This had been confirmed by the vessel's captain as well as the loading agents in New Orleans.

The young Nigerian was anxious to make contact with the vessel before he could attend the daily berthing meeting at the Harbour Master's office where he would report the arrival of the ship in order to secure early docking. True, the port was not as congested as it used to be a few years earlier, in the late seventies, during the crazy Nigerian cement rush. Justin wanted to impress by expediting the turnaround of the ship. The *time is money* adage was certainly true of shipping. But how could he report a ship that had not yet arrived? Was the ship's radio out of order? Could she have sunk in bad weather? There was a severe storm in the area the night before. Justin began to sweat. He was more concerned with his promotion than with fate of the ship.

It was almost ten-thirty in the morning. The working day was by now in full swing. The office building of Trident Shipping Agency in downtown Apapa was bustling with activity. In the main operations room, agency supervisors attempting to look important, were desperately trying to make sense out of their near-flat-battery walkie-talkies, trying in vain to hear and be heard by equally frustrated counterparts at the other end, perhaps colleagues on board docked ships trying to communicate the daily loading and discharging reports. Others on the busy ground floor were having shouting matches on scores of claims and counter-claims amidst the clattering noise of the archaic Olivetti manual typewriters. In a small adjoining room the continuous rattling noise emanating from the non-stop telex machines added to the pandemonium. There was a contrasting mixture of half-a-dozen able seamen who had come to shore waiting for the agency to arrange transportation to local markets so they could replenish their provisions before their ships set sail for the open seas. Another small group of seamen were sitting patiently waiting to be taken to hospital, to the dentist, to the optician, some doing their best to look unwell. A day out in town for medical reasons also meant a full day's pay with no work.

There were others, from various ships and nationalities enduring the frustrating procedure of attempting to contact their families abroad by phone, assisted by patient agency staff knowing that this was easier said than done. Koreans, Philippinos, Greeks, Indians all talking, all shouting, trying to convince the Lagos telephone operators that their particular call was the most urgent. It would be some time before any of them would get their international calls through. In this part of the world it was hard enough to phone across town. An international call was something of an experience.

In all the daily mayhem and the usual state of organized chaos taking place in the premises few people, if any, noticed the slim tall young-looking man in khaki pants and a beige shirt walk straight into the Swedish General Manager's office, clutching to a large, thick manila envelope. It contained one hundred thousand American Dollars.

It was the first day of September yet the mid-morning temperature had already climbed to 34 degrees on the Celsius scale. The stench of sweat hovering in the building was more imposing on the nostrils that morning. The combination of humidity and heat associated with Apapa, Lagos along with the added discomfort of the habitual breakdown of the air-conditioning system was clearly showing on the young Nigerian's face. Justin wiped his forehead, moistened his lips and tried again.

'Iphigenia, Iphigenia this is Trident Shipping Agency calling from Apapa, Lagos, do you read over?'

'Don't you give it a rest now oga. Man, your ghost ship it no here now, you hear? There is ader people you know trying to call reeal ship on this channel!' The familiar voice pouring out of the radio, deliberately accentuated with local Pidgin English painted a broad smile on Justin's face. He did not get the chance to respond, as his unseen older brother Daniel who worked for a rival shipping

agency, went on. *'Santa Clara, Santa Clara this is Oceanic over?'*

'Oceanic this is Santa Clara at Lagos Roads. Switching to channel eleven.'

As soon as channel 16 became momentarily free again Justin started to call his *ghost ship* again when the familiar accented voice of his Swedish boss was heard behind him.

'Forget it *Yiastin*. The Lagos Port Harbour Master as well as the Chief Pilot at Tin-Can Island confirmed to me that the *Iphigenia* is not on Lagos Roads. In fact she cannot be found anywhere within 50 miles of Fair-Way-Buoy.' Lagos Port was divided into two ports, Apapa, where ships berthed alongside and midstream, and Tin-Can Island. The latter, considered a little safer against pilferages, was being almost exclusively used by container ships.

'How can they know that, sir? Good morning sir, I... I mean it could be a radio fault or engine trouble, it would not be the first time. The ship will show up I know it will.' Justin was trying hard to reassure himself. 'How can they *confirm?* Fifty miles is a long way out.'

'Now you know why it is necessary for us managers, especially expatriate managers, to entertain port officials every now and again. They can be difficult at times but they can also be very useful.'

'What do you mean, sir?' Justin knew only too well about so called favors, *dash* and *kick-backs*. In Nigeria, that was a way of life. He was still paying one third of his salary to a colleague for introducing him to the agency. The enigmatic look on his face had more to do with the ship's fate than with any *gratuities* extended to corrupt officials.

His General Manager anticipating this carried on. 'A container ship that left Tin-Can this morning reported a couple of stowaways on board. The Harbour Master sent a patrol boat out to collect them. Ten, perhaps twelve miles beyond Fair-Way-Buoy. The Harbour Master feeling more obliged than accommodating had already penciled in the *Iphigenia* for priority berthing this morning. Naturally he started to feel rather uncomfortable when the ship did not arrive and did not respond to your calls all morning. He therefore instructed the patrol boat to venture outwards for a while. No luck though. No visual or radio contact was made.'

'The HM did that? It pays to… pay sir!' Justin grinned but quickly turned serious again as he shuffled through some papers. 'One moment, please sir,' he said.

'What is it?'

'It is very mysterious.' Justin gave his boss a piece of paper. 'Although this cable was delivered to us, oh, two hours ago, it was actually transmitted noon yesterday and it is in line with previous ETA's. If anything, this last cable brings the ship's arrival at the anchorage forward.'

Lars Bergman, the Swedish born General Manager of Trident Shipping Agency in Lagos, Nigeria took the green coloured cable received through Nigerian Telecommunications. Green is the national color and almost all official stationery is green, one way or another. The fact that this makes difficult reading, seems to be of no concern to the authorities. The fact that the particular cable was delivered almost twenty-four hours after it was transmitted was considered good going by local standards. Bergman read it.

WED AUG 31 83 – 1145 HRS:
TO: TRIDENT APAPA LAGOS NIG
DEFINITE ETA LAGOS ROADS 0130 THUR 1 SEPT 83STP

CARGO 13,765 MT US BULK CORN NO. 3

ARRIVAL DRAFT BRACKISH WATER 26 FT 2 INCHES

PLS ARRANGE BERTH SAME DAY A.M.

DELIVER 15 MT FRESH WATER AND 50 MT MDO STP

NOR TO BE TENDERED TO CGO RCVRS A.M. 1 SEPT

RGDS MASTER MV IPHIGENIA

END ++++

The small room, which housed the main radio on the second floor, was at the back of the large house turned office. In the port area of Lagos known as Apapa, office blocks could be counted on one hand. Most businesses rented or purchased ordinary one level or two-floor houses and converted them into offices. The Swede went to the open window and looked out, squinting at the bright light. He seemed lost in thought as he stared at the mid-morning sky. The black clouds that caused the heavy rainfall the night before creating storm conditions were nowhere to be seen. The sun was beating down, feverishly working on the pools of water that covered most of the ground surface only a few hours ago. Another hour and the streets would be completely dry. He thought how difficult it would be for people with no first-hand knowledge of the tropics to look at the morning after the night before and fully conceive what had taken place. In his hometown of Helsingborg whenever the skies opened up, the town and the streets would remain pretty wet long after the rain stopped – even with the assistance of modern drainage systems. Drainage was, of course, totally alien to Apapa but such was the power of the equatorial sun that evaporation alone seemed to be more effective than the most effective drainage system. But with the heat and evaporation comes humidity, the ideal conditions for the *pigeon*-sized mosquitoes to go to work.

Bergman turned to Justin who was looking at his boss, wondering what was going through his mind. 'Send an immediate telex to the owners of the ship. Maybe they can throw some light on this mystery. Keep the line open and demand a live reply, there and then. Also call the receivers of the cargo and tell them what we know.'

'More like what we don't know,' added Justin as he was leaving the radio room for the telex room downstairs. He was bitter and angry at the way things were developing. This was his ship and his chance for a better job, a promotion and a better tomorrow. He was going to get to the bottom of this mystery one way or another.

Bergman looked out of the back window again, at the narrow unpaved alleys that crisscrossed the low roofed huts and makeshift houses of the shantytown neighborhood, rife at the back of every main street in downtown Apapa. Two-three hours earlier these same alleys resembled small streams and ponds. Half-naked children and half-grown up adults in plastic bathtubs and anything else that could float were pretending to be out at sea, navigating their makeshift crafts in the muddy water that was the source of so many unpleasant viruses. Now clothing of all sizes, shapes and colors were hanging, dangling on trees, out of windows, on sticks or simply stretched out facing the sun. The locals had finished with their ablutions, their fun and games over.

He hated all this. It was his second year here but he could never adjust to Nigeria. Having spent eleven months out of work, waning his redundancy money to alarming levels, he jumped at the chance for a change when offered the job, without fully realizing what Nigeria was all about. He was not totally alien to harsh living and working expatriate conditions. Trident Shipping Agency is part of the powerful multinational T&S International Enterprises Group, Bergman's previous employers. He worked for the Group as shipping operations manager for three years in the Middle East Gulf region. But the Iran-Iraq war put an end to that. It wasn't the South of France, but he survived. True, he was younger then and could adapt without too much difficulty. Nigeria proved to be a different proposition, worse than he could have ever imagined. However, he was approaching fifty and his options were somewhat limited. The pay was good and it was about to get better. Much better.

He lit up a cigarette. The thought of early retirement in luxury made him feel good. He took out a handkerchief and wiped his forehead. It was hot, very hot. He allowed himself a chuckle as he headed for his office.

***

Athens, Greece, 1983

It was just after nine in the evening in early September but still hot and humid in the center of the Greek capital. The young couple walking hand-in-hand were both casually dressed in shorts and T-shirts. The athletic looking young man sported a picture of the rock group Police on his T-shirt, while the blonde young lady had the iconic black and white image of Che Guevara on the front of her own T-shirt. Two tourists among thousands nonchalantly walking in Syntagma Square pondering on where and how they would spend their last Saturday night in Athens before they return to England and to their studies.

'Jimmy, I am not sure they will let us into a posh club dressed like this. Why don't we find a nice taverna beneath the Acropolis for a bite and a drink?'

Jimmy put his arm around his girlfriend, looked lovingly into her eyes and said.

'Miss Rachel Yates, I promised you a last good night in Athens and a last good night we shall have. I've got a few Drachmae left and I am told that the place is swinging, posh, stylish, classy and crazy. Just like us!'

'Yes but dressed like this? At least let us go back to the hotel first and change into something more appropriate.'

'I will tip the doorman. Trust me Rachel. Let's go and have some fun. If my street map is correct the place is only five minutes away from here.' Jimmy gave Rachel a kiss and they headed for the club a few streets away. Ten minutes later they were going down the steps of The Red Gallery Club. Jimmy had generously tipped the doorman and asked for a dark corner table as they were not appropriately dressed. He obliged. The main room of the club was large with low, soft lighting and impressively decorated in black and red shades. The ambience felt good. At one corner a four-man jazz band was playing Henry Mancini's Lara's Theme from the sixties film 'Dr. Zhivago.' The place was half-full, but it was still early for Athens by night. A waitress ushered them to a corner table. She asked what they would like to drink.

'Champagne please! A bottle of Bollinger.' Jimmy did not hesitate while Rachel was nervously kicking him under the table.

'Are you *sure* Sir?' The waitress looked at the young couple almost in disbelief before she carried on. 'It costs 22,000 Drachmae per bottle.'

'In that case bring us two bottles,' said Jimmy with a grin on his face. He then took out of his pocket two one thousand Drachmae notes and gave them to the waitress. 'One is for you; the other is for the band. A request, if I may. Please ask them if they can play Midnight in Moscow, or Moscow Nights if they prefer it by that name. *Efcharisto. Spasipa.*' Jimmy thanked her in Greek and in Russian.

The waitress looked meaningfully into his eyes, thanked him – in English and went about her business. Meanwhile Rachel was stunned. She hit him on the shoulder.

'Are you crazy?' she hissed. 'That is almost one hundred pounds per bottle.'

'Yes I am,' said Jimmy. 'I am crazy about you. I saved for this night. I can afford it so let us enjoy it.

'I love you Jimmy Scargill, I really do.' He kissed her passionately.

The waitress returned with a bottle of Bollinger on ice and two glasses. She then passed an envelope to Jimmy telling him that it is a coupon for half-price cocktails for next time they decide to visit the club. Jimmy opened the envelope as the waitress engaged in friendly, meaningless, conversation with Rachel. Inside the envelope there was a numbered seat ticket for a second division football match at Stamford Bridge in London, between Chelsea and Cambridge United for the following Saturday 10th of September. There was a note too which read:

Your contact will take the seat on your left 5 minutes before kickoff. He has top/top clearance.

Jimmy lit a cigarette and burnt the note.

Chapter 5

Seventy-five feet beneath Downing Street in London's Whitehall is the starting point for a labyrinth of tunnels, which connect the residence of the First Lord of the Treasury, that is the British Prime Minister, to the Ministry of Defence and other key government buildings. Scattered in these tunnels are numerous secret rooms. These are not the old wartime tunnels that accommodated the PM's bunker and housed the War Cabinet shelter rooms. These are newer, deeper, wider tunnels. They not only provide the PM with an escape route from aspiring assassins and terrorists but also provide the PM with an escape from the public eye.

Work on these tunnels commenced slowly in the nineties and was completed at a more pressing pace soon after the 9/11 attacks on the World Trade Centre in New York. Different sections were completed at different times by different teams of workers and specialists. For most of the early work the men and women working on the tunnels were under the impression that they were digging auxiliary support tunnels for the Jubilee Line of the London Underground train system. However, for the later stages and the finishing touches on work directly beneath Numbers 10 and 11 Downing Street, the workforce was not only carefully screened but was also bound by the Official Secret's Act. C-Branch of MI5, the section responsible for the security of sensitive government installations, safeguarded the secrecy of the project.

Scraps of information were deliberately leaked here and there, especially within Parliament, suggesting the possible existence of such tunnels and secret rooms. Disingenuous elements at work circulated rumours that these new tunnels and secret rooms were constructed for one reason only. To withstand a nuclear attack, thus ensuring the survival of a functional British Government in the aftermath of a nuclear strike on London. Humbug! The tunnels exist, so do the secret rooms, but they serve an entirely different purpose.

Outside a few insiders with privileged information and top security clearance, nobody really knows for sure just how far these tunnels go or, indeed, what purpose the underground rooms serve. One particular person knew. An elderly gentleman. A man knighted by the Queen for outstanding services to his country. A man who had little or no personal life. A man who was completely devoted to his job, married to his job in fact, until he quietly slipped into enforced retirement a few years ago. A man with a seemingly routine job, yet a job that was full of lies, deceit, conspiracies, and clandestine operations. He did what he had to do for the greater good of his country, to protect the British *way of life*. A man whose main purpose in life was to protect the British Premier from being compromised from within. Sir Robert Ross knew. He knew that the tunnels extend all the way from Downing Street to Thames House, Millbank and Vauxhall Cross on the banks of the River Thames, the official Headquarters of MI5 and MI6, Britain's home security and international intelligence services. He also knew the dark secrets of the secret rooms.

In such a room, beneath Downing Street, a meeting between two men was taking place. One of the men was Timothy Blythe the British Prime Minister, the other James

Marlow Scargill, JMS to his friends, the current Director of SIS, the British Secret Intelligence Services formerly known as MI6. Two sturdy men in civilian attire stood outside the black, steel-reinforced, door. They were dressed in dark grey suits and each held an automatic rifle. The bulge under their white shirts betraying the presence of bulletproof vests. An identity card was pinned to their lapels. A thin, coiled wire coming out of the breast pocket of their jackets disappeared in their left ear. The only person who could authorize use of this particular room was the Prime Minister himself through a verifiable directive. In his absence, the Director of MI5 and the Director of MI6 could each issue such a directive, as long as the Prime Minister's Chief of Staff was informed in advance.

The last time a Prime Minister used this particular room was in early July of 2003. That was a period when public outcry caused the government much concern and discomfiture. The issue was Iraq's possession of weapons of mass destruction, chemical and biological, as well as Iraq's projected capability to deploy such weapons. A supposition vigorously defended by the U.K. and the U.S.A., both nations having used the threat as their main excuse to go to war against Saddam's Iraq. The room was also used on July 11th 2005 following the July 7th bomb attacks in London. Eleanor Bishop, the Director-General of MI5, Anthony Cross the Chief of London Police and Home Secretary Cecil Cox attended. The Prime Minister authorized the meeting.

The room itself was modestly furnished. A round table with six chairs, four armchairs and two side tables. On one of the side-tables there was a bottle of mineral water and two glasses. The walls and ceiling were painted in brilliant white. The floor was covered with Italian marble. There was no other décor and no ornaments. No phones, no computers, no equipment of any kind. Nothing. Once the steel reinforced door was shut, no cellular phones could function and no electronic devices could penetrate the secure and sterile conditions inside the room. Concealed jamming devices, silent acoustic correlators and acoustic sound generators ensured that nothing and nobody could possibly listen to what was being said. As an extra precaution, the thick walls were lined with a double wire mesh preventing electromagnetic information going in or out of the room. The only evidence that something was at work besides the lighting was the soft droning noise of the air purification and ventilation systems. Before and after meetings, the room was electronically swept for possible violations. This was considered to be the most *sterile* room in the United Kingdom. Whatever was being said in this room remained in the room. It was not documented, had nothing to do with official government policy and it was never discussed again.

'Are you telling me that with all the resources at our disposal there is nothing else we can do? No way around it?' Timothy Blythe, the Prime Minister, casually dressed, leaned back in his armchair, his eyes fixed on the Director of MI6 sitting opposite him wearing a chic Armani summer suit.

'I wish there was another way Tim. Based upon the hard evidence we have provided you with, you requested a solution. I am presenting you with one. If you have gangrene on one foot you do something about it. You don't wait and see.' James Marlow Scargill, the youngest ever post-WW2 Director of MI6 and a polyglot, was not known for mincing his words or beating about the bush. He was fluent in French and Russian and had a reasonable working knowledge of German, Greek and Arabic. He had risen through the ranks, was considered a brilliant analyst and had the confidence of a man who knew what he was talking about. Throughout his rise to the top, it was as if he had divine assistance, a guardian angel, keeping him clear of potential career banana skins and out of dark political alleys. He had made all the correct moves.

'Gangrene? If you were to do something about the gangrene in the service there wouldn't be enough people left to run a service,' said Blythe. 'But then again, I suppose that in the land of the blind the one-eyed man is king.'

Scargill, completely ignoring the PM's comment, carried on. 'So far our ghost surveillance has been effective. He is being monitored, but to openly confront him is to alert him. We may lose him in the wind. I dread to think how far he would go or what his ulterior motives are. We know for a fact that in the mid-nineties he had close ties with China's PLA Second Department, that is the Chinese Military Intelligence Department. A *hard stop* is the best option, in fact the only option. He is beyond salvage, believe me.'

'Jesus, man! Can't you speak in plain in English for once?' Tim Blythe was quite animated by now and somewhat irritated. It was not that he resented the man seating across him. After all, he was the one who appointed him Director of the British Secret Intelligence Services. He was the one who followed his career with interest. But he infrequently did take exception to some of his methods and the impossible jargon in his vocabulary. However, the government, the country, the nation could not afford another scandal, another uproar and definitely not another inquiry. He stood up and walked about for a while. 'Shut him up. *Kill him*. Is this what you are telling me? Murder a man knighted by the Queen?'

'If he gets his way and he talks, I am sure Her Majesty will regret giving him the knighthood.'

'The Palace is rather nervous about all this.' Blyth took a deep breath. 'The implications of his alleged revelations regarding the death of Diana will hit the Royals hard.'

'It could hit you, Prime Minister, even harder.' Scargill delivered the words with a lot of frost and ice. Blythe shuddered.

'What the hell do you mean?'

'W.A.G.' Scargill whispered the letters but there was enough venom in his tone, thus ensuring that Blyth got the message.

'WAG?'

Scargill smiled. 'The Way Ahead Group,' he said. 'A bit like the SIS of the Royals. Do not underestimate them.'

'How do you want to handle this then?'

'I will cancel Ross. This is the right moment in time.' The answer was simple and cold.

'Just like you cancelled that FSB defector with your brolly games last year? I am still not clear about the real motives behind that assassination.'

'You can have answers on that from our allies across the Atlantic,' said the MI6 Director.

'I am aware of the existence of the so-called Beluga or Moby Dick, or whatever operation code names spies have for their dirty work. Mark my words, this will come back to haunt us one day.'

Scargill was unmoved. 'This time, with Ross, it will be a believable accident. As for the knighthood, you know I am to be knighted sooner or later and I can assure you I am no saint.'

'Well, at least this time it will not be another suicide. My God, I don't know, I, I don't believe we are having this conversation. I really don't.' The PM sat down again.

'Officially we are not.' The Director made an attempt to smile, trying to lower the levels of adrenalin in the room, but his stern expression took over again. 'Whether you like it or not, I am also saving your skin. He knows too much, far too much.'

'There are times, JMS, when you are a cold so and so.'

'Thanks, it goes with the job. That is why you are having this chat with me and me alone. Strictly speaking you should have been addressing this issue with our lady friend at Thames House.'

'I don't trust the cow any more than you do. But you are right,' said Blythe. He sighed deeply, raising his hands in the air in a gesture of exasperation. 'It is just that I have known this man, personally, for what? Ten, eleven years? He is a good man, he is no traitor and I am sure that in his own mind he thinks, no, he believes that by doing this he is doing a service to his country, a service to democracy.'

'Too much democracy is bad for your health. You do not successfully defend the realm by being *democratic*.' Scargill meant every word.

'What I'm trying to put across to you is that he is not doing this for himself. He can't be doing it for money and he's definitely not doing it for publicity either. I don't believe for a minute that he's turned. That much I am sure about. It must be a moral thing with him. But why now?'

'Or something personal. Revenge? Retribution perhaps?'

'Revenge? Revenge for what?' Blythe was puzzled.

'Two things spring to mind. One is Paris, the other the death of his spy *mistress*. Maybe he has the misconception that we were involved.'

'Were we? Were you?' Blythe's expression was hardening up.

The Director of MI6 leaned forward in his armchair and looked at Blythe straight in the eyes. 'On Christmas Eve 1988 I had been with the service for just nine months, nine short months as a junior analyst. My access to classified information was extremely limited. There is nothing on our records now to suggest that the death of his lady-boy Cabus, on that night, was not an accident.'

'As there will be nothing on record to suggest that Ross died from anything but an accident. Just like Paris in 1997. An accident.'

'Was it not?'

Blythe simply stared silently at the Director for a few seconds. Then he spoke. 'You tell me. Was it an accident Jim? For I have no idea. You were SIS Chief of Security and Public Affairs at the time. I am not interested to know what your official records say on the matter. I want to know what you know. The truth. What really did happen in the tunnel that night in Paris?'

Scargill's stance hardened somewhat. 'Let us stop playing games Tim. You know very well where you should be addressing this particular question. My own conscience is clear. We all serve Queen and Country, we mustn't forget that.' He took a deep breath. He was calm again. 'Look Tim, the problem facing us now is Ross and not how or why Diana died. I am sure that amongst the many things he wants to tell the world will be his own account of events regarding Paris. You've heard of his absurd theories on the subject. He will destabilize the country and the Monarchy. He has to be stopped.'

'Absurd theories? What about that ex MI6 agent who suggested that Diana's driver was blinded by some ultra-strong light beam or whatever?'

'Theories. Unsubstantiated theories…'

'If they were only theories I would be able to sleep at nights. I, I don't like it. Not one bit.' Blythe shook his head slowly from side to side, countless thoughts as well as niggling doubts pestering his mind. 'However,' he added, 'We do live in difficult and dangerous times.'

'Yes, we do.' Scargill, seating motionless, sensing that the Prime Minister was softening up seized the opportunity and pressed on. 'I agree with you. He may not be an apostate but he is a whistleblower and we both know that he probably has the evidence to substantiate at least some of his stories.'

'We don't need another GCHQ scandal…' Blyth was almost whispering. Scargill shook his head.

'You will have no choice but to resign and the country will go to the ballot. That is the easy part. The difficult part is restoring public confidence in the intelligence and security services and carrying on with our home and foreign policies without having to publicly justify our every move. And that's not all.'

'There's more? I can't wait.' Blythe felt uncomfortable.

'If he wants to, he can damage you, personally I mean.'

'He could have done that years ago and you of all people ought to know that.'

Scargill was undeterred.' He can really damage you beyond repairs with more up to date events. Read Iraq and the WMD fiasco, the enquiry into the scientist's suicide. Read Iran, nukes, oil and the Euro. Collaborating with the Americans against EU interests! The terror paradox. Blindly accepting and adopting the US government's version of the 9/11 attacks. Need I go on?'

'Iraq is already haunting me. We harvest what we sow. Thousands have died this year alone and thousands will die in the future. We turned the place into a bloodbath. This will escalate. They will eventually bring the war to our doorstep, here, in Europe. You saw the backlash when the Danish press published drawings of the Prophet last year. We can't take anything for granted anymore. We've opened Pandora's Box with our interventions in the Middle East. It is irreversible. We have created a *Hydra* monster.'

Scargill listened but said nothing. Tim Blythe's tall body momentarily shuddered as if an electric current had passed through it. He looked at the surreal environment around him. He closed his eyes for a while before he carried on. 'You know, you can keep the truth from surfacing, hide the truth, but you cannot hide from your own conscience. Remember that Jim. That is if you still have a conscience.'

'I do get a scruples attack every now and again but I soon think of the greater good. I sleep easy at nights. I take pills!' Before the PM could respond, Scargill carried on. 'In a perfect world we live not. A few months ago we, the so-called civilized West, succeeded in persuading the International Court of Justice to rule that the killing of around 7,000 Bosnian Muslims by Bosnian Serbs in Srebrenica amounted to genocide. It suits our agenda. Yet we turn a blind eye to the real genocide committed by the Americans on the American native Indian and we refuse to acknowledge the Armenian genocide by the Turks – because it suits our agenda.'

Blyth shook his head in disbelief but said nothing. Scargill carried on with his monologue.

'For over half a century the Americans have been hiding the fact that they were nuking their own troops, exposing them to deadly radiation, all in the good cause of science and national security—debunking the UFO phenomenon, the vaccines used on unsuspecting human guinea pigs, the man-made viruses, our own tolerance on addictive food additives. The controlled media

72

brainwashing the masses. The lies never end. Fracking is another ticking bomb. Profit today, fuck the earth tomorrow. Our society lives a lie.' Scargill was in full swing. 'Do not talk to me about conscience and hypocrisy. I am what I am and I have to live with it. Boy, I am really happy I am not a politician. Rant over.'

'Sometimes you really scare the shit out of me,' said a worried PM. 'Thank God you are on my side!'

'God? What about God? Religion is another lie. The biggest. How many wars have started because of religion? What do you think will happen if the world wakes up one morning to find out that the church has been deceiving people for two thousand years, that Christianity and other religions are only man-made, fabricated supposedly for the good of the living souls on this planet? When in fact all it does is to control the masses and start the odd holy crusade if economic necessities dictate it. Chaos and anarchy. There goes your control. The world we live in has been built on lies and half-truths.'

Blythe was mildly stunned. 'These are your own extreme views,' he said. 'But let us not drift away from the subject.'

'Let us not,' snapped Scargill. 'More often than not the truth has to be buried. Deep. A view obviously not shared by Ross.'

'What about the reporter? How much does he know? And what if Ross has already made other arrangements, in the event of his sudden demise? An insurance, a back-up of some sort.'

'A reporter without his source has nothing to report. We shall rough him up a little and ridicule him if he attempts to disclose something. The reporter is not the problem. Ross is. As for any possible post-demise arrangements, we have a lead on that. A couple of people connected with his past. We are monitoring the situation and if need be we shall intervene.'

'Intervene? I am not sure I want to know what that implies.'

'Acting in the country's best interests. That's what it implies,' said Scargill.

'Why not *ridicule* Ross as well?' Blythe was just being hopeful and he knew it. 'Hold on, let us think about this for a minute. What if we let him know that we are on to him and if he goes ahead and hangs out our dirty laundry for all to see we shall discredit him. You are supposed to be the experts on this sort of thing.'

The Director laughed nervously. 'With all due respect Tim, you say you have known this man for over fifteen years? You cannot discredit a man like Ross. The man is a legend. It would be easier to discredit Mother Theresa!'

'We could have him arrested under the Official Secrets Act. He would have already broken the law if, and I do say if, he has already divulged classified information to this TV reporter.'

'It is not just the reporter. He is also planning to publish a book.'

'A book?' Blythe was startled.

'Yes. We have fresh video evidence of his meeting with a publisher just three days ago. They went jogging together. We have fragments of his conversation on tape, recorded using laser technology for voice vibrations. He was not discussing the weather.' The Director was getting impatient and he was showing it.

Blythe was undeterred. 'If he is the intelligence legend we all say he is, don't you find it rather odd that he allows himself to be caught on video, *scheming* against his country?'

'He is either getting careless in his old age or he simply doesn't care anymore.'

'Or he is suicidal…' Blythe was being sarcastic.

'It transpires, from the transcript of his conversation with the publisher that our man has even thought of a title for his pending book. *Whitehall After Dark*. I am sure this will have nothing to do with Central London clubbing.'

'Well, you have got to hand it to him. He's got class!'

'He has got to be stopped, Tim. Now.'

'His demise may do us more harm than good. Have you considered this?'

'I hate to use old clichés, but dead men tell no stories.'

Blythe was not convinced. 'There must be another way. He was, he *is* one of us you know. What if I talk to him, alone? That is what I should have done when the problem first appeared.'

'NO.' The Director was abrupt and uncompromising. 'It is not a good idea. He will use it to his advantage; he will buy time so he can slip through our net.' He lifted his arms in the air, gesticulating at the impasse that was facing them. He looked at Blythe, sitting across him, lost in his thoughts. His short-lived outburst was overcome by his usual relaxed manner. If anything, his voice softened and sounded more sympathetic. 'Look Tim, you are the Prime Minister. The final choice is yours and yours alone. I'd hate it to be in your shoes right now. I mean it. However, you did request of me that I come up with a minimum damage solution. From where I am standing that is the best I can offer, for the good of the government and that of the country. I cannot see a way around this. He needs to be decommissioned. Permanently. Tim, the man is a walking bomb.'

'I know,' said Blythe. He looked straight at the man across him. 'Perhaps, in retrospect, the decision to shut him down was taken in haste. How do you see it now?'

Scargill smiled with a sense of satisfaction. 'Can't really comment on this one. The person who shut him down is in this very room and it is not me Tim'

'Irrelevant. You are evading the question. Was it a wise decision? Should I have kept him on, kept him close and in control?'

'He shut himself out. He was getting out of control, he had lost the plot. He was doing things without clearance and justification. He was becoming a liability. A rogue unit, operating a mercenary wing. The Hub. The *Hub?* What kind of a name is that? A centre for what? His private clandestine games? He was detrimental to the people he was supposed to serve. He and his cronies were becoming a government within the government. The unofficial and unauthorized centre of government policy. You of all people know that.' Scargill's retort was uncompromising.

'Yes, according to the reports that *you* and your service compiled. But, that is not entirely true. He was only doing what he had always done, what he was asked to do from day one and not without success I might add.'

Scargill shook his head. 'He had no divine right to fabricate unauthorized events and scenarios – not without official approval from the PM's office and approval from SIS. He was a black sheep, harbouring ambivalent views, always going against the flow. Even our *cousins* across the pond were wary of his activities. Twice the CIA warned us about him. Frankly I'm surprised that he was tolerated for so many years.'

'The same could be said of us.'

'He sanctioned the killings of innocent people and now he wants to tell the world about it? Really, where's the logic in all this?'

'Whereas *our* killings are legal. Is that it?' The Prime Minister helped himself to a glass of mineral water. 'He is not the first insider to take his tongue for a walk in Fleet Street you know and he will not be the last.'

'Precisely,' snapped Scargill. 'That is why we have to send a clear message to our inner community that we shall not tolerate this anymore. He ought to have got a life years ago.' He paused for a while and then meaningfully looked at the PM. 'What was it that someone once said? You only require two things in life. Your sanity and your wife! Well, Ross has neither.'

'At least there will be no grieving family left behind, this time.'

'Well he does live with his housekeeper, Mrs. Porter.'

'Not blood family though.' The Prime Minister was barely audible. He buried his head in his hands. A few moments later he stood up, composed himself and without saying another word, gently shook his head signifying his approval.

The Director got up and shook hands with a reluctant PM. 'It will be OK,' he said. 'Five days, six at the most. We have done our homework.'

'Spare me the details will you?'

'We have been down this road before. We shall try to overshadow this with some other event.'

'I'm sure you will. You are not unlike Ross in this sense.'

'Is that a compliment or an insult?'

The PM for the first time in the meeting allowed himself half-a-smile as he recalled a certain event, which Ross himself had confided to him. 'Wilson,' he said. 'His shock resignation and Princess Margaret's divorce. One event overshadowing another. The Queen was extremely concerned of how the press would react to her sister's divorce announcement. This was 1976 and the blue-blooded tried to act the part. Ross negotiated an *understanding* between Downing Street and Buckingham Palace. Wilson shocked Fleet Street with his resignation announcement and Margaret's divorce had a soft landing. The Royals were happy and Ross gained points.'

'He did have his good moments I suppose.'

'He had class. He wasn't known as *The Rolls* for nothing you know.' Blyth meant it. He did like Ross.

'I thought he was known as The Rolls because of his initials,' said Scargill.

'Yes, that too. A *good moment* is what I need. If I am to believe the various polls in the tabloid press I do not seem to be very popular right now.' The PM tried to smile but could not manage it.

'Leave that to me Tim,' said a smiling Director. 'What we need here is another terror alert or perhaps an environmentally caring Prime Minister, or both! Start a save the planet campaign. Do something to boost the NHS and the inner cities. Help unemployment. The American President has damaged you. Show that you are British. Put some distance between you and the yanks. Show your human face Tim.'

The PM was not impressed. 'I don't feel human anymore. In fact, I don't really feel proud for what I have done. My policies, decisions, leadership. I believed I did what I did for the good of our country. No other reason. I may have been wrong.'

'Thought about early retirement?'

'All the time. Maybe now is the right time to step down, while the going is still relatively good. I cannot see myself lasting till Christmas, not to mention my full term. The last few summers have not been good to us, Jim. Not good. July's not a good month. I have a feeling this one will be no different.'

'Oh, I don't know about that.' Scargill looked at his watch. 'There's always Wimbledon. Still time to catch some doubles action.'

The Prime Minister shook his head in mock disbelief. 'Ever considered running for office Jim? Be legally elected? A minister of Her Majesty's Government?'

'If we take it as a given that the credentials one needs for one to be elected is rhetoric spiced with lies and more lies plus some cooked statistics then, yes, I would qualify. But not to be just a Member of Parliament to be woken up whenever there is a vote in the House. You know I aim high.'

'Of course you do,' said Blyth. 'In fact I honestly believe that with your international intelligence background and knowledge, you would make the ideal Foreign Minister for this nation. Even Prime Minister.'

'I'll sleep on it, but first there is work to be done. Thanks for your time Tim.'

Blyth smiled and said nothing more. He walked to the door and pressed a button on the door. A buzzing sound was heard and a green light flashed on the other side of the door. Within a few seconds the armed guards outside opened the armoured door and the two men walked out. Now it was the turn of the sweepers to enter the room and ensure that security had not been compromised in any way. The meeting that lasted for forty minutes never took place.

***

Sir Robert Ross was sitting in his favorite antique chair, a century old original English Chippendale mahogany library armchair. He was near the window in the front room of his third floor apartment and enjoying his mid-morning hot beverage. Contrary to general belief, this respectable old English gentleman did not care much about England's national hot drink. In fact he hated tea. He was a coffee man. Black and strong. That is how he liked it. He also liked his cigars, the best the world had to offer. And he felt like puffing on one right now.

'Daphne, where are you old girl?' He slowly turned his head around, as best as he could, looking for his housekeeper and companion.

'I am in the bedroom Sir Robert. One moment please.' The housekeeper slowly shouted the words out from somewhere within the apartment.

Daphne Porter was approaching her fifty-seven birthday. She was Greek by birth and still quite handsome for her age. She had been looking after him ever since he was knighted, some fifteen, sixteen years ago. At first she used to come round to Sir Robert's flat three times a week to clean up and do his laundry. However since his involuntary retirement he became something of a recluse, spending a lot of time indoors, reading and writing most of the time. The only time he ventured outside with some regularity was for his early morning jogging exercise at Regent's Park twice a week and a monthly visit to Bayswater for a Chinese food night out. He was in his late sixties but he kept fit. He was married to his work so he never had time for marriage. He had no family and no close relatives. Soon it became obvious to both of them that he needed help on a daily basis.

Six months after Oliver Porter, Daphne's husband, an ex-Royal Navy Midshipman died following a two-year battle with cancer, Sir Robert asked her if she would like to live in his flat. She had no other relatives in London. Her only son, Nick was at boarding school and later studied political sciences and philosophy at Oxford but soon became an environmentalist and a passionate believer of renewable energy concepts. He was making a success of his career with the United Nations in Geneva, thanks to Sir Robert who not only introduced him to the right people but also wrote a first class reference letter for him. Sir Robert was fond of Nick. He was his mentor. He was the son he never had. They had spent countless hours together, discussing philosophy and world politics. Sir Robert encouraged Nick to learn at least one foreign language. Nick thought Greek would be good, but Sir Robert suggested Russian. Know your enemy he said with a wink. Daphne had been away from her hometown of Sparta in Greece for far too long to return there. She was alone and the daily commuting on the Jubilee Line from her own modest flat in Willesden Green to Bond Street station was beginning to enervate her. So she was only too happy to accept his offer. He was being looked after and she had company. Their lives acquired a new meaning.

'What is it?' she asked standing next to him.

He looked at her. His eyes somewhat magnified through his bifocal gold-rim glasses depicted the affection he felt for her. To him she was an ancient Greek Goddess, tall, dark with long wavy hair and eyes that were still full of fire, full of life.

'I am wondering,' he said, 'really wondering if I'll ever see the day when you'll get up one morning and call me Robert, Bob, Bobby, love, handsome, punk, bum, gorgeous, anything but *Sir* Robert.'

'I'm pretty sure this is not the reason you called me,' she said smiling.

'Pretty you surely are my dear, but, if this is how you want to play this, get me a cigar then, would you?'

'You are getting old, *Robert*. You drink too much coffee and you smoke too much. Poor George has given up on you.'

'George? George you said? He calls himself a doctor? He's not even sixty and looks older than I do. What does he know? He asks me to quit puffing my cigars and he smokes like a bloody chimney. Cigarettes, that's what he smokes, cigarettes! Move over I say…'

'What do you expect him to smoke, lamb chops? Not everybody can afford these, these Cuban cigars you know. What was it now that they charged me at Selfridges the other day?' Daphne looked at the ceiling trying to remember. 'Seven hundred and eighty pounds for a box of twenty fives! That is a full wage for some poor man. Now you move over I say…'

'No, no you misunderstood me when I emphasized the fact that he smokes cigarettes. You see a cigarette smoker inhales the smoke. Some, like George, keep it in their lungs for a few seconds before they blow it out. Disgusting habit. That is when and where the damage is done. A proper cigar smoker never, but never inhales the smoke. It's not cricket you know. He tastes it and just puffs it out. No harm to the lungs. Now you see the difference.' Sir Robert finished his coffee.

'I see,' said Daphne. 'Now I can eat lobster.'

'What? Lobster you said? What's that got to do with anything? Anyway, you are allergic to shellfish, are you not?'

'It is all right. I will eat it like you smoke the cigar. I will chew it, taste it in the mouth and then spit it out!'

Sir Robert smiled. A broad, beaming and happy smile. Daphne could picture in her mind the dashing handsome young man he must have once been. He still had a good posture and remnants of his clean-cut good looks. He was still as good-looking as he was seventeen years ago when she first met him when a Royal Navy Commander, an acquaintance of her husband, introduced her to Sir Robert for housekeeping work.

'What is it going to be today?' she asked affectionately.

'I feel like something quick and strong. A *robusto* please and some more coffee. And Daphne, please fetch my binoculars.'

'Old habits die hard,' she whispered. Daphne kissed him gently on the forehead and went to a small cupboard in the next room. Sir Robert had the cupboard converted, years ago, to a fully functional humidor. This is where he kept his prized cigars, in great numbers. She picked up a short thick cigar with a yellow label and black and white squares and a matching cigar cutter. She then went to another room, which Sir Robert was using as his office and picked up his old racing binoculars.

'Cigar, scissor, glasses and long matches' she said quite loudly as she handed him the items. 'No coffee. Later perhaps.'

He laughed. 'OK then, coffee after lunch and this, this I told you is not a *scissor,* it is a cigar cutter and this, this is... oh, never mind,' he said. He cut the cap off the Cohiba cigar and used a long Davidoff match to light it. He leaned back in his chair and relished the moment. 'You know what Daphne? I'd say this is probably...'

Daphne quickly interrupted him. 'Yes, yes I know,' she said. 'You are going to say that this is probably the best cigar in the world. I told you, you sound like that beer commercial on TV!'

'I've said this to you before?'

'Not that many times,' she said smiling.

Sir Robert's apartment was situated on the southern side of Manchester Square in Central London. He had made a habit of having his mid-morning coffee whilst observing the small picturesque park in the center of the square below him. The park, or the gardens as it was known, was for the private use of the local residents. He liked to observe the birds nesting on the trees and perhaps catch sight of the odd squirrel running up and down. To get a closer look he often made use of his old horse racing Miranda 10 X 50 wide-angle binoculars. He was fond of horse racing and he missed the racing tracks. He frequently remarked that watching the races on television was like having sex from a distance! He was not much of a gambler but he did enjoy the odd flutter on the English Classics every now and again and once in every blue moon he succeeded in persuading George Clayton, his doctor and friend of many years, to go racing at Epsom or Ascot with him.

This time though he was not pointing his binoculars at the tree-tops but lower at street level, focusing on the white-shirted occupant of a dark blue saloon car parked on the far side, the northern side of Manchester Square, in front of Hertford House. He had seen the same car with the same driver the day before. Finding a parking space in the square was a trying experience as most of the spaces were reserved for local residents. Those that had the right to park their cars in the resident bays had City of Westminster parking permits with the letter F displayed on their windscreens. There were also a few paying bays for nonresidents but were always in great demand, with Oxford Street less than two minutes' walk away. The car that drew his attention had no permit displayed; yet it was parked in a space that was reserved for residents. What made him take serious notice the day before was the fact that when a burly traffic warden approached the driver, presumably with the intention of asking him to move on or issue him with a fine, something odd happened. The driver, though trying his best to be inconspicuous, appeared to flaunt something that could have been an ID card and the warden simply nodded and walked away.

'What is it some new bird?' Daphne was curious.

'What was that?'

Daphne raised her voice somewhat. 'Is it a new bird that you are watching?'

'No bird this time. More like a rat,' Robert replied, without breaking his observation.

'A mouse? Ah, you are joking with me. What do you want for lunch?'

'Is there any fish?' Robert lowered the binoculars, stood on his feet and drew the net curtains across the window.

'Only smoked kippers.'

Robert grimaced his disapproval.

'I know what,' said Daphne. 'I could get us some Dover sole from Selfridges. I will grill it with mushrooms and serve it with boiled baby marrows and new potatoes. I shall also buy some squid for a Greek dish tomorrow. How is that?'

'I say, that sounds great. We'll wash it down with a nice Chablis, what?' he smiled at the idea as he walked towards her.

'You'll never learn…'

Robert put his arm around her. He lowered his voice, almost to a whisper. 'When you go out I'd like you to do something for me. Let us sit down for a few minutes and I'll explain in detail what it is you have to do. But first, please put some music on.'

Without questioning his motives, she placed a CD in a portable CD player that was nearby. Music from Kenny Ball and his Jazzmen filled the room. She then sat very close to him and listened.

Fifteen minutes later he watched Daphne walk to a public phone booth on an adjacent street corner. She made a short call. She then looked for and approached a female traffic warden patrolling the square and said something to her, raising her arms in the air as if in despair, protesting and pointing to the general direction of Hertford House, the imposing building housing the Wallace Collection. From his third floor vantage point, Ross observed the two women approach the dark blue saloon. The warden appeared to talk to the occupant and then gesturing that he should move. Daphne was close by looking on. In an instance, the driver quickly glanced towards the apartment window, not for long, just for a split second. But that was enough to give him away before he drove off in a hurry. Bad form! An incompetent wheel artist thought Ross. A casual could have done a better job. Sir Robert Ross, the legendary *Rolls*, was sending a clear message to the Secret Intelligence Services. A soft target he was not and it was game on. He needed to find out, quickly, why he was the subject of a surveillance exercise and who it was that actually authorized it.

Meanwhile, Daphne had turned away in a mocked huff and walked down Duke Street on her way to Selfridges. Ross, impressed by what he saw, thought that she could have been a first class pavement artist. He went to the kitchen cellar, picked up a bottle of white wine and placed it in the fridge.

'Well what the hell,' he whispered to himself. 'There won't be any jogging for a while. At least, not in London.'

Chapter 6

The sunrise was reassuring. It was tranquil, serene, soothing, calming. It was the beginning of a new day and with every new day there was new hope. To witness it in all its glory meant that one had survived the day before, the night before. Life!

Zoe Coburn, wearing a long white T-shirt and nothing else, was looking out of the caravan window. She was around thirty and she had a good figure and her facial features could have easily graced any glamour and fashion magazine cover. The sparkle in her blue eyes successfully hiding the anguish and pain she suffered in years gone by. For at long last, she was a happy woman.

Her gaze was focused to the east where the fiery oval ball was beginning to rise over the Aegean horizon gradually waking up the morning skyline over the sea with happy explosions of bright orange colors. She could see a flock of seagulls, already at work following a couple of fishing boats in the distance. Life! She adored the morning sun. Darkness had been with her, a part of her, for too long. The memories of a past life, the nightmares from another world had scarred her in more ways than one. She shivered. She swiftly turned her attention to her Garfield coffee mug, cupping it with both hands. She drunk some coffee and then affectionately grinned at Garfield, her favorite cartoon cat that seemed ready to pounce at her. Her life was getting better though. Everything that was haunting her had been gradually erased from every cell in her body. Staring at the horizon she could just about see the reason. A thin mirage-like silhouette swiftly moving across the low sun-disc. A windsurfer taking advantage of the early morning breeze, the *meltemi,* the endemic summer wind blowing from north to south in the Aegean Sea.

She impulsively waved at George Anderson, a keen windsurfer, her lover and future husband. She smiled, realizing that he could not possibly see her from that distance. The caravan was parked on an isolated spot on Keros beach on the Greek island of Limnos in the northern Aegean Sea. It was early July and the few mainland tourists that infrequently camp on this particular beach do not usually make their presence felt before late July-early August, the traditional holiday period for the Greeks. The off the beaten track island, beautifully simple with acres of virgin beaches, was not as commercialized as some of the better-known islands in the Aegean, mainly due to the intense military presence of the Greek army and air force, a legacy of the ever-stretched Greek-Turkish relationships. The sandy beach at Keros Bay stretches for about three miles and is horseshoe shaped. It is on the eastern part of the island, the less developed part. In the early hours of the morning, just before and after sunrise, the meltemi wind creates perfect windsurfing conditions and every day at the crack of dawn, George, was out enjoying his favorite sport. The rest of the day, and all of the night, he was devoted to Zoe. The love of his life.

It was her lover's idea to come to the little-known beauty spot for a ten day holiday. He told her that he had been there twice before and knew the area well. They rented a caravan, a sailboard with the necessary accessories and a motorcycle from Thessaloniki on mainland Greece and then took the ferry to Myrina, the capital port of

Limnos. Keros Bay is less than an hour's drive from Myrina. Access to the beach is through Calliope, a tiny farming village with less than two hundred inhabitants. George and Zoe often visited the village with their motorcycle in order to replenish their provisions and to occasionally have the odd drink and meal at the local taverna.

They met each other in group therapy sessions in London just three months prior to their coming to Limnos. She attempted to end her life and he was suffering from acute depression. Depressed or not he could not help but notice her stunning beauty. He made his move, their chemistry clicked and a passionate relationship soon evolved. It proved to be the perfect therapy. Happiness was instantly born out of their misery and hardship. Inside three short months she felt happier and safer than at any other time of her entire, tormented, adult life. There was no turning back now.

Zoe was a fully qualified pediatrician and nutritionist and used to work for the World Health Organization (WHO). Her last posting with the WHO was in Iraq. One spring afternoon in 2004 she was driving with Paolo, an Italian colleague, on the outskirts of Karbala, south of Baghdad, when their car was ambushed and they were both kidnapped. On the fifth day of their captivity, her colleague was taken away and was never seen again. She was told that he was executed. Her captors told her she would have the same fate unless she conformed to their demands. Demands which she never understood. She was kept inadequately fed, naked, in total isolation and in total darkness confined to a small smelly room. She was not really physically hurt but she was touched all over her body, at times hands were feeling her breasts. She was more mentally abused than anything else. Her naked body was frequently photographed, in detail and two hooded men, one flashing a torch light in her face the other brandishing a gun, kept asking her for hours on end, in fairly good English, the same questions over and over again. Questions on subjects that were totally alien to her. Questions regarding the whereabouts of a microfilm or a compact disc containing classified information on how the British Intelligence Services fabricated the case for war against Iraq. On other days they wanted to know what she knew about events leading to the 9/11 attacks in New York, Osama Bin Laden fund accounts and something that they referred to as DJNO. Even more mystifying was the fact that her captors wanted to know if she believed in any of the conspiracy theories surrounding Princess Diana's death. Infrequently she would be asked to narrate the story of her own life. Her every answer, her every word was recorded and they made sure that she knew it. She was at a total loss, at breaking point. She was losing her sanity. She tried, in vain, to convince her captors that she had no idea as to what they were talking about, that they must have kidnapped the wrong person. It was futile. She had come to terms with the fact that she was going to die. Then suddenly, twenty-one days into her captivity, she was unexpectedly released, abandoned in a side street in the southern Iraqi city of Basra. A British patrol had found her late at night, scantily dressed, wandering bare-footed in a general state of shock.

The World Health Organization reported her and her colleague missing the morning after they vanished but nobody claimed responsibility for the kidnapping and no one had made any demands. There was nothing to go on. For this reason the case did not receive extensive worldwide publicity. Her only living relative Alexandra, her twin sister who lived and worked in Fairfax County,

Virginia in the States, only found out about her ordeal once Zoe was back home in Southgate, North London, where she was escorted to a few days after her release. Her sister immediately visited her in London where she stayed for a while, offering support and comfort. After receiving treatment for malnutrition and counseling for a few weeks, she then tried to piece her life together again. She quit her job with the WHO and managed to find a job at a private clinic near Russell Square in Central London.

One week into her new job and she encountered her second traumatic experience, one that scarred her for life, literally. It was a summer morning and Zoe was on the Piccadilly Line underground train, commuting from her home in Southgate to her work near Russell Square. She was seating near the middle of the second carriage. A couple of minutes before arriving at her destination a bomb exploded at the rear of the first carriage of the train. Pieces of mangled metal and broken glass had cut her badly around the torso. Her right breast was almost severed. But she was rescued in time and she survived, just. She spent five weeks in hospital. Apart from extensive counseling she had to have major plastic surgery on her breast. Three days after the casualty lists were made public her sister was again by her side along with Iphigenia, their childhood friend, comforting her and offering whatever financial support she could. She pleaded with Zoe to move in with her, to live in Virginia. No, London was her home. She was staying. She would, somehow, manage. The day after her sister left, something unexpected happened. A very polite and soft-mannered man, in his sixties with thinning grey hair and dull grey-blue eyes, visited her in hospital and insisted that he cover all expenses, including the expensive cosmetic surgery she had to have. Unknown to her he also deposited ten thousand pounds in her bank account. He said that he was a friend of her father, a father that she hardly remembered. A father who died under bizarre circumstances, dressed as woman, on the London Underground a long time ago on a Christmas Eve. He said he had something to tell her about her father, something that her father entrusted him with the day before he died. He promised to contact her as soon as she was better. He didn't.

It took time but Zoe once more gradually recovered and became totally absorbed in her work. She sold her flat in Southgate and rented a small studio flat within walking distance from her work near Russell Square. She coyly started to go out in the evenings and even attempted dating. She was becoming a new person.

One evening she returned home after having a few drinks with colleagues from the clinic. She found her studio flat turned inside out. The furniture was badly damaged, her bed-mattress torn apart, lampshades smashed, clothes everywhere on the floor, draws and chairs turned upside down and her fitted carpet torn from the floor. The place looked like a disaster area. She screamed. Her neighbor Mikel Bengochea, a thirty-six year old Spanish lecturer at London University living on the same floor, rushed to her aid. After he ensured that nobody was still in her flat he told her not to touch anything and that she should call the police. Wise move. She went to the phone and that is when she saw it. A large manila envelope with her name on it. She didn't know why but she felt like fainting. Mikel got her a glass of water. Contrary to his advice not to open the envelope before the police arrived she went ahead and ripped the envelope open. She froze. There were ten may be twelve, large photographs of her, showing her sitting on a dirt floor, filthy, undernourished and totally naked. The horror of Iraq was coming back to haunt her. Before Mikel could ask what it was all about she lost consciousness and slumped to the floor. He called for an ambulance and the police.

She was hospitalized for three days suffering from shock. Crime detectives visited her in hospital the next day where they asked if she had anything of value or of importance at home. She hadn't. They said that the intruder must have been looking for something specific. However, they did not have much to go on. Forensics could not recover any evidence from the intruder. Mikel and his English girlfriend dropped in to see her. They offered to help her put her studio flat back in order.

Later on that day another man visited her. A man with shifty eyes in his early forties dressed in a dark blue suit. He introduced himself as Ian Cross and explained that he was assigned to the Special Branch of the Security Services. He gave her a card and asked her if she could visit him at his office when discharged from hospital. He said that it was a security matter and that it was extremely important. She did call and went to see him four days later. The address on his card read *Thames House, 11 Millbank*. The MI5 HQ. There she was asked about her terrible experience in Iraq and what it was exactly that her captors were after. She patiently explained that British Army Intelligence in Iraq had documented all the details relating to her ordeal. The same was done by the Foreign Office when she returned to London. Ian Cross insisted and persisted with his questions. Questions about matters that she knew nothing about. The same questions her captors in Iraq were asking. Zoe's nightmares were coming to life again. She felt as if she was being interrogated. She was intruded, abused. She felt dizzy. She felt like vomiting. She felt as if she wanted to die. She could not take the *abuse* for much longer. Her stomach was tied up in knots, she couldn't breathe, her head ached, and her eyes felt like bleeding. She asked to be left alone, she *screamed* that she be left alone. She knew nothing. NOTHING. She felt persecuted, she trusted no one. She became suspicious of everybody and everything. In a state of daze she got up and left.

She arrived at her studio flat by taxi. A couple of somber-looking girls, probably students, were sitting on the steps of the main street entrance. She recognized the one with tears in her eyes. It was Suzan, Mikel's girlfriend. Zoe managed to find the strength to ask what was wrong. The sobbing girl said that Mikel had an accident a few hours ago. He was hit by a car in Gower Street as he was walking home from University College. A student who witnessed the accident told her that he was conscious and talking when an ambulance finally arrived and picked him up. She was therefore shocked when a doctor at the hospital informed her that Mikel died on the way there, apparently from internal hemorrhage. Zoe wanted to scream but she couldn't. An *accident?* How convenient. She was confused. She wanted to explode. She felt as if the whole world was conspiring against her. She asked Suzan, no, she instructed Suzan to go home to her parents for a few days. That she would be safe there. She did not bother to explain why. Suddenly she was calm. The anger had gone. She was at peace with herself. As if in a trance she walked into her flat, went to the bathroom cupboard and took out various small plastic bottles and containers. She emptied the contents in her palm and started to swallow them. Painkillers, barbiturates, amphetamines, sleeping pills, anything and everything. It was a deadly cocktail. Her eyelids suddenly weighed a ton. She went to sleep before she reached her bed. Luckily for her, a few minutes later Suzan followed her, curious about what Zoe had said to her earlier. The door was still open and she saw Zoe lying on the floor. She called an ambulance. She saved her life.

Five weeks after her last ordeal Zoe began to attend group therapy sessions. She finally realized that she needed to share her terrible experiences with other people. She needed to get things off her chest, out of her system. She needed to be cleansed. That was when she met George. He was going through a bad patch. He was totally confined within himself, and he was suffering from chronic depression. George was around her age but very well built and athletic. He took part in the Atlanta Olympics of 1996 representing Britain in windsurfing. He was not amongst the medals but he was surely a world-class windsurfer. He had recently lost his treasured seventeen-year old daughter Janet in a motorcycle accident. He felt that his life had become meaningless. He raised his daughter alone, his wife having left them both when Janet was four. She had moved to France with her young lover and never heard from her since. He did not remarry. It did not take long for George and Zoe to be attracted to each other. Happiness born out of their misery.

Her past life now seemed light years away. She was happy. This was bliss she thought. If only they could stay on the beach forever. Still, they had another three days left. She stepped outside the caravan and made herself comfortable on a deck chair. The beach was deserted. Deserted and beautiful. She watched her lover's bright orange sail in the distance surf beyond the southern tip of the bay and out of sight. She did not like it when he ventured that far out but after a week she got used to his daily routine. It was just after seven in the morning and George would be back within thirty-forty minutes ready to devour a full English breakfast. She was in love and it showed, her mind racing forward to happy scenes of family life in an English country-house with lots of kids running about. She adored children and she definitely wanted her own. She was at an age where it was now or never. She started thinking of possible names and what their first day at school would be like. She closed her eyes and smiled, thinking happy thoughts.

A while later her thoughts were interrupted by the familiar rattling sound of an outboard motor-engine heard in the distance. She could see the old fishing boat coming into view around the southern tip of the bay, laboring towards the beach and the familiar figure with the large straw hat at the helm. She smiled. Old Mitsos, the local fisherman used to drop by every morning for a cup of coffee and offered Zoe first choice of the morning's catch before selling the rest to the local taverna at Calliope. And why not? The English couple paid well for fresh fish, especially for red mullet.

A short while later the old fisherman secured his boat, as he always did, on a mooring point on the beach about seventy-eighty meters away from the caravan. The early morning sun was behind him as the shadowy figure with the large straw hat walked towards the caravan. He seemed to have a spring in his step that morning as he waved to Zoe with his left hand, his right hand holding the fishing basket. The catch must have been good she thought. Zoe waved back and went inside the caravan. She quickly donned her bikini under her T-shirt. Maybe it was her imagination but the old fisherman seemed to take a much closer interest in her that was acceptable and she did not want to push her luck by being provocative. She liked him, but she also kept a discrete distance – just in case. She started to prepare the traditional Greek coffee for Mitsos. The old man loved his morning coffee and by the time he took to drink it and smoke a couple of cigarettes, she always managed to negotiate the price of the fish in her favor, or so she thought. His English was relatively good and she enjoyed a mild altercation with the man with the husky voice.

There was a gentle knock on the caravan door. Zoe, with coffee in hand turned round and opened the door with a smile. In a flash her jovial expression was replaced by one of perplexity and bewilderment. Her eyes widened, bulging out of their sockets, the hot coffee spilt all over her. She was in shock and felt no pain as the cold steel blade of a large kitchen knife plunged into her abdomen, again and again. She felt sluggish but tranquil as she fell to the floor and was slowly engulfed by a soothing darkness. At long last she had found eternal peace. Nothing and no one could do her anymore harm.

Chapter 7

'Pass the salt will you please Daphne?'

'Too much salt is no good for you. You are not twenty-one anymore. You are not even sixty-one.'

'Ah but you, you my dear make me feel as young as I've ever been.'

Sir Robert Ross and Daphne Porter were having their usual banter over lunch.

'I say, this is quite agreeable old girl.' Robert took another bite of food and chewed on it with obvious pleasure. 'If I didn't know better I'd say you've been attending cookery courses at Le Cordon Bleu around the corner.

'I have,' she said, 'but not in Marylebone Lane, in Sparta.'

'A Greek dish is it? Heavenly taste. What exactly is it?'

'Calamaria gemista.'

'Which is?'

'Stuffed squid!'

'Well, that has taken the stuffing out of it!' Robert grimaced with mock disappointment. He raised his wine glass. 'But I suppose it has its moments. I'll drink to whatever this is.'

'OK,' she said. 'You asked for it. This is how it is done. You take a few large squids, boil for five minutes. You make them dry, err, how do you say, strain them that's it, then you cut off the head and, and the, the little legs...'

'Tentacles?'

'Yes, that. You chop them into little pieces and make pilaf with them. Then you add crushed almonds, raisins, garlic and onion, a little Greek olive oil, black olives finely chopped after of course you take the stone out, a little tomato puree, a sprinkle of oregano and black pepper and the last, a generous portion of pure Greek feta cheese. That is what gives the good taste. You stuff all of these into the squids and close the opening with, with a cocktail stick and put in the oven for one hour, adding a little lemon and olive oil every fifteen minutes. You serve with boiled baby carrots and green salad. Now I will drink to that! Anything else? Cheers.' Daphne seemed pleased with herself.

'Amazing! My God, you are wonderful! I can eat this for hours.' He quickly showed his gratitude by planting a kiss on her.

'This Chablis is good,' she said pointing to the wine bottle, 'but with this dish you need to drink retsina. A real man's wine or ouzo may be.'

Before Robert could respond the phone rang. He picked up the cordless set.

'Hello?'

'Good day, sir. This is Stan from downstairs. Begging your pardon Sir Robert, for the intrusion I mean.' Stan was the long-serving cockney old porter at the building's main entrance. Robert often used to say that he'd been there longer than the building.

'That's OK Stanley, what is it?'

'There is this delivery lad from, err, let me see now, Dreamfood Pizza at the front door here and he says that you've ordered takeaway food. Shall I let him up Sir?'

'Takeaway food? Oh yes. Ask him what the order actually is.' Robert looked at Daphne. She was sitting motionless, listening and not looking surprised by the prospect of takeaway food arriving in the middle of their ongoing lunch.

'Yes, hold on a minute please, sir.' After a few moments Stan was back on the phone again. 'Well sir, according to this invoice, it is a large thin and crispy summer special pizza with extra mushrooms and olives. Is that the right one?'

'Thank you Stan, that is the right one. Send him up would you?'

Daphne got up and went to get her purse. 'It is a long time since we had one of these,' she said. 'They could have sent it a little earlier; it would have saved me all the cooking.'

'And miss your exotic dish? No way,' said Robert.

She opened the door, paid for the delivery and placed the pizza box on the table in front of Robert.

'Old habits die hard,' she murmured.

'What was that dear?'

'Oh nothing,' she said. '*Kali orexi!*'

He opened the box. The pizza looked inviting. He carefully lifted the pizza out of its box and found what he was looking for. A folded aluminum foil with a note in it. He read it. Suddenly his face hardened up, his appetite gone in a flash. His lower lip started to tremble, he was short of breath, he was also furious and it showed. There were tears forming in his eyes. He removed his glasses.

'What is it? You look as if a man just walked over your grave, like you have seen ghosts.' Daphne was alarmed. She hadn't seen him like this before. She got him a glass of water. He took a sip.

'I, I have…' his voice was breaking up, he quivered, his eyes flooded with tears and his head shaking, moving from side to side. Daphne rushed to him, embraced him and wiped his tears away with a soft paper tissue.

'What is it love, what have they done to you? What did that note say?' She kissed him on the forehead. She did not know how to console him. She was at a loss.

'I have never been a father to anyone,' he said swallowing hard. 'I have no children of my own, but, but I guess that this... this is how it must feel to lose one.' He gave her the note. She put her reading glasses on and slowly read it aloud.

Zoe murdered yesterday morning in LXS. Missing local fisherman implicated. Must meet ASAP. Gladys.' She looked at him, puzzled. 'LSX?'

'Don't ask. Please, don't ask anything. This is war. The less you know the better, believe me. If any harm comes to you because of me, I, I will kill myself.'

'But who...'

'No, don't ask.'

She persisted. 'Does this have to do with yesterday and the man watching you?'

'Daphne, you are the only *family* I have. Please don't.' He was polite, gentle but also quite uncompromising.

She started to clear the table. She was not at ease. She wanted to say something but didn't. She dropped a plate on the floor. *'Anathema se satanic,'* she cursed. She did not curse often but when she did it was always in Greek. Robert was lost in his thoughts. He seemed miles away, years away. He attempted to smile but tears filled his eyes once more.

'The masks are coming off,' he whispered. 'It is time to clean the house.'

'Robert.' Daphne could not hold herself any longer. 'I do not understand what this is about, but you are in pain. I feel for you and I worry about you. You are not a young man anymore. Please not do something you'll regret or start something you cannot finish. Please Robert. You scaring me, I worry.'

'I, my dear, have started nothing. I had no desire to start anything, but others obviously, have, did. It has nothing to do with politics or state secrets anymore. This is personal, very personal. It will go all the way. It is irreversible.'

'What on earth are you talking about? I, I never seen you this shaken before. I am afraid for you.'

'Don't be,' he said as he composed himself. 'It is like pieces of dominoes you know.'

'Dominoes? The game?'

'Yes, dominoes. Hundreds of them, thousands of little pieces, lined up, one behind the other. Places, events, people, all interlinked, all connected and yet not truly connected. All in harmony, balanced, defying the passage of time. Well, somebody knocked the first one over and it was not I who did it. What do you think it is going to happen?' Before Daphne had a chance to respond he carried on with his monologue. 'The whole damn lot are going to be knocked over. Every one of them, right down to the last one. Nothing and nobody will be left standing. Yes Daphne, dominoes and masquerades. It is time to remove the masks and look people straight in the eyes. There is a rogue unit in our midst. A traitor who wants me in the fray. Well, pick up the gauntlet I surely will.'

He looked at her standing in the middle of the dining room with dishes in her hands, silent, listening to him, looking totally confused and trying to make sense out of what he was saying. She finally spoke.

'Would you like a cigar?' She didn't know what else to say.

'Yes please, get me a torpedo.'

'A what?' She put the dishes back on the table and sat close to him. She held both his hands.

Robert finally smiled at her response. 'A Monte Cristo Number Two, on the lower shelf to the left.' he said. 'Commonly known as a torpedo because of its shape. And that is exactly how I feel right now. Ready to explode. Take the ship down. I'll have a brandy with it. I'll have a Greek brandy, one of your *Metaxas* Special and a Greek coffee. It looks as if I shall be going Greek for a while.'

Daphne was more puzzled than impressed. 'What shall I do with the pizza?' she asked.

'Throw half of it away, the other half give to Stan. He's a good man.'

'Robert, I never ask about your work. Not then and not ever. I never question you, I never doubt you, but this, this, how you say, this is different. I am worried. What is it? Who is Zoe and what is *LXS*? Who is this *Gladys* woman that keeps sending you messages with pizzas? Who was that man in the blue car yesterday?'

He looked into her eyes. She was strong but she was also worried. He kissed both her hands.

'LXS is the IATA code for Limnos airport. Something terrible has happened on the island.' Robert let go of her hands, got up and strolled around the room.

'Limnos? The Greek island?'

Robert was motionless.

'Gladys? Who is she? Should I feel jealous? Robert! Talk to me.'

He looked into her eyes. 'After what, seventeen years is it? You should know that I trust you with my life. These last few years you must have also realized that I love you more than my own life. You are all I've got in this ugly world and I want us to grow even older, together. Some things you need not know. Not now, later perhaps when this is over. And believe me it will be over, one way or another. Sometimes what you don't know cannot harm you.'

'All right, you know best.' Daphne was not convinced. 'It is just that you are not a young James Bond anymore. Not even an old James Bond. Just be careful.'

'That I promise. I also need to go away for a few days. Alone. If I'm suddenly gone, do not worry. I'll be in touch one way or another. Trust me.'

Twenty minutes later Robert was sitting in his antique chair in his front room staring out of the window. He had just finished his coffee and he was now enjoying his cigar and brandy. He was staring at the square below but he wasn't really looking. He hadn't even noticed the unusual movement on the pavement on the next street corner. His inner eye was looking at something completely different, his mind and soul being in another country, in another town, in another century. Two angels, two little girls with bright blue eyes smiling at him, laughing with him, chasing him around the room, asking him if he had brought them any *chocolat Anglais.* He could see their proud father playfully ticking them off, telling them to leave *Uncle Bob* alone, that chocolate was not good for their teeth. But he always had some chocolate in his pockets for the little angels. He felt bitter, bitter with himself. He felt inadequate, he hadn't done enough.

Ross finished his Metaxas brandy and puffed his Havana cigar. Brandy, French Cognac actually, was the favorite drink of an old friend from France that was no longer around. The distinctive flavour of his Monte Cristo cigar stirred his memory further. Distant images of Cuba entering his mind. His thoughts were now making U-turns, going back and forth. He cursed at himself thinking that he was becoming slow and senile in his old age. He cursed again and again. He was angry with himself but gradually he let his mind relaxed and mentally analyzed recent events.

Ross slowly realized that he should have picked up the signals that something was not right when Claude Duval, his old Surete friend and Hub collaborator apparently committed suicide in Paris a few weeks ago. He attended the funeral of the old friend who once saved his life and that was only the second time Ross traveled abroad since his retirement.

The first time was to the USA to attend the wedding of Zoe's twin sister, Alexandra. He had a few words with Claude's trusted aid and one of the last Hub conscripts, Jacques Petit, who under the grooming and guidance of Claude has now risen to second in command in the DCRI, the French equivalent of MI5. Petit told Ross that should he ever need anything in France to contact him. He had made a mental note to do so. Claude's death happening only days after two other trusted Hub collaborators in Cuba, Jose Guerrero, *Pepe* as Ross called him, and Domingo Ramirez were killed in a road accident with Pepe's eldest grandson at the wheel outside Santiago de Cuba, not far from Guantanamo U.S. Naval Base. Coincidence? Not bloody likely he thought. And now Zoe? What can she possibly have known? How was she implicated if indeed she was? Could her father have passed something on to her before his death? But she was only a kid at the time. Was it made known that his death was not an accident?

He was furious as images of Ian Coburn – alias Fabian Cabus, his closest friend and colleague filled his mind. He started to sweat. He had failed to see the writing on the wall. Zoe's kidnapping in Iraq must have been no freak random exercise. He was slow off the mark. But he was now going to put that right. Starting right now. He must contact Alexandra, Zoe's twin sister. He froze. Alexandra Coburn was Zoe's next of kin. What if she had already been contacted and was on her way to identify the body. She could also be in danger. He must also contact all the other living members of his old section. The *fisherman* mentioned in the pizza note could be no other than Cabus's old contact *Gitanes.* He must meet with Gladys immediately. Someone was *decommissioning* his old team. This was a total *deletion* exercise. But why? Why now? Suddenly he realized that he, too, must be a target. The next on the list perhaps.

An unwelcome event suddenly gave a new meaning to his life. Now he had a purpose, a mission. He put pen to paper and scribbled some notes. He then placed the note in an envelope, sealed it and phoned Stan, the porter and asked him to come up. A little later a surprised Daphne let the old soldier in the apartment.

'Good day Mrs. Daphne, the Guv'nor wanted to see me,' said Stan.

'Sir Robert? When?'

'He phoned me a couple of minutes ago.'

'Come in Stan,' said Ross who had just walked in the hall leading to the front door. Daphne retreated to her kitchen.

'Stanley, please take this letter round to the doctor's and make sure that you hand it to George personally.' Robert lowered his voice as if to give a sense of importance and secrecy to Stan's mission. 'It is sensitive and confidential, if you catch my drift.' He slipped a crisp ten-pound note into Stan's jacket pocket.

'Mom's the word Sir Robert. You can rely on Sergeant Stan Morrissey to deliver the goods.'

'Thank you Stanley and no need to get on the blower to confirm delivery. If for any reason you cannot find Dr

Clayton, please take the trouble to return the envelope to me, in person.'

'Loud and clear, sir.' Stan excitedly winked at Robert and was about to leave when Daphne showed up and handed him an aluminum food container.

'It was too large, the pizza I mean,' she said. 'No way could we eat all of it.'

'Bless you Mrs. Daphne,' said Stan. 'I'll enjoy this with a jar of bitter in a couple of hours when I come off duty. Bye for now.'

Robert watched Stan from his front room window go across the square and into Spanish Place where George Clayton, his doctor and friend of many years, had his doctor's practice as well as his apartment. He felt better. Things were set in motion. He picked his daily paper and turned his attention to the horse racing pages. There was an evening meeting at Windsor that day. Perfect he thought.

***

On a pavement at the corner of Hinde Street and Manchester Square a couple of telephone company engineers were working on underground cables. One of them had a phone plugged in on a board attached to the cables and was talking to someone. That someone was his *control* and was in a room above him, on the top floor of a building in Hinde Street. The control was peering through the half-opened venetian blinds, looking into Manchester Square, focusing his attention on the front door of the building where Robert Ross had his residence, no more than sixty yards away.

'There was no outward call made from the apartment to any pizza joint,' said the engineer on the pavement. 'Just the one to the porter a few minutes ago.'

'And the scanners detected no cellular call either. It must have been a drop then. Stay with it for another hour or so.' The control on the top floor turned to another man in the room who was zooming a concealed camera on Robert's front room window. 'Arrange with Field Ops for the deliveryman to be picked up by *SO13* citing the anti-terror yarn and have him taken to Paddington Green. I'll take it from there myself.'

'Anti-Terrorist Branch?' The operator with the camera was a little surprised. 'I thought we had specific orders not to involve home security forces, to keep Elle's thugs out of it.'

'We are keeping them out of it. We are giving them nothing. It is not the deliveryman I am after. I am certain he knows nothing. I want to ruffle the feathers of a bigger bird.' The control focused his large binoculars on Robert's third floor window. 'The rabbit across the road is obviously not alone. Whoever is feeding him information is probably still active in the service and, if he is, he should be of primary concern.' He turned round and faced his assistant with the camera. 'We have a mole somewhere. JMS will rapture his balls over this one.'

'What about the porter?' asked the man with the camera. 'He took a stroll to the doctor's after he was summoned by the target.'

'Our assignment is to observe and report on Ross and if need be intervene to prevent him doing an overseas runner. There's a different team monitoring the good doctor. Call Chapman and ask him to find out who manages the particular pizza branch. Better still let's get a run down on the whole staff, full profiles and records. I want to know the full works right down to what time they take their daily leaks. I hope Chapman did follow the delivery man.'

'Yes he did. The pizza store is in Wigmore Street. He called a few minutes ago to confirm it.'

'Good,' said the control. 'Let's pay them a visit. I fancy a free lunch. Don't you? Call for *eye* replacements, *pronto.*'

***

About half an hour after Stan returned, Dr George Clayton's old black Bentley pulled up right in front of Robert's apartment. Stan swiftly opened the passenger door and Robert, wearing white slacks and sporting a collarless black shirt under a navy blue blazer got in the car, holding his horseracing binoculars in clear view. He told Daphne that he was going evening horseracing at Windsor Park with the doctor and that she should not expect him back early. What she did not know could not harm her.

'Good luck Sir,' said Stan as the car drove off.

'I sure hope that you have a good enough reason...'

Before Dr Clayton could finish his sentence, Robert Ross signaled to his friend that he should keep quiet. Ross then turned the car radio on and placed a handwritten note on George's lap. George silently read the note:

"Let's keep the chat trivial. Your car may be bugged. Drive to Charlie's at Queensway."

The black Bentley headed westward in Wigmore Street and when it reached Seymour Street, just after the Marylebone Police Station, Ross signaled to Clayton that he should stop by a public telephone booth. He quickly got out of the car and made two phone calls: one to a restaurant in Bayswater, the other to a trusted friend. When he replaced the receiver he produced a pair of sharp pliers from his jacket pocket and while trying his best to be discreet, he severed the cable rendering the phone inoperative. As he was about to return to the Bentley, a car's horn began to sound continuously. Ross instinctively turned around and saw the driver in a dark blue car, parked about fifteen yards away across the road, slumped forward onto the steering wheel and seemingly unconscious. A policeman emerged from the police station further down the road and cautiously walked towards that car. Ross hurried back to the Bentley and gestured at George to step on it. Ten minutes later they parked in Bayswater's Queensway in front of *Kowloon Palace,* the posh Chinese restaurant owned and managed by a larger than life friend from the past. Charlie Chow.

'It has been quite some time since we've had the pleasure,' said Chow as he personally greeted the two men. 'Usual table?'

'Hello Charlie,' said Ross as he firmly shook hands. 'I am getting old my friend, George is losing his hair as well as his teeth and you, you are getting, well, larger!'

'It's the wife,' said Chow. 'She feeds me all the time. That is how she keeps tabs on me. With this body how far can I go?'

The three men had a good laugh as Chow escorted them to a table away from the front door.

'What was that all about?' asked George once Chow went away. 'Back at Seymour Street?'

'Poor chap must have fainted,' replied Ross. George was not entirely convinced but did not press the point any further as Chow showed up again and handed each of them a menu. He also gave Ross a wine list.

'I strongly recommend the wine of the day on page three,' he said meaningfully. 'It goes perfectly with Cantonese duck.'

Ross leafed through the wine list and saw an attached note:

"The car is at the back. Olive green MG number 208. Untraceable accessories under the seat."

'That would be fine,' said Ross. 'We'll have a bottle. I'll visit the gents while George decides on the order.' He turned and looked at his friend and smiled. 'Take care of things George, would you? Thanks old friend.'

Chow retrieved the wine list and followed Ross at the back of the restaurant and guided him through the kitchen towards a back service door where they could have some privacy.

'You didn't give me much time but all's ready. What is it boss?' Chow looked genuinely worried.

'I have no idea,' replied Ross, 'but it looks as if someone is trying to erase all traces of our old section, including its living members and their relatives. And, I am talking about people that no one knows they even exist. People like yourself.'

'But who and why?'

'SIS most likely but I cannot be certain. Why? I intend to find out. Look Charlie, take good care of yourself and be alert. There may be a passive probe on your doorstep or we may have been followed here. Either way be prepared to face some flak from the spooks, may be sooner than later. If they push you, I need you to buy me some time. Then give them the car. Nothing else.'

'Don't worry, I can handle these amateurs. Here's the jacket and cap.' Although Chow returned to normal life after Ross was retired and was living the good life in London's Bayswater, he still yearned for some action and was missing the good old days.

'Please do look after George if things turn sour, would you? He is out of his depth here.'

'Don't worry. Where will you go?'

'A safe house to begin with so I can recollect my thoughts,' said Ross. 'I'll contact you when I can. Thanks Charlie.'

'Yes, do that. Anything I can do. Go, go, go now and do call me. Good luck!'

Ross quickly removed his navy blue summer jacket replacing it with a white one. He transferred his leather cigar case, wallet and passport from the old jacket to the new and donned a black baseball cap. He then went out the back service door that led into Inverness Mews at the back of Queensway and got into the MG that was parked there. The ignition key was in place. He retrieved a plastic shopping bag from under the seat. There was a cell phone with a sticker attached to it that referred to the PIN code, and a wad of currency notes, pounds and euros. There was also a hand pistol, which Ross instantly recognized as a Chinese made double action 5.8 mm QSZ-92, a firearm almost exclusively used by China's Military Intelligence, the PLA. He instinctively checked the ammunition and the safety lock. He then removed the battery from the mobile phone. Good old Charlie he thought. He knew he could rely on him. There was no turning back now. He was on the run. Literally.

Chapter 8

Ross left Bayswater driving the MG west towards Shepherd's Bush and as far as he could tell he was not being followed. However he had to double check. When he reached the Holland Park Roundabout he went around it twice ensuring that he had no tail on his back before he headed for Goldhawk Road. He glanced at the time. Ten minutes past three. There was adequate time to make the three-thirty rendezvous with Gladys, a rendezvous fixed earlier when he made the calls from the public booth. At Goldhawk Road he turned right into Lime Grove where he found a parking place. He sat in the car for a while, his eyes meticulously sweeping the area around him, looking at passing cars and pedestrians, searching for that little something, that little clue that would give away anyone that could be tailing him. Nothing.

It was almost three-thirty. He placed his leather cigar case along with his wallet and passport in the plastic shopping bag with Chow's *accessories*. He then took off his white jacket and black cap and placed them in the boot of the car along with the ignition keys. He had no intention to return to the car. He walked to the end of the street clutching the bag in his hand and before he turned left at Goldhawk Road he took a last look at the MG and the surrounding area. Nothing out of the ordinary. What he could not see was the small tracking device that was inconspicuously attached beneath the car. Under the railway bridge just outside Goldhawk Road train station across the street, Ross spotted a tall slim man, with a cigarette in his mouth. He had thinning grey hair dressed in blue denim trousers and jacket. He was standing there, apparently browsing at a copy of the Sporting Life. Their eyes made contact and Ross discreetly nodded in acknowledgement. This was no blind date. He then casually walked around the corner into the busy Shepherd's Bush Market and went inside a café. He knew that this was probably the last time that this trusted rendezvous location would be used. His eyes instinctively scanned the room. His last visit there must have been a good few years ago. Not much had changed. The air felt more *breathable* as the no smoking campaign was gathering ground and the smell of greasy food was not all that apparent as extractor fans were now in full use. The place was small and crowded with frequenters, most of them old, taking a break from their shopping perhaps. There was also a table with three lads in their teens, two of them sporting Chelsea football shirts while the third wore a QPR football shirt. They seemed engaged in deep, serious football talk. Ross smiled. Some things never change he thought.

The café appeared to be staffed by a skinny man in his thirties behind the coffee bar and a somewhat younger waitress wearing a miniskirt that left little to the imagination. He found a free table at the far end of the room from where he could clearly see the entrance door. He ordered black coffee and placed Chow's plastic bag on the empty seat next to him. Although there was a large no smoking sign on the wall, he held a cigar to his nose, smelling it with obvious pleasure. Suddenly the waitress approached him and politely pointed out that smoking was not allowed in the premises. However he could have a quick cigarette if he wished as long as he stepped to the back of the café near the window.

'I suppose cigarettes are better for everybody's health,' joked Ross.

'What can I tell you,' replied the smiling waitress. 'I only sniff coke!' She winked at him, then giggled and went to get his coffee.

'I was born half a century too early,' he whispered to himself.

A few minutes later the man in the blue denim outfit walked into the café and went straight to Ross who stood up and greeted him.

'Am I glad to see you old chap,' said Ross as he warmly shook his hand. 'It has been some time old friend.'

'Hello Bob, nice to see you too,' said the man. 'It has been too long if you ask me. Five, six years? Anyway, time seems to have been kind to you.'

'Oh, I don't know about that. You don't look too bad yourself.' Ross was just being polite. His friend looked tired and pale and much older than his age. His grey eyes were almost lifeless. 'What will you have?'

'The usual please.' He started to cough, a deep chesty cough.

'You could have something stronger if you wish,' joked Ross.

'Excuse me. An old chest cold. Something stronger you said? Thanks but no thanks. You know me. I haven't changed, still teetotal! Tea and a scone would be fine.'

Ross rested the plastic bag on his lap and ordered. The two men sat there and just looked at each other for a moment or two. Although they had kept in touch, one way or another, they hadn't actually met, face-to-face, for over five years. The other man placed a cigarette between his lips but did not light it. He coughed heavily before he spoke again.

'I do have my vices, as you very well know.' He pointed at the cigarette. 'These will be the death of me,' he added. 'Remember that.'

'I should have convinced you long ago to turn to Havanas old boy,' said Ross.

'On my salary? A little late in the day for that I'm afraid. Anyway. Let's talk shop.'

'Yes, let's, but one thing at a time,' said Ross. He held his hand up, gesturing to his friend that he should wait a moment. Knowing how softly spoken the man was, Ross adjusted his hearing aid accordingly. 'Despite your earlier comment, I am not getting any younger.'

'Come on Bob, it is me. You know you don't need that.' Ross ignored the remark so he carried on. 'Look, Bob, I am sorry about Zoe,' he said somberly. 'Terrible. Thank God her poor dad is not around to bear witness to this atrocity.'

'We'll come to Zoe in a jiffy. But first tell me. What the hell is going on Gavin? What have you managed to find out?'

'It has only been a day since Daphne left the message on my answering machine regarding the surveillance so I don't have much to go on.'

'Come on now,' snapped Ross. 'Twenty-four hours is more than enough for Gladys and all the resources at your disposal.'

'I am afraid Gladys is dead!'

'What do you mean,' asked a puzzled Ross.

'I was officially retired six weeks ago, quite unexpectedly, really and without warning.' Gavin Addice alias Gladys, a close friend of the deceased Fabian Cabus, Hub collaborator and ex-Intelligence Officer with the DIS section of the Ministry of Defence, smiled coyly and shrugged his shoulders.

'What? Why? Who authorized it?' Ross was stunned.

'What difference does it make? Now, I mean. However, I believe that...' Addice cut his sentence short as the waitress approached their table. She served the tea and scone.

'Oh I'm afraid you cannot smoke that in 'ere Sir,' she said pointing at the cigarette Addice was holding.

'Don't worry sweetheart,' said Addice. 'I'll smoke it when I get out in the open.'

'Sorry Sir, I don't make the rules. Silly, but what can you do? Can I get you anything else?' she asked smiling.

'Another coffee for me please,' said Ross. 'Black.' He paused for a second till the waitress left and faced his old friend. 'You believe what?'

'Nice legs!' said Addice observing the waitress as she walked away. 'The barman is not too bad either,' he joked. He then turned to Ross. 'I was going to say that I believe Bishop was directly behind my enforced departure from the MoD.'

'Eleanor Bishop? The Director-General of MI5?'

'Yes, the lady herself. Fucking bitch!' Addice was being laconic and enigmatic. Also it was not like him to swear in a vulgar way.

'That's it? No explanation?' Ross gestured his bewilderment at him. 'What are you holding back Gavin?'

'You know I have no secrets from you. Let us not waist time on me. You are the one we should be discussing.'

'Fine,' said Ross. 'What can you tell me? After more than three decades in the service I am sure you have an abundance of sources at Millbank and Vauxhall.'

'Whatever it is, it must be very hush-hush. Just scraps of information doing the rounds on the rumour-mill. A clue here, a word there. Nobody's in the know for sure and those that may know something remain tight-lipped. Only rumours.'

'What rumours?' Ross was getting impatient and Addice seemed reluctant to respond. 'Gavin, what fucking rumours?' He said that louder than he wished and a few heads turned around. He lowered his voice. 'Well?'

Addice finished his scone and sipped some tea. He then drew an imaginary drag from his unlit cigarette, coughed some more and then looked Ross straight in the eyes. 'The word is that you turned. That you are working for the Chinese.'

'What?' Ross didn't know whether to laugh or cry. 'What a load of horse manure!' He then shook his head in annoyance. 'I have access to nothing. Don't they know I am retired? What am I supposed to have done?'

'You've opened Pandora's Box! All hell is breaking loose.'

'Can you be more specific? Please, Gavin.'

'You are selling what you know to the PLA and they in turn use the information to blackmail our own.' Addice dished the rumor out with a dose of apathy, thus registering the fact that he did not really believe any of it.

'What do you mean by *selling what I know?* What exactly?'

Addice crashed the unlit cigarette in his tea saucer, moved closer to Ross and lowered his voice. 'The British Government's illegal black operations over the last thirty, forty years.'

'No kidding! Such as?'

'Paris, Lockerbie, Iraq, Sakhalin, Saudi, illegal accounts for funding terrorists, assassinations, military support to rogue states and dictators, Gaddafi, Saddam. Shall I go on?'

'Lockerbie? The Pan Am flight that exploded over Scotland? What does that have to do with the price of butter? This is bullshit. What a farce!' Ross was losing his composure, he was angry. 'Does this have anything to do with Zoe and the others?

'What others?'

'Claude Duval and our Cuban friends died recently? Did you know that?'

'I knew about Duval but not of the Cubans.' Addice took a deep breath. 'That's not all,' he said. 'As I have mentioned in my note, Dimitri Vlahakis, your fisherman, is missing, accused of murdering Zoe, his own godchild, how preposterous! Totally outlandish, and, if that wasn't enough, *the Ferret,* Christos Leonardou washed up on a beach in Crete a couple of weeks ago. He was shot once in the head at close range. The right temple. A professional hit.'

Ross was stunned for the second time inside five minutes.

'I had a feeling that the *fisherman* mentioned in your note was *Gitanes*. But the *Ferret*? My God! They had both long retired before I did. I talked to both of them on the phone recently, during the Greek Easter holidays. Why? Christos said he would be sending me a present, a package, the contents of which would make a lot of people lose a lot of sleep...' Ross was flabbergasted. Then realization set in. 'Oh my God! Is this why he was killed?'

'You talked to them? On the *phone? Any phone?'*

Ross was not listening. His eyes were beginning to water. 'They are blaming Mitsos, our *fisherman* for Zoe?'

'*Mitsos?'*

'It is a local pet name for Dimitri. A suspect for Zoe's death? Poppycock! If he's missing, he's dead you know. Unless he's gone to ground on the Holy Mount.'

'We had a young operative in a monastery up there, did we not?' Ross said nothing. Addice frowned and then leaned forward, close to his friend. 'I've got to ask you this Bob. Are you involved in any way? Is there any truth in the rumours?'

Ross said nothing once more. He was being overwhelmed with emotions of anger, emotions of nostalgia for his friends and associates, emotions of bitterness for Zoe's death. He had failed her as he had failed Ian, her father. He felt uneasy. He seemed a million miles away.

'No. There is no need to reply. I am sorry I asked.' Addice patted his friend on the shoulder. Then he placed another cigarette between his lips, followed by the usual coughing. 'Filthy habit, I know but if I cannot smoke in a public place I will pretend I do so. Be sure that whoever is behind this will eventually accuse you of being responsible for the deaths of our old friends. It ties in well with the rest of the plot.'

'What are you saying Gavin? What plot?'

'Well, several of our ex-associates died under questionable circumstances in the last few weeks.' The ex-MOD Intelligence Officer was carefully choosing his words. 'At the same time the story on you was being leaked, ingeniously circulated and you were placed under surveillance. Yes, I may have had a few question marks, because you and you alone had the whole picture of our covert network. You've set it up. However all doubts were instantly evaporated yesterday morning, following Zoe's murder. I knew she was like a daughter to you. You could never harm her. Not her and not her sister. Their father was like a brother to you. You cared so much for Zoe that you did not even visit her in hospital during her horrible ordeals. You did not want to implicate her in any way. You kept away.'

'But you didn't. I still have my sources and I know that you've been to see her in hospital. That you have helped her, financially. That was a bad move.'

'She was helpless. I did it in the spirit of friendship, out of respect to her father.'

'I know,' said Ross. 'Do not think that it was easy for me to do nothing. But the killers may have made the connection, discovered her real identity and that was what really got her killed. Did you ever consider that?'

'The thought did cross my mind,' said Addice. 'And if that is the case I have to live with it. And, die with it. But they, whoever *they* may be, were on to her long before that. The abduction in Iraq and most of what followed was obviously orchestrated. But what were they after?'

'That is what I intend to find out.' Ross was quite emphatic.

'Ian Cross.'

'Ian Cross?' Ross looked at his friend with a puzzled expression.

'Special Branch. He works at Millbank.'

'MI5? What about him?'

'Remember the name. I believe this is the man that can shed light on Zoe's death, Bob.' Addice drew a long breath before he continued. 'He visited Zoe in hospital and later quizzed her at Millbank. About her ordeal in Iraq.'

'Why?'

'I don't really know. However I do know that this guy belongs to Scargill. MI6,' said Addice meaningfully.

'The SIS Director and close friend of the PM?' Ross shook his head, a million thoughts flooding his mind. He seemed somewhat lost. He felt somewhat unsure about things he thought he was sure about.

'I have not been entirely open with you Bob. I was afraid of what you might have done. There are things that I should have told you before, thoughts that kept me awake at night and haunted me during the day. I am referring to the demise of a dear friend to us both. But...' Addice turned his attention to his unlit cigarette for a couple of seconds, toying with it and then looked Ross straight in the eyes, as he always did when he wanted to make a point. 'Maybe that was what triggered this off.'

'I am listening.' Ross was feeling uneasy. There was something that bothered the old intelligence legend but he could not yet fathom what it was. Tiny drops of sweat were beginning to form on his forehead. Maybe it was a premonition on what was about to be said.

'I suspect that the reason I was fired from my post had something to do with my recent probing in classified Home Security and SIS reports and files regarding the Pan Am crash at Lockerbie, a few days before Christmas in 1988. Can you remember who was responsible for counter terrorism at the time?'

'My God,' said an astonished Ross without thinking twice. 'Eleanor Bishop!'

'Eleanor. She was involved in the investigation and was instrumental in influencing the then Director of SIS and the Prime Minister to lay the blame squarely on Libya. The killing of the policewoman, a few years earlier, outside the Libyan Embassy in London was still a painful memory. She didn't have to try all that hard.'

'But Libya was guilty. They conceded to the fact years later and paid compensation for bombing the plane, didn't they?'

'Yes they did, but whether Libya was actually guilty or not is not the issue here. Our own intelligence suggests that another country was involved.' Addice was being

122

enigmatic once more. 'Libya paid compensation in order *to buy peace* as they put it. To enable Gaddafi to return to the international community, at least for a while. Gaddafi is now relaxed and he will be caught off guard with, supposedly, revolutionary rebels. Not really *rebels* but armed gangs which we and the yanks are currently funding.'

Ross was not completely following his friend's train of thought. 'But, where's the connection? With what's happening now I mean.'

'A few days before I was fired, I managed with the help of *Joe 90*, a trusted friend, a computer whiz kid, to break into well protected MI5 and Special Branch computerized files kept on The Hub and its official dismantling. There was also an appendix file requiring additional security clearance on one Robert Ross. Only Bishop and her Deputy Director have access to this appendix.' Addice stopped talking expecting a reaction from Ross. A reaction that did not materialize. He cut his cigarette in half and threw it in his tea saucer. He cleared his throat before he carried on. 'Do you understand what I am saying?'

'So the MI5 kept and keep records on me. I would have been surprised if they hadn't. My own existence was not all that secret towards the end, neither was most of our work. Home security did get to know about us. When Blyth became Prime Minister he made us obsolete and you know why he did that. Our field operators and overseas collaborators on the other hand, yes, they should not exist. Again, where is the connection with Lockerbie?'

'Your file also incorporated data on two other names. Fabian Cabus and Arantxa Abasolo.'

'My God! NO. They knew about Ian? Is this how they got to Zoe?' Ross began to tremble. Panic was setting in.

'No. No mention of Zoe or Alex. No mention of kids. Not in that file anyway.'

'Arantxa? My God! Is she OK? I've got to warn her. She has the dossier on Blyth. How could they know about her?'

Gavin Addice lowered his eyes for a second or two. He evaded the question for he knew that Ross used to be very close to her. He also knew that Arantxa had what was described as a fatal house accident a few days earlier. Her house was burnt to the ground, with her in it. He sighed and carried on. 'Fabian was on to something. He apparently uncovered something of horrendous enormity and magnitude regarding the actual bombing of the Pan Am plane. He had also conveyed his conviction that there was a traitor in our midst, but needed more time to be sure. You were in Spain at the time, so he contacted me instead. He asked me to urgently check on some facts for him and a meeting was set up. We were supposed to meet a few days later, here, at this place.'

The ex MoD intelligence analyst moved even closer to his friend, cleared his throat and carried on. 'He wanted to confide something to me and share some serious concerns. He thought that all the information he had gathered led to an unthinkable conclusion. He wanted to explain his thinking process and data analysis that led him to believe what he believed. But alas! He never made it. He was on his way to me, in his female disguise, when he ended up under the train. He was definitely on to something and I believe that what he eventually uncovered cost him his life and possibly the life of his daughter, Zoe years later. His death was no accident. He was coming to meet with me when he was killed. Murdered. Accident my arse! I should have briefed you on this back then, but I was afraid you'd act irrationally, being Fabian I mean.'

Ross listened but said nothing. He was staring into empty space. He seemed oblivious to everything and anything around him. This was the third time he was stunned inside twenty odd minutes. He was one very short step away from total shock. His breathing gradually became heavier, his heart was pumping faster, much faster than he would have liked. He could not control his thoughts. His lower lip began to tremble. He removed his glasses and rubbed his eyes. He did not have the mental strength he once had. He was not a young James Bond anymore. Daphne's words hit home. He was reaching breaking point. Anger turned to suspicion. He felt betrayed, he was being set-up, framed, but by whom? And why? He felt entangled in a web of conspiracy. He could trust no one. He felt threatened, like an animal being cornered. He put his glasses back on and picked up his coffee cup. It was empty. He suddenly realized that he had not been served the second cup he ordered. He looked around for the waitress in the mini-skirt but could not see her. Where was she? He was furious. He waved his empty cup at the man standing behind the coffee bar, ten yards to his left.

'She's forgotten my coffee,' Ross shouted angrily. 'Well? Where the fuck is she?' His eyes were on fire and he had a *do not fuck with me* look on his face. He was taking no prisoners.

Suddenly there was an eerie silence in the café. Over a dozen pairs of disapproving eyes were staring at him, turned on him like blinding interrogation lights. He felt hounded, cornered. Images of a previous life coming back to him, being chased, hunted in a jungle somewhere in Africa, eons ago. His brain overloaded. His vision began to blur. He couldn't breathe. He felt paralyzed. God! Was he poisoned? Was there something in the coffee? He was not going down without a fight and he was definitely not going to be taken alive. His right hand slipped inside the plastic bag that was resting on his lap. He could not think clearly.

The barman, taken by surprise by the outburst, managed to stutter a reply. 'I, I am so sorry sir, she, she forgot, she, she err went off duty. Her replacement, she will err, get your co-coffee, now. It is coming.'

The barman was stuttering. This is no speech impediment thought Ross. The barman was nervous. Very nervous. He was hiding something. *A replacement waitress was getting his coffee?* He swiftly turned to Addice and spoke with some venom.

'Gavin there is something wrong here. Were you followed? Tell me, were you followed?' Ross felt for the gun inside the bag. He released the safety catch on the Chinese QSZ-92 and positioned the index finger of his right hand on the trigger.

'Calm down. No, of course I was not followed,' said Addice as he nervously looked around the room. Gladys was never a field operator. He was not a man of action. He delegated the action but never took part. He was more analytical, more administrative. An intelligence data collector and feeder, an analyst. However he was experienced enough to lose a tail if there was one.

Ross hissed angrily at Addice. 'Get up! We must leave, right now.'

At that moment an austere-looking middle-aged woman with ice-cold eyes was suddenly approaching the table. An assassin? Ross was about to point the gun in the woman's face when she spoke.

'I am sorry, sir. Kate must have forgotten your order. She was in a hurry to go home I suppose. What can I get you?'

Ross was in a daze, motionless, sweating and speechless. His eyes fixed on the woman, his sweating hand still gripping the gun inside the bag on his lap.

'Sir? Are you all right?' Still no response from Ross. She then looked at Addice.

'Yes he's all right now thank you. He's had a rotten day. Get him a black coffee please and I'll have another tea. I am sorry about this,' said Addice. The woman attempted to smile and went away.

'Bob. Bobby, snap out of it. You are making a spectacle of yourself.' Addice gripped his left arm and shook it firmly. He wanted to placate him. Ross slowly moved his head up and down and took a couple of deep breaths.

'I am sorry. Sorry Gavin. I don't know what got over me. I'm all right now.' Ross secured the safety catch on the gun and placed both hands on the table. 'Let us finish our drinks and go, shall we? I need some fresh air and time to think.'

'We also have a lot to talk about.'

'Yes. Yes, we do,' said Ross as he repeatedly filled his lungs with air. He placed the plastic bag on the floor by his feet and suddenly stood up. He held his hands up and looked around him at the people in the café.

'My apologies,' he said aloud. 'I am a couple of years short of seventy. My wife is sixty. We have been married for forty years, and suddenly this morning she decides to leave me for a man ten years her junior. My pride was hurt. I must have had a drink too many earlier on. Once more I apologize for my inappropriate behaviour just now. God bless you all and may you never experience such a misfortune.' He sat down. The Rolls was back and rolling again.

'You should thank your lucky stars mate,' said an old unshaved punter at a nearby table. 'I've been trying to get rid of the missus for as long as I remember, but no such luck!'

There were a few laughs and some more banter amongst the customers in the café. Order had been restored.

***

Alone in a sterile office room located at one of the underground levels at Vauxhall Cross, the imposing edifice housing the Headquarters of the British SIS, Director James Marlow Scargill was busy talking on a secure phone.

'If he turns into a shadow or, worse still, if he manages to flee the country, you'll spend the rest of your miserable life in Afghanistan, counting raindrops and collecting camel shit. Have you got that?' He listened for a while. 'Shake them down. Invent whatever story you want and find out how he got out of the restaurant. He must have a collaborator there. Also put pressure on the doctor. You have twenty-four hours.'

There was a knock on the door. Scargill finished the call, got up and unlocked the entrance to the room. The burly figure of Raymond Wise, his trusted aide and bodyguard appeared escorting a man in the room.

'Thanks Ray,' said the Director.

Wise left closing the door behind him. The man that was shown in was dressed in a dark blue suit. His name was Ian Cross, a Special Branch Officer assigned to MI5.

'It is almost nine o'clock. I expected you earlier,' said Scargill as he ushered Cross to a sofa. 'What have you managed to find out?'

'What? No coffee?'

'Talk,' said Scargill abruptly. 'We don't have much time.'

'OK,' said Cross and shrugged his shoulders. 'I had to await the outcome of the tests. It looks as if your man was taken out on Seymour Street by one of our own.'

Scargill's eyes widened with astonishment. 'What are you saying?'

'Robert Ross is protected by MI5. To be more precise, Elle Bishop is keeping him alive. That much I can say with certainty.'

'Why?'

'I have no idea,' said Cross. 'But one thing I am sure of. It was a professional hit and by that I mean by an outsider. Probably imported from the Far East.'

'Ballistics proved that?'

'Yes. Five-point-eight millimeter pointed bullet.' Cross leaned forward towards the Director. 'A single shot to the right temple from close range. One Christos Leonardou an ex-Greek air force officer was shot in an identical manner recently. Probably by the same person.'

'The ferret? *Ross's ferret?* I don't believe this.' Scargill got up and paced around the room. He had an elastic band between his fingers, which he turned and twisted as he always did on those rare occasions when he felt nervous and unsure. He stopped in front of Cross who was still sitting on the sofa. 'How sure can you be that this was the work of MI5?'

Cross leaned back in the sofa and smiled. 'Elle hushed up the killing,' he said. 'She had her thugs at Marylebone Police Station bullying the local bobbies within ten minutes of the shooting. She ordered a complete clean-up operation and media shut-out, in the interest of national security as our American friends would say!'

'Leonardou. What's the connection? What's MI5's interest in him?'

'My sources tell me that he was about to send a hot package to Ross when he was taken out on a local ferry off the island of Crete and then dumped overboard. That info was of primary importance to Elle. However the package was never retrieved. Bishop's rage went off the charts. A few heads rolled, some quite senior.

'MI5 took the ferret out?'

'It seems so.'

'What was the package about?' Scargill's anxiety was increasing by the minute. The elastic band snapped between his fingers. He cursed.

'I don't know. What I do know is that Leonardou aroused Bishop's interest from an intelligence report suggesting that he acquired damaging information regarding the death of a certain Fabian Cabus and the bombing of the Pan Am plane over Lockerbie. That was back in 1988, the two incidents a few days apart!'

'Cabus? Ross's *mistress?* God Almighty! What a fucking mess. It is worse than I thought. The bitch is playing spy games in our own manor.' Scargill said nothing for a few moments. He just stared at his planted mole within MI5 as if he was sizing him up. He then instructed his developing prodigy. 'All right Ian. Try and find out why Bishop is apparently protecting him, if she really is. I want to know what she's after. This whole exercise is backfiring.'

'I could take a long look into Eleanor Bishop's dirty laundry if you wish. I know some people who may be encouraged to talk.'

'Do that. Discreetly. Try to keep costs to a minimum this time will you? Even I have difficulties accounting for *non-disclosed* expenditure."

Ian Cross got up and held open both his palms.

'Ten thousand? You have fifteen but I want the full works *A-S-A-P*. I want to take the bitch out. She's not really interested in Ross. I have a gut feeling she's after me and the Prime Minister!'

Ian Cross was neither daunted nor impressed. He simply shrugged his shoulders once more and without saying another word got up and was about to head for the door when he paused. He turned round and faced Scargill. However he said nothing. A change of heart perhaps as to what he was about to say.

'What is it?' The Director sensed this and pressed on the point. 'Well?'

'Since you are so generous, this information is for free.' Cross paused again.

'Yes, I am still here,' said Scargill.

'I think I know who *Gladys* is and it is not a she but a he and he's closer to home than you think.'

'Well?'

'Gavin Addice. A senior MI5 officer within DIS at the MOD.'

'You *think*?' Scargill was intrigued but wanted proof.

'Bishop fired him recently. He was prying into her past and she found out. But most importantly, for you I mean, he was also very active in counter intelligence information gathering during the days leading to the invasion of Iraq as well as being involved with plans to overthrow Gaddafi in the coming months.'

'Iraq? Libya?' The Director of SIS suddenly sounded and looked concerned.

'Yes Iraq and the *real* reasons behind the US and British intervention. That could implicate ex-Prime Ministers, the present Prime Minister, as well as yourself.'

Scargill felt as if he was kicked in the balls. He also felt like kicking his mole in the face but promptly ignored his last remark and pressed on, ignoring the Iraq implication. 'Yes, but how sure can you be that this Addice chap is Gladys?

Cross smiled cynically. 'It is so simple it is ingenious. His full name is Gavin Lovell Addice. When he was at school, he used to sign his name using the initials of his first two names before his surname. G L Addice. Phonetically, *Gladdice!* The rest of the boys in his class were soon on to him, so much so, that his mother transferred him to another school.'

'Where he dropped his middle name I suppose. So much for our Mata Hari theory,' said Scargill. 'Thanks Ian.'

'You are welcome. I am sure you can access his file at the MOD. Make the transfer to my Lux account. First thing tomorrow.' Cross turned round and left.

A few moments later the Director of SIS was on the phone again.

'Ray, a change of plan. Cross should be leaving the building soon. Now's the time to give him his cancellation documents. Then come back here. There is something else we must do. It is going to be a long night.' A few moments later he was dialing 192, the directory enquiries number.

Chapter 9

After they had left the café in Shepherd's Bush Market, Ross and Gavin Addice each bought a daily travel card from Goldhawk Road Station and boarded the Hammersmith and City Line. This was the first time they defied an age-old tradition of not being seen together in the open, of not catching different trains from different stations, following a pre-arranged meeting at the market café. It was not that they were careless, but nothing seemed to matter anymore. They were out of the closet, out in the open. Their adversaries, whoever they were, were on to them by now. As if the dismantling of their previous lives were not enough, they were now deleting their retired ex-colleagues. They were mopping up.

The two men spent a couple of hours traveling on the London Underground. They were not really going anywhere but they needed to talk, often changing trains. Ross was taking no chances. He knew that any would be listener would have a hard job documenting their conversation amidst the noise that is associated with a moving underground train. A good part of the time was spent discussing the events surrounding the deaths of two dear friends. Fabian Cabus and Christos Leonardou. Zoe's brutal murder was discussed but as this was very recent, Addice did not have much information. Recent international events were also discussed. Addice did most of the talking, close to Ross's ear. Ross was taking mental notes. A *talented* hairdresser was also mentioned. A business card changed hands.

At Goodge Street Station in Central London they parted company after a warm and rather long shake of the hand. A little earlier Ross had suggested that they should somehow keep in touch. However, he had a bad, gut feeling, that Addice was saying goodbye. Gavin Addice stayed on the Northern Line and headed northward towards Burnt Oak where he lived alone in a single-bedroom bungalow. Ross got off the train. At street level outside Goodge Street Station he turned left and then left again into Tottenham Street. He followed the back streets leading towards the general direction of the British Telecom Tower, still clutching the plastic bag with Chow's accessories.

The weather was changing, dark clouds rapidly covering the early evening sky. It would not be long before the fresh breeze would bring the first raindrops. A summer shower loomed ominous. Ross suddenly felt cold. Cold and curiously lonely. Within a few minutes he hurried past the imposing Telecom Tower and walked into an old block of flats on Clipstone Street. He used the keys Addice gave him earlier to enter a specific apartment on the third floor. This was a safe house that was privately funded by Addice himself. No official record of it existed anywhere. He would spend the night there, recollect his thoughts and plot the next course of action.

The two-bedroom apartment was very modestly furnished. The living room window was facing BT Tower. For some reason Ross always referred to it by its original name, the GPO Tower. Different times, different games. A strange, if not a bold location for a safe house he thought. With dozens of security cameras in the neighborhood, the possibilities of being caught on video as well as the possibilities of eavesdropping from the Tower must have been countless. However he did trust Gladys. He had to. He drew the curtains halfway across the window and snooped around. There was no working telephone line in the flat but there was a small television set, a refrigerator and an electric kettle. Ross scoured the kitchen cupboards and was relieved to find what he was looking for. Coffee!

A few minutes later, with coffee in hand, he made himself comfortable, sinking his body in an old armchair in the small living room. He thought about lighting up a cigar. He decided against it. He realized that he had nothing to eat since he left home. It had already been a long day. He felt tired but sleep was not an option. Not yet. He had things to think about and things to do. Addice had entrusted him with useful information. Information that would help him comprehend what was happening to him, what has happened to his old section associates and what might be expected to happen in the future. Information that might, just might, keep him alive. Some of it was hard fact and some conjectural. Hypothetical or not, it had to be very close to the truth. On-going international events and rhetoric from the leaders on both sides of the Atlantic proved the point. Addice was a master in data handling and information analysis. He removed his hearing aid from his left ear and leaned back, deep into the old armchair, half-closed his eyes and thought about his conversation with the legendary Gladys. Too much data had been given to him. He felt very tired but he had to mentally process the information and make sense of it all. He was lost, deep in thought.

Suddenly he was shaken by the sound of what he felt was a loud blast and then another and another. A series of light flashes filled the darkness around him and then more blasts and more flashes. He momentarily froze. Gunshots? Where was he? He could not see anything. He jumped to his feet and soon realized that he was in the safe house. He went to the window and looked outside. A summer thunderstorm in all its glory was taking place. The dark sky was being dissected by lightning, the spooky silhouette of the Telecom Tower switching on and off with each flash. He secured the window and closed the curtains. He switched on a lampshade that was on a table next to the armchair. His cup of coffee was still there. Untouched. He instinctively looked at his watch. He couldn't believe it. It was five-fifty in the morning. He must have dozed off for the best part of six hours. He felt somewhat stiff. He stretched his body as he always did after a nap. Daphne! She must have been expecting him back from the races a long time ago. She must be worried to death. Unless George, George! Is he all right? He panicked! What a fucking situation he thought. He was not a young James Bond anymore. He realized that he could not go through with this alone. He had come to terms with himself that he did not have the mental nor the physical strength he once had. He needed help and he needed it fast. Help he could trust. Nick Porter sprung to mind. Daphne's son. However he was in Geneva and he needed to get out of the country undetected. He dare not use any of his own passports. New travel documents were urgently required. Addice had given him a trusted contact, a contact that would be expecting him first thing in the morning. A contact that he could trust one hundred percent. He trusted no one, one hundred percent, not even himself. But what choice did he have? He retrieved a business card from his back pocket. He looked at the name on the card.

'MICHEL – HAUTE COIFFURE'

Addice had told him that this unlikely contact could and would help him with just about anything, including a new passport. Ross was getting a hairdo first thing in the morning. But first a hot shower followed by hot coffee was required. He checked the small cupboard in the bathroom. There was a full set of toiletries and disposable shaving razors. Good old Gavin, he thought.

***

The striking blond woman with the dark sunglasses, dressed in black slacks and a tight fitting black blouse was the first to emerge through the automatic sliding doors that separate the luggage collection room and the main arrivals and departures area at Limnos Airport on the little Greek island in the Northern-East Aegean. She had arrived on the early morning domestic flight from the Greek capital of Athens and as this was an internal destination there was no immigration control. She had no luggage other than her small *Hartmann* mobile traveler. She hurried through the exit doors, totally ignoring a handful of taxi drivers outside who were touting her for a ride into town. Without breaking her stride she headed for the parking area, no more than sixty meters away from the main airport building. Her eyes were now scanning an area to her right, focusing on a light green VW Beetle with its engine running. As she approached the car, the driver, an attractive woman with an athletic figure and jet-black short-cropped hair, got out of the car and warmly embraced and kissed the arriving passenger on both cheeks. The two women looked at each other for a few seconds before they got in the car and drove west towards Myrina, the picturesque seaside capital of Limnos.

***

Ross frowned and grinned somewhat as he splashed a generous dose of Old Spice aftershave on his freshly shaven face. He went to the living room and turned on the television set. He zapped through the channels till he found one with the early morning news. He felt much better after a much-needed hot shower. He made himself another cup of coffee. It was still far too early to venture outside. He had to buy some clothes and visit St. Christopher's Place just off Oxford Street, where Michel had his hairdressing salon.

Daphne was an early riser. He decided to risk calling her. He was about to connect the battery to Charlie Chow's mobile phone when he felt a cold chill go up and down his spine. He felt short of breath as his eyes caught a glimpse of what he thought was the picture of a familiar face on the television screen. The TV set now had his full attention. A young female news reporter was now reporting on something or other from a street pavement while onlookers were being ushered away from the scene by police and firemen. A house appeared to be half-burnt. Ross quickly fitted his hearing aid to his ear and adjusted the TV volume.

'...a neighbour has already told the police that the deceased was a chain smoker and a heavy drinker. He appeared to be extremely depressed since his recent retirement from the civil service. Police say they have no evidence of foul play. A cigarette was the most probable cause of the fire. Gavin Addice was not married and he lived alone. Back to you Anna.'

Ross seemed unable to move. He wanted to scream but couldn't. His relaxed face was breaking into spasms and sweat drops were forming on his upper lip. He just stood in front of the TV, as if in a trance, his eyes fixed on the screen listening to the studio anchor reporter, mechanically, narrate the next news story.

'The drowned man found floating in the River Thames near Vauxhall Bridge last night has now been named by the police. He is Ian Cross, a civil servant. Medical documents found on his body certifying that he recently tested positive for HIV suggest to the police that he may have taken his own life...'

Two blows in quick succession. Ross was about to scream and take a wild kick at the television set but, as if by magic, his early life training and life-long experience took control of his mind and body. His eyes turned steely and his face hardened. He went into a *sixes* mode, a succession of slow deep breaths. His thumping heartbeat reversed to normal. In less than a minute he was transformed from a kind and helpless old gentleman to a cold-blooded ruthless killer and conniving underground operative. The *Rolls* was now in command of his mind, body and soul. He switched the TV set off and headed for the shower. Again. But this time what he needed was a cold shower. Forty minutes later he was out on the street.

Chapter 10

Iphigenia Nicolaou, *Efi* to her friends, sat patiently at a table beneath the shade of a palm tree in the front garden of the Castle Beach Hotel in Myrina enjoying her *frappe* coffee. She was looking at the hill five hundred meters to her left, home of the imposing ruins of the eight-century-old Byzantine era castle, built on the pre-existing Pelasgian Walls overlooking the sea. She was killing time by trying hard to spot one of the deer that roam the hill freely. No such luck. She guessed she was too far away. She then looked straight ahead, letting her gaze wander towards the west, far across the sea at a point in the horizon where the blue summer morning sky seemed to caress the deep blue water, embracing it, becoming one with the Aegean. A truly beautiful sight she thought. She felt relaxed. She removed her sunglasses and looked again, focusing harder this time. She could just about make the faint outline of Mount Athos on the Halkidiki Peninsula on mainland Greece in the distance, some thirty-forty miles away. Suddenly she felt uneasy. She shuddered. Her face twitched, her patience seemingly gone. She quickly looked at her watch. It was just after nine-thirty in the morning. She instinctively looked behind her and saw the blond woman whom she met earlier at the airport walk towards her with a smile.

'I'm sorry Efi. I just had to have a shower.' Alexandra Coburn sat next to her friend. She looked stunning dressed in a long blue summer dress with an open back.

'Don't even think about it Alex,' said Efi, returning the smile. 'You have been traveling for almost a full day.' Efi became a little concerned as she studied Alexandra's dress. 'That is a beautiful dress. However, don't you think that something simpler and black would, perhaps, be more suitable? For today I mean.'

'I thought about it but I am not mourning yet. Not until this is over, one way or another.'

Efi smiled. A reassuring and affectionate smile. 'That's fine. We still have plenty of time before our appointment at the hospital. Have some coffee will you? It will do you good.'

'Thanks. I'll do that. I'll have an espresso, *frappe* lasts forever in Greece!'

Efi summoned the waitress and ordered. She then reached out and held Alexandra's hand before she spoke. 'Are you ready for this? It is not a pretty sight.'

'Nothing is pretty. In fact it is going to get uglier, I can assure you.' Before Efi could respond, Alexandra carried on, the harshness in her voice not gone unnoticed by her companion. 'Look Efi, let us get the identification formalities over and done with and then let's sit down and talk. Exchange ideas. Plot our next move.'

'Yes, we must do that.'

'I know where I stand with my sister, but you must be worried to death. You know your dad is probably dead, murdered, don't you?' Alexandra was more sympathetic now.

Efi's eyes momentarily watered as she looked away from her friend and towards Mount Athos in the distance.

'Either that or he's gone to ground, hiding out there on the *Aghion Oros.*'

'The Holy Mount?' Alexandra's eyes widened with anticipation, and hope. '*Dum spiro spero.* I hope he did manage to get there, for our sakes as well as his.'

'If he's there, he'll get word to me. It has only been forty-eight hours…'

Efi stopped talking as the waitress served Alex her coffee.

'Charge whatever we had to my room please,' said Alex.

The waitress looked at Efi, as if awaiting a confirmation.

'You can buy me coffee when I come to America,' said Efi as she handed the waitress a ten-euro bill. '*Efcharisto Katerina.*'

'*Ego efcharisto kyria Iphigenia.*' The waitress thanked Efi and left.

'You seem to be popular. Unlike your namesake, the notorious *Motor Vessel Iphigenia!*' said Alex.

'Well, it is a small island and I am a doctor and my husband is the county coroner. As for the good ship *Iphigenia*… her time will come. Vindication is around the corner.' Efi then frowned, her expression hardening somewhat. 'You know, no person on the island really believes that my father killed Zoe. Only the police officer in charge seems to think so and I am sure that he has been definitely influenced by that British Embassy man who arrived from Athens yesterday.'

'What's his excuse for being here?'

'A British national has been brutally murdered and another is missing.' Efi shook her head in disbelief. 'Normally it is the next of kin who requests embassy assistance when something like this happens overseas…'

142

'I certainly requested nothing of the sort and as far as I know Anderson has no next of kin,' said Alex.

'People like him are probably recruited early on, from orphanages…'

'Either that or serving long jail sentences and are given a way out.' Alex smiled at her friend before she carried on. 'Regarding Mitsos, I could put the record straight once and for all but that would blow us away. I don't suppose they know that your father was-*is*, Zoe's Godfather, do they?'

'Not even my husband knows that. What's the point…'

'The fact that the *lover* has also disappeared seems to leave the police unimpressed from what you've said on the phone.' Alex looked at Efi in the eyes, her composure beginning to desert her as she raised her voice in obvious anger and frustration. 'Really, what are they saying about *him*? Do the police know who he *really* is?'

'Alex, shh… easy now. Not here. Later. Finish your coffee and let us go.' Efi sounded uncompromising, yet she felt uneasy as she looked around her, perhaps to see if anyone was eavesdropping on their conversation. There were a few men looking in their direction from nearby tables. Efi thought, or rather hoped, that they were more interested in Alexandra's looks than in what the two women were saying.

Tears began to flood Alexandra's eyes. 'They've got the *wrong* sister,' she said sobbing. 'They've got the wrong sister…it should have been me…me! It's all my fault. I should have been there for her.'

'How can it be your fault? Alex, please. Don't do this to yourself. I need you to be strong.' Efi hugged her and Alexandra cried.

'They will pay Efi, they will pay.'

'Sure they will. You have my word.'

Alexandra suddenly sat up straight and used a paper tissue to wipe her beautiful blue eyes dry. She finished her coffee before she spoke.

'Do you have the coroner's report? Perhaps I can have a quick look at it before we get to the hospital.'

'I am afraid you can't have it. Not before formal identification of the deceased.' Efi sounded sympathetic as well as apologetic.

'But the coroner, Stelios, he is your husband Efi!'

'The report is written in Greek. It has not been translated yet. Anyhow, I wanted us to play this by the book. I do not want anyone to say that we have bent the rules in any way for obvious reasons. At first, the police and the British Embassy man, especially the Embassy man, wanted to fly in an independent coroner for the autopsy, citing personal emotions, family involvement and conflict of interests and all that bullshit. After all, the main suspect happens to be the coroner's father in law. But Stelios kicked up a fuss and the hospital administration supported him, with some major help from the Health Ministry in Athens. We had to pull a few strings.'

'In the light of what you have said, I guess you did the right thing,' said Alex. 'At least we know that the autopsy results do tell the truth.'

'It is more or less as what I told you on the phone.'

'Can you give me some more details? Please Efi.'

Efi sighed and held her friend's hand. 'Why do you do this to yourself?'

'I, we, have to piece the puzzle together. Every scrap of detail helps.'

'Fine. Cause of death from severe hemorrhage from at least five stab wounds in the abdomen by a large kitchen knife. Six inch blade. The murder weapon was at the scene of the crime.' Efi had gone into her doctor mode. 'The liver was punctured twice. Zoe probably fainted from shock before she passed away, so she did not suffer.'

Alexandra's blue eyes were now on fire, angry and she was ashen-faced. She retrieved her hand from her friend's grasp. Efi was mildly startled.

'Are you all right Alex? Are you sure you want me to carry on?'

'And the rest of it. All of it. The bit that will not become public knowledge.'

A reluctant Efi continued. 'The killer then cut open both of the victim's breasts as well as her vagina and rectum.'

'He was looking for something wasn't he?' Alex sounded distant and cold.

'Yes, he probably was. However, it was done in such a way that most people would think that this was a sex attack by a deranged person. A psycho. And it almost fooled the police...'

'Till the idiot from the Embassy turned up. What is the incriminating evidence? From what you said on the phone, there were no finger prints on the knife.'

Efi sipped her iced coffee and then opened her handbag and retrieved a packet of non-filter *Gitanes* cigarettes. 'This is the main evidence,' she said. She took one out and started to smoke it.

'Efi, I'm shocked,' said a surprised Alex. 'I didn't know you smoke!'

'Neither did I! But I do now. It is only the second day.'

Alex pressed on. 'What about the cigarettes?'

'A couple of cigarette butts, Gitanes, were found on the floor of the caravan as well as my father's straw hat. Everyone on the island knows that Mitsos smoked this brand for years.'

'What? Is that all?'

'Plus the fact that he has not been seen since. Also, his fishing boat was moored on the beach not far from the caravan with the day's catch still on board.'

Alexandra was not convinced. 'So we are led to believe that your dad killed my sister and then he made sure that everyone knew he did it by dropping cigarette butts near the body, leaving his straw hat behind and his boat moored on the beach. Morons!'

Efi simply nodded her head in agreement and grinning in disbelief.

'What about this Anderson character? He's also disappeared.'

'Yes, he's vanished but his sailboard was found yesterday afternoon, damaged and entangled in some rocks a couple of miles away from the caravan.'

'Has it been forensically checked?' enquired Alex.

'I wouldn't raise any hopes on that front. However, we've had some interesting developments last night, regarding Anderson' said Efi. 'Apparently he had purchased a ferry ticket the day before from a travel agent here in Myrina for Thessaloniki. The ferry sailed from Myrina at one-thirty in the morning. A good six or seven hours before Zoe's murder.'

'What?' Alexandra was astounded, bewildered. 'Was he on board? Was the ticket used?'

'We don't know yet. We are coming into the high season for tourism. Things are a bit hectic with the ferry lines. Police are looking into it. We should know soon.'

'But even if there is proof that the ticket was in fact used, there is no way to guarantee that Anderson was actually on the ship. Right?' Alexandra's mind was working overtime. 'Do they match I.D.s against the name on the ticket for domestic ferry destinations?'

'No. Not really,' said Efi.

'Could Zoe have been murdered earlier? Were there any early morning flights into Limnos from Thessaloniki that morning?'

'I have been torturing my brain over these same questions.' Efi shook her head. 'No early inbound flights that morning and Zoe definitely died sometime between six and nine. Stelios is pretty sure about that. She was found just after ten o'clock by Petros, a young boy who usually asked the couple if they wanted fresh baked bread from the village. He would bike into Calliope and back and they would tip him.'

'Was the crime scene tampered in any way before Stelios got there?'

'It is hard to say,' said Efi. 'But I can tell you this. As of this morning I have a few friends, scuba divers, checking out the rocky area and the numerous underwater caves along the southern tip of the bay, the *Kavallaris* area. Something might surface.'

'But, shouldn't the police do that?' Alex was more astonished than angry. Efi smiled at her.

'Look Alex, this is Limnos. An out of the way small island with about 20,000 people. It is up to us to solve this. The police will give the verdict they will be instructed to give. Do you understand what I am saying?' Efi took a deep breath and extinguished her cigarette. 'If only I knew she was on the island. If only… if only my dad would have told me.'

'How could you have known? The last time you spoke to her must have been over a decade ago.' Alexandra suddenly stood up. 'Come on. Let us get it over with. Also, I would like to meet with this British Embassy man. Check him out and see what he is up to. I have a feeling that he is a drone and his controller is somewhere in the corridors of power, probably the upper echelons of the British Government.'

'*Echelon* is a dirty word here,' joked Efi as she stood up. 'But if you want to talk shop, I also think that the embassy man is probably a *playback operative,* sent here to misinform and confuse the situation.'

'Bury the truth you mean. Well, we'll be waiting for him on the other side of the fence.' Alexandra's helplessness was suddenly replaced by motivation, her sweet girl appearance giving way to a hardened and determined professional.

'That's my girl!' said Efi.

Well? Who is this man? Is he young? Old?'

'He is around sixty, I think. His name is George Webb.'

***

Ross, donning a pair of dark glasses and a blue jockey cap, courtesy of Gavin's wardrobe, kept his head down and consciously avoided looking up as he leisurely walked in a westward direction along the length of New Cavendish Street. He wanted to avoid Oxford Street and the scores of security cameras. There were not many people out and about at that early hour. It was a bright morning but the streets were still wet from the storm of the previous night. Ideally he should have ventured out an hour or so later. But he could not confine himself in the safe house. Not for another minute. He was like a lion in a cage. He had things to do. He would, however, return to the safe house. He decided to leave the plastic bag and all of its contents there, including the Chinese hand pistol. He would meet the hairdresser and then buy some clothes.

A few minutes later he turned left into Welbeck Street and then went across Wigmore Street and into St. Christopher's Place, a one hundred and thirty meter long paved alleyway with a variety of shops, restaurants and cafes. Its other end connected with Oxford Street. Ross knew the area well as it was in very close proximity to his apartment in Manchester Square. He felt uneasy as he subconsciously lowered his blue jockey cap.

Halfway into the alleyway, he spotted Michel's Hairdressing Salon to his right. He casually walked passed it. A tourist, checking out the shops. It was still closed. He looked at his watch. It was eight fifteen. Adjacent to Michel's there was a café that was open and had tables outside on the pavement. He was hungry. He picked a table with a vantage point and sat himself down under an umbrella. He removed his dark glasses but not his cap. He put on his gold-rimmed bifocal reading glasses. Before he had a chance to look at the menu, a youngish blond waitress that looked as if she just got out of bed was on top of him with pencil and paper.

'Good morning Sir. We have breakfast special with two eggs, bacon, baked beans and grilled tomato, oh and two toast with real butter. English tea or French coffee. You like?' She recited that almost mechanically with a heavy central European accent.

'Real butter eh? What happens if I wanted three pieces of toast?' asked Ross smiling.

'I am sorry?' The waitress seemed puzzled. 'You like the special or you want from the menu?'

Ross realizing that the young lady was not in the mood for friendly banter, presumably because of not enough sleep – or the lack of it altogether, immediately succumbed to the *special*. 'The special is good, with coffee. Black coffee please. Thank you.'

She looked at Ross for a second or two, then at the number on the table, scribbled something on her pad and turned away without saying another word. 'Thank you very much,' he whispered to himself as he discretely scanned the area around him. He was not actually familiarizing himself with the area, which he knew well but was scanning the area for faces, trying to spot something out of the ordinary.

By this time the sun was drying up the wet streets and although the morning had been crisp, it was beginning to warm up. The number of people going about their business was increasing by the minute as Central London was gradually waking up to a sunny July morning. Still, there was no apparent life in Michel's salon.

'Coffee, sugar and milk,' said the waitress as she served Ross.

'No milk, thank you. I drink my coffee black.'

'Your coffee *is* black, no? What is the problem?' She was taking no prisoners.

'What I meant…' Ross held his hand up and added. 'Never mind. No problem. Yes, it *is* black thank you.' The young waitress shook her head in annoyance and was about to turn away when Ross spoke to her again. 'Excuse me! Where are you from? If you don't mind me asking, that is.'

'European Union,' she said flatly, eyeing the customer with a suspicious look on her face. 'Why do you ask? Something wrong?'

'No, just curious. Your accent sounds familiar that's all. Where in Europe?' Ross was beginning to wonder why he got involved in such a conversation in the first place.

'Poland. And you?'

'I'm from England. I live here. You've been here long?'

'Six months in London, five months working here. What do you do? You are police or taxman? Immigration?'

'No, no, not at all. I am, err, I am a writer. I write books,' replied a reassuring Ross. 'My name's William.' He managed a smile.

'I am Paulina. William, eh? Like William Shakespeare? I thought maybe you are an American.'

Ross raised an eyebrow. His smile had gone. 'Why in heavens did you think that?'

'The English, they only drink tea, no?'

'Well I am English and I am a coffee person,' said Ross as he warmed up to the girl. 'Tell me, Paulina, do you happen to have any of this morning's newspapers available in the premises?'

'Newspaper? Yes. Do you want to read?' She leaned forward, lowering her voice. 'My boss buys the Sun. He likes page three. Shall I get it for you?'

'The Sun?' Ross was mildly shocked. 'No, no that's OK, thank you.' The waitress was about to turn away when Ross, once again, spoke to her. 'Just one more thing…' He did not finish his sentence as the Polish girl suddenly snapped at him.

'Please. I am busy. Also, even you are nice man, I think you are too old for me! I am only twenty-four you know.' She turned round and vanished into the depths of the café. Ross was left staring at empty space, hoping that other customers on nearby tables did not hear what was said. *How easily can one be misunderstood* he thought. Twenty-four? He did not think so. She looked a bit older than that. Five minutes later Paulina returned with Ross's breakfast. 'More *black* coffee?'

'Yes, please,' said a wary Ross. When she returned with the coffee, Ross tried to explain himself. 'Look, my dear, I was not implying anything, I simply wanted to ask…' He was cut short again.

'I know, I know. You are making chitchat. But if I talk too much with customers, I lose my job. My boss is Italian! What do you want to ask? My phone number?'

Ross was at a loss. He did not know what to make of this young girl. Maybe he was out of circulation for too long, he thought.

'No, no. I am too old for you, remember? I just wanted to ask if you know what time the hairdresser, next door, opens up.'

'The hairdresser? But, that is for ladies only, no?' Her face flushed somewhat and appeared to grin with embarrassment. 'Oh, I am sorry, now I understand. It is *Michel* you want. He has many older friends. *Men* friends. Some like you! He comes around nine. I know because I serve him a glass of milk and a chocolate croissant, every morning.' She giggled and left.

Ross shook his head in disbelief and then tucked into his breakfast. Thirty minutes later a tall, tanned, balding flamboyant man in tight white pants and a loose blue shirt with a pink silk scarf around his neck, was unlocking the front door of Michel's salon. A few minutes later Paulina was on her way to the salon with Michel's breakfast. She winked meaningfully at Ross as she went passed him.

'Well, they do say it takes all sorts...' Ross was whispering to himself and allowing himself a smile. Paulina was on her way back when he gestured at her that he wanted to pay.

'Four fifty,' she said as she readily handed him a receipt.

Ross gave her five pounds, got up from his seat and faced the girl. 'Was that Michel, the owner?'

'Yes and he is expecting you right away Sir Robert.' She said that in a low voice and in a perfect London accent.

Ross was stunned. 'Do hurry, will you and good luck!' she whispered.

He moved forward, in a state of confusion and muttered a thank you to the waitress.

'Have a nice day sir. Please come again.' Paulina reverted to her foreign accent once more and went about her business.

Chapter 11

Sir Robert Ross was sat in the old armchair back at the safe house recollecting his thoughts from the extraordinary meeting he had earlier in the day with an extraordinary man. A meeting that lasted for the best part of three hours. Michel was definitely not what he seemed. He was an intelligent covert operator recruited, years ago, by Addice and trusted by Addice. Ross had no choice but to trust him too and trust him he did. Paulina, the young waitress in the café next door to his salon, was working for Michel. She was his niece.

The hairdresser appeared distressed over Gavin's death but said that he did expect it. Gavin had confided in him that his days were numbered. He recently said to him that he did not know what or who would get to him first. The lung cancer from which he was suffering or the dark forces, as he called them, within the British Intelligence Services? He was snooping around, asking questions that annoyed certain people. He was getting close to the dark forces and their agendas. Yes, Michel was definitely distressed with Gavin's death but he did keep his composure. He had to. Apparently he and Gavin Addice had been lovers for years. Ross was not really surprised. He suspected that Gavin was homosexual.

Ross had his hair dyed a light shade of brown and an optician summoned by Michel measured his eyesight and later supplied Ross with dark brown contact lenses. He had to get used to them for he was doing away with his gold rimmed glasses. No more blue eyes. Photographs were taken for a new passport, which Ross was to pick up from Michel late in the next day along with a flight ticket for the South of France, plus a hotel reservation. Richard Alexander Taylor, born in Manchester. A name that he had to get used to. A name that he had to use from hereon. Sir Robert Ross ceased to exist. He was not impressed with his new initials that spelled RAT. Michel either had a very dry sense of humor or he had good reasons for putting this name forward. At least he was kind enough to make him a few years younger. Michel also gave Ross something else. A valuable and trusted contact in the British Embassy in Athens. He assured Ross that he would get solutions to the puzzle from this contact.

He suddenly got up and looked for Chow's plastic bag. He inserted the battery into the mobile phone and dialed a number.

'Daphne? Is that you old girl?' Ross embraced himself for the expected response.

'Robert! My God! Where in heavens are you? Are you all right? My God Robert! Do you know what I'm going through? Are you safe? Robert, what is happening? Robert, talk to me. Are you all right?'

'I am all right my love. I am sorry I could not...' Ross was interrupted by Daphne, the austerity in her voice not gone unnoticed.

'How dare you do this to me? You are gone missing one day and one night. What am I supposed to do, or think? I cannot think. Nothing. George phoned me to say that he was arrested for God knows what and that he is, he was asked... err how you say, interrogated about you. What is happening? Talk to me Robert. Do you hear me? Are you there? Hello?'

'Yes, I am still here. Look old girl, they've got nothing on George. They will have to let him go.' Ross paused for a few moments, choosing his words carefully. 'Daphne, listen to me. This is something I have to do. I cannot talk for long. Do not worry, I will contact you soon. I am in Belgium. If you are asked anything by the police, tell them what you know. You have nothing to hide.'

'Belgium? In Europe? What is in Belgium? Robert, please…'

'I'm thinking of you. See you soon.' Ross did not wait for a response. He disconnected the call and removed the battery from the cell phone. He then took a piece of paper and started making notes.

***

A distraught Alexandra and a comforting Iphigenia walked out of the main doors of the Myrina Hospital and were heading across the road where Efi's green VW beetle was parked. Alexandra had just formally identified her sister's body at the hospital morgue. She did not handle it as well as she thought she would and wanted to head back to her hotel. As they were about to get into the car a speeding motorcycle screeched to a sudden halt next to the two women. A young man in swim shorts and a lose shirt removed his helmet and looked at Efi who immediately recognized him. He was one of the divers that were searching the Kavallaris area.

'Antoni? What is the matter?'

The man took a deep breath before he spoke. 'I am sorry Mrs. Efi. Your phone, the phone is switched off. I came as soon as I could.'

'Antoni, talk to me. Did you find something?' Efi's concern was growing by the second. She tried to prepare herself for the worst.

'I am sorry. We found your dad. He's dead Mrs. Efi, he's dead.' It was now the turn of Alexandra to comfort her friend. She hugged Efi, wiped her eyes and took over.

'How?' she asked. 'Where?' Antonis not knowing who Alexandra was looked at Efi. She nodded.

'In one of the caves at Kavallaris. He is tied to a rock underwater.' He paused and breathed hard again. 'Mrs. Efi, someone killed Mitsos. His throat is cut. I am sorry.'

For the first time since this ordeal begun Iphigenia Nicolaou lost her composure. She let out a scream and then buried her sobbing face in Alexandra's arms. They both cried. Two women emotionally drained by a sudden and unjust loss. Two women entangled in a web of deceit and political conspiracies. Two women unwillingly acting the part in a book that was written by dark and twisted forces, that linked years gone by with the present in a very uncompromising manner. A past that had nothing to do with the two protagonists, a past that was unknowingly inherited and a present that is being forced upon them by invisible, grey and emotionless people who are daily playing with people's lives on a political chess board, supposedly for the protection of the realm and in the interests of national security.

***

Two levels below ground in his personal sterile office room at Vauxhall Cross James Marlow Scargill, the Director of the SIS was listening on a secure phone. The fingers on his right hand were busy, turning and twisting an elastic band. He was listening, saying nothing, his facial expressions motionless. The elastic band suddenly snapped in his fingers and he snapped into life.

'When you get the nod, do it right. No lose ends. Do what you have to do and you go up two notches. Georgy, fuck up and you are on your own. You know the rules. Make sure you are at the location tomorrow.' He did not wait for the response. He disconnected the call and instantly dialed an internal number.

'Ray, summon our fat friend. Find a busy public place near Arnos Grove Station tomorrow night at eight sharp, within proximity of your target. We'll go together, we come back separately. Have the girl taken the moment she comes off work tomorrow afternoon and do what you have to do.'

***

About fifteen hundred miles south-east of Vauxhall Cross in Myrina, the capital of Limnos Island in the northern Aegean, George Webb sat in the back seat of a taxi inconspicuously parked opposite the main gates of the Myrina Hospital observing two women in grief drive away. He had just finished an overseas telephone conversation with his boss. He knew what he had to do. He tapped the cab driver on the shoulder, handed him a crisp one hundred euro note and asked him to find out what the young motor cyclist had said to the two women. He then stepped out of the taxi and casually walked to the seafront.

At the same time, some thirty miles west of Myrina on the Holy Mountain on the Halkidiki Peninsula on mainland Greece, a monk from the St. Panteleimon Monastery had also just finished an overseas telephone conversation. He would be making arrangements to visit the island of Limnos the next day.

Chapter 12

Sir Robert Ross, alias Richard Alexander Taylor, walked out of the Perpignan Llabanere Airport in the South of France and headed towards a car park nearby. He was accompanied by an employee of a car rental firm.

'*Il s'agit de votre voiture, M. Taylor. Avoir un bon voyage,*' said the car rental man as he handed him the car keys and the relevant documentation.

Ross thanked him in French and got into his blue Renault Twingo. He placed his small cabin luggage on the passenger seat and pulled out a local road map. Fortunately for him he got used to wearing the contact lenses without too many problems. He allowed himself a few moments to familiarize himself with the controls of the car and he mentally reminded himself that he had to drive on the *wrong* side of the road. He then drove off, heading north on the motorway towards Narbonne and Montpellier.

It was late afternoon on a warm July day. He wanted to reach his destination before dark. His brain was working overtime, thinking what he had to do, where he was going and why. Michel had been more than helpful. In addition to his new passport and new driver's license, he supplied him with a credit card under his new name with a ten thousand pounds spending limit. He also gave him clean, unmarked cash money, ten thousand euro in large denominations and asked him to hand over the cash Chow had given him. Precaution. Michel also advised him to leave the handgun at the safe house, to put the battery back into the mobile phone and leave it under the seat of a bus a few hours before he headed for Stansted Airport. Precaution again. Ross took a liking to this flamboyant character. In fact he respected him for his professionalism. Addice had recruited well. He therefore followed Michel's instructions to the letter. So far.

Before he reached the town of Narbonne, Ross left the E15 motorway near Sigean and took the coastal road for the small picturesque town of Port-la-Nouvelle. One hour after he left Perpignan he parked the rented car somewhere in a side street off the Avenue de la Mer near the port. He switched off the engine and scanned the immediate vicinity. It was getting dark but there were plenty of people walking about. A few of them were entering a fish restaurant directly across the road from where he had parked. He spotted a half-lit neon sign of a hotel further down the road. He retrieved some papers from his luggage and looked at them for a minute or two.

Port-la-Nouvelle was not really a town. It was more like a village with a resident population of less than seven thousand. However, being at the height of the summer season it seemed a lot more crowded. The nearby sandy beaches did attract tourists. The place was better known for its relatively busy commercial port and its imposing grain silos. Michel had made a reservation for him at the Hotel Mediterranee in the tourist area in the Boulevard du Front de Mer. He was not going there. Precaution. Never trust anyone one hundred percent. His early life training was gradually coming back to him, guiding him, protecting him. The legendary Rolls was rolling once more.

Ross took his hand luggage and walked to the hotel down the road. Annie's Hotel was the name on the sign. It was small and more like a bed and breakfast joint than a hotel. It suited Ross fine. The lighting at the small reception was dim. At the reception desk sat an attractive dark skinned woman in her mid-forties. When he approached her he could not help but notice her stunning green eyes.

'Bonsoir Monsieur. Bienvenue,' she said smiling.

'Bonsoir,' said Ross returning the smile. 'Do you speak English?'

'Yes, I speak a little English. How I can help you. You need bedroom? For one people?'

'Yes I do,' said Ross. One room for two nights please.'

'Please give passport. It is 160 euro for two nights but please pay before. Breakfast downstairs from seven until ten. Sorry but no room service and please Sir no girl in the room from outside. Sorry.' She smiled.

'I am too old for girls... from outside.' Ross smiled back at her meaningfully as he handed his passport and the money. 'Where are you from, if you don't mind me asking?'

'I am born from Marseilles but mother from Senegal and father from Catalonia.'

'That then explains why you are so beautiful,' said Ross. 'Your English accent is very sweet, just like you and your eyes. They are divine.' The woman blushed a little as she handed Ross his passport and the receipt for the room.

'Merci. Your room is number 33 on floor three Monsieur Taylor.' She handed him the key.

'Your husband is a lucky man. You are married I assume?' As soon as he asked the question he felt uneasy and he was about to apologize.

'He *was* lucky but also not lucky. He died in automobile accident two years ago. *C'est la vie.'* She grimaced.

'Oh I am so, so sorry.' Ross felt genuinely embarrassed. 'Please forgive me, I did not mean to intrude…'

'No worry Monsieur Taylor.' She smiled at him and he felt better.

'Thank you… miss… your name?'

'Mariama, but my friends call me Marie.'

'Well goodnight Marie. I am tired so I will stay in. Where can I get some water to drink from?' asked Ross.

'There is fridge with mini-bar in room Monsieur. Also television with BBC World Service channel and CNN if you believe Americans. Goodnight.'

Ross smiled and went for the elevator. Mariama was indeed an exotic beauty he thought. The room was small and modestly furnished but adequate. The window faced the front road where the entrance to the hotel was. He opened it and popped his head outside. He could see his car parked in the distance, opposite the fish restaurant. He looked inside the mini-bar refrigerator. There were several bottles of Evian water, some soft drinks, juices and two half bottles of white wine. The brand was unknown to Ross but it was local wine. He decided to have a glass and his hands instinctively reached for his cigars in his luggage. However the large 'No Smoking' sign on the door restrained him. He sat in the only armchair in the small room and took a sip. Not bad he thought. It had only been three days since the pizza delivery with the message from Gladys regarding Zoe. In a curious way, Zoe's murder had given him a new lease of life. A purpose. He did miss Daphne's company but at the end of the day he thought that was a small price to pay. He wanted to call her but he was afraid that the phone call would be traced to his hideout. His stomach started to make funny noises. He realized he hadn't eaten much since the snack he had at Stansted

Airport. He looked at his watch. Almost nine o'clock. He finished his wine, changed into something more casual, washed his face and went downstairs. Mariama was not at the reception. There was an old man there instead. He left his key on the desk

'I just checked in,' said Ross. 'Mariama?'

The man looked at him for a second or two before he spoke in a very distinct Geordie accent. 'A Brit are you? I come from Newcastle myself. Andy's the name.' He extended his hand and Ross shook it.

'Richard. Ric. You are a long way from home.'

'Been here twenty-five years. Annie is my wife. French. We own the place. Thatcher's *economic miracle* drove us out of the U.K. Couldn't pay the mortgage on the house, so we sold and moved out here. Annie has family here.'

'How is it going?' asked Ross.

Andy shrugged his shoulders. 'Can't really complain. We are doing all right here even though we only work five, six months a year. But, it does put food on the table. You asked of Marie. You just missed her. She finishes work at nine. Nice lady. Been with us for seven years. Like most people she has her own problems.'

'Who doesn't,' said Ross. 'Oh, it is nothing really. We exchanged a few pleasantries while I was checking in. Nice talking to you. I am just going out to stretch my legs. See you later Andy.'

'Right on. Try and stay on the main streets. We do get some weird characters visiting us during the summer holidays.' Ross thanked him for the advice and stepped outside on the road. Marie was standing a few yards away on the pavement talking rather angrily on her mobile phone. She saw him and Ross nodded. As he walked passed her she ended her phone call and called out to him.

'Monsieur Taylor!'

Ross turned around. 'Hi Marie.'

'Your room is good? You want to buy something outside?' She was being helpful and polite. Ross eyed her for a moment. She was almost as tall as he was with long wavy hair and a very sexy body for her age. He warmed up to her.

'To tell you the truth, I feel a little hungry. Is there anything that serves seafood nearby?'

'There is a good restaurant that can serve... err, *fruits de mer* there,' she said pointing to the restaurant up the road. 'But I have to tell it is very expensive, is how you say, *de premier qualite, de premiere classe.* High-class! That is too much money.' She giggled and her beautiful green eyes lit up in the dark. Ross was pleasantly stunned. He started to experience feelings for this woman, feelings that deserted him a long time ago. He felt his heartbeat quicken a tick or two. He was going for it.

'Marie, please do not take this wrongly, but if you do not have a pressing engagement and you have the time, would you please accompany me to the restaurant? I would be very happy to buy us both a nice meal.' She stood there saying nothing. She was probably a little surprised by the offer. Ross was not deterred. 'Please, I do not speak French and I would not know what to order.' He lied. His French was as good as his English. She finally spoke.

'You are sure? We can go another place much better prices? When I do not work for hotel I work for restaurant not far from here.'

'Is the food good here? At this one I mean?'

'But of course. It is the *Pecheur.* The best in Port-la-Nouvelle!' She smiled again and each time she smiled Ross found her even more attractive.

'The Pecheur it is then.' They started to walk towards the restaurant. Marie paused for a moment.

'Monsieur Taylor…'

'Richard, please call me Richard, or Ric,' he said.

'Ric? All right. Monsieur Ric, after we eat I must go straight home. Not far but home. OK? I am working morning time in hotel tomorrow. OK?'

'OK.'

***

Scargill, the Director of SIS was sitting at the front of the second carriage of a Piccadilly Line train in the London Underground railway system heading north. He was dressed in plain casual clothes and he was reading a tabloid newspaper. It was a few minutes before eight in the evening, well after the early evening rush-hour and there were not many passengers on board. As the doors closed and the train was pulling out of Bounds Green Station, Scargill lowered his newspaper and looked at a man sitting a few seats away from him. The man looked back at him and gently lowered his head a little, acknowledging the eye contact. Although it was a warm July evening the man was wearing a baggy, light raincoat, thus concealing the gun that was secured in the holster strapped to his chest. He was also holding a DIY plastic bag that had various tools in it. That man was Raymond Wise, Scargill's trusted aid and bodyguard. He was also an assassin.

The next stop was Arnos Grove. This was their destination. Wise got out first. He walked up the stairs to the exit of the old station building and turned left. Scargill was about ten paces behind him. Fifty yards down the road there was a pub. Wise went in while his boss remained outside pretending to read his newspaper. Two minutes later Wise came out of the pub and walked passed Scargill on his way back to the station. The brief eye contact between the two men was enough for them to proceed with their next move. Scargill looked at his watch. It was six minutes after eight. He wasted no time. He threw his newspaper in a bin nearby and went into the pub. The smell of freshly cooked food hit his nostrils. It was not really a pub as such; in fact it was an inn and it served excellent food. The place was therefore favored by the locals and it was fairly crowded but he quickly spotted what he was looking for. At the far end of the premises in an out of the way corner, an obese man was sitting at a small table sipping a glass of white wine. James Marlow Scargill approached the table and sat down. The obese man offered his hand for a handshake, a gesture totally ignored by Scargill.

'Hello Charlie. Long time no see.' Charlie Chow, ex Hub recruit and current Chinese restaurant owner said nothing for a while. He took another sip from his wine glass before he spoke.

'Nice to see you too JMS. Care for a drink?'

'I'll have whatever it is you are drinking,' said Scargill. Charlie summoned the waitress, a young foreign thing but her English was good.

'Good evening gentlemen. Are you dining tonight?' She offered them the menu and smiled patiently.

'I will have whatever he has,' said Scargill as he refused to take the menu. 'As you can see from his size he is an expert on food and drink.' The waitress smiled politely but said nothing.

'Please bring us two fillet stakes, medium to well done with whatever vegetables you serve.' Charlie then looked at the wine list for a moment or two.

'We have a nice Bordeaux to compliment the steaks if you are interested,' said the waitress.

'That will do thank you.' It was Scargill who spoke, his impatience showing.

'What have you done with your goon?' JMS was mildly surprised with Charlie's question. 'Come now JMS. I've seen him come in a few minutes before you did, checking if I was here.'

'He's getting old and careless, but he has served me well. He's part of the furniture now.'

'Don't know him at all but if he's half as good as his young half-brother, then he's good enough.'

'You are well informed Charlie.'

'That is why I am still in the game. That is why you recruited me. That is why you trust me.'

'You are costing me a fortune. And for your sake I sure hope you can deliver.' Scargill's face hardened a little. 'You'd sell your family for money wouldn't you?'

'Everything has its price, even you Director.' Charlie laughed out loud. 'I don't mind if you want to ask your bouncer to join us.'

Scargill shook his head negatively. 'He has things to do. Now, tell me about Ross. Who's monitoring him?'

***

'Thank you Richard, the food was good, the wine very good and I have very good evening. But the two vodka shots in the end made me, made me like my feet not on the road. Floating. My English is getting more good, no?' Marie and Ross were standing outside the front door of Marie's apartment. He had just walked her home, a few streets further down from the restaurant.

'Ah, the vodka. The devil's drink! Marie, it was my pleasure. I am extremely grateful to have had the pleasure of your company. I had a very nice time and I hope that you did too.'

'Yes. I did. *Merci.*' They were standing there looking at each other for a moment or two, saying nothing. Marie looked at her watch. 'Richard is late. Midnight. *Merci beaucoup.* Thank you.'

She planted a kiss on his lips, turned round and went in. Ross felt as if he was struck by lightning. He liked Marie, he liked her very much. There seemed to be some good chemistry developing between the two. She talked about her life and how difficult things were without her husband. This was her second marriage. She married her first husband when she was twenty-one. He was a French truck driver and the marriage ended within three years when he lost his job and started to drink. She had a son with him, whom she raised alone, a twenty-four-year old who is training to be a pilot with Air France. He lives in Paris and she sees him every two or three months or so. She also told him how she was attacked by a drunk one night as she walked home alone and that ever since she managed to acquire a Taser stun gun for protection, which she always carried in her handbag and always kept it fully charged. Ross tried to tell her that use of such stun guns by civilians may not be legal but she laughed it off saying that in Port-la-Nouvelle nothing is legal. Ross told some half-truths about himself. He wanted to tell her more, he felt that he could trust her but held back. He definitely liked her.

There was a spring in his step as he walked back to his hotel. He needed to rest for the next day was going to be a busy day for him. Early morning he had to be at a specific place so he could be contacted by one of Michel's people. The plan was to get Nick Porter, Daphne's son to come to

Port-la-Nouvelle, safely and undetected from Switzerland. To Ross, Nick Porter was like the son he never had. He knew that he could trust him. They shared the same values and beliefs. He was not a young James Bond anymore. He needed assistance.

***

Ray Wise was loitering in the vicinity of Arnos Grove Station, constantly keeping the exit to the station in his sights. He looked at his watch. It was 8.35. He cursed under his breath. He was about to light up a cigarette when he saw what he was looking for. A tall balding man in tight trousers and a large lose silk shirt came out of the station and turned right. He was walking towards the Arnos Grove Roundabout with the grace of a super model walking the catwalk. Wise casually followed him.

Chapter 13

Ross parked his car at a parking bay on the Quai du Port, directly opposite Rue de la Mairie and waited. Michel told him that at precisely 10.15 local time in the morning a man on a motorcycle wearing a black helmet will contact him and will speak to him in English. Ross was to remain in the car, smoking a cigar and pretending to read a local newspaper. He picked up the newspaper at the hotel at breakfast time. Marie was there, she actually served him his breakfast. Events permitting he did want to see her and perhaps take her out again in the evening. He checked the time. It was 10.05 a.m. He did come out much earlier ensuring that he found the place and that he could secure a parking slot at the designated rendezvous spot. Each time he heard the engine sound of a motorcycle he could feel his heartbeat go up a beat or two. He leafed through the newspaper for a few minutes. There was nothing of interest. He puffed on his Montecristo cigar and he suddenly realized that he had smoked more than half of it. He looked at his watch again. It was 10.27. Unavoidably anxiety started to set in. He felt uneasy. He then remembered that he did not check into the hotel booked by Michel. Could this have any bearing on why the contact was late? He was going to wait another fifteen minutes and then he was on his own.

A few minutes later there was a gentle knock on the window on the passenger side. A tanned middle aged, athletic looking man, wearing jeans and a summer shirt was gesturing to unlock the door. In his left hand he was holding a black *Shark* motorcycle helmet while a strapped small sports bag was hanging from his right shoulder. Ross looked at him and then looked around him. He could see no motorcycle. He spoke.

'*Oui?*'

'Mr. Ross, please open the door,' said the man pointing at the helmet.

Ross rather reluctantly unlocked the door and the man sat in the car.

'My name is Gerard Ambroise. I was Michel's assistant in his salon in London for six years.' The man placed his helmet on the back seat of the car. He then opened the sports bag and offered Ross his passport.

'That is all right. No need. I am sorry; I was expecting you on a bike.' Ross was being apologetic.

'I did come with a bike, it is parked further down. I am sorry I am late but there was some confusion because you did not check into your hotel last night and I got worried. I contacted Michel this morning to let him know but he did say that I should come here anyway.'

'What next?' asked Ross.

'Do you have your travel documents on you?'

'You mean my passport?'

'Yes, I need it to organize flight tickets,' said Gerard.

Ross was bewildered. 'I am going somewhere?'

'Change of plan. We are flying you to Switzerland. Nick Porter will meet you there.'

'My passport is at the hotel. Why did Michel change things?' Gerard seemed to notice the tiny trace of concern in Ross's voice.

'No idea, but when we get to the hotel we shall call him from my mobile. Let us go.'

'What about your bike?' asked Ross.

'I will pick it up later, no time to waste.'

Ross disposed of his cigar, and tossed the newspaper on the back seat. He started the car and headed back to his hotel. His instinct was telling him that all was not well.

'Your English is very good Gerard. Hardly any trace of an accent.'

'Thank you,' replied Gerard. 'I grew up in London and went to various hairdressing schools. I had my own unisex salon but the rent was too high. I was lucky to have met Michel. I was his assistant for six years.'

'Yes, so you said…'

Ross looked in his rear view mirror. He had the feeling that he was being followed by another car. He parked opposite the hotel but did not get out. The car behind him kept going. No slowing down, no change of speed.

'Is everything all right?' asked Gerard.

'Gerard, why did you call me *Mr. Ross*?'

Gerard looked at him in the eyes. A cold, steely look which soon disappeared as he smiled. 'Very good. Michel said if I use your real name, then you'll know for sure that I am his man. He does not want you to worry. We'll talk to him soon.'

The two men got out of the car. Ross retrieved the helmet from the back seat and handed it to Gerard. They crossed the road and entered the hotel. Marie was at the reception. She smiled at Ross and gave him the key to his room.

'Thank you,' he said. 'This is my friend Gerard. Gerard this is Marie.'

'Bonjour Monsieur.'

Gerard said nothing. He simply acknowledged the remark with a gentle nod of the head.

'Gerard, please be kind enough to wait here for a few seconds. I left something in the car, back in a jiff.' Ross did not wait for a response. He was out of the door in a flash, crossed the road and went to his car. He desperately wanted to see what the small piece of paper was that fell out of the helmet and onto the back seat. He picked it up and his eyes widened with shock as he looked at it. It was a sales receipt for the helmet. It was purchased at 09.37 in the morning, less than hour before Gerard met him. He had been compromised. He had to act fast and decisively. This was for real. He could feel his heart pump faster. That is what he needed. The adrenalin flowing again. He picked up the French newspaper and hurried back to the hotel. Marie was at the reception talking to an elderly man, a resident of the hotel perhaps. Gerard was nowhere to be seen.

'Your friend is gone to toilet.' Marie pointed to a sign saying *Toilettes* with an arrow on it pointing towards a downward staircase. He had to act fast. Marie was saying goodbye to the old man. Ross mumbled his excuses and gently pulled a surprised Marie to one side. He spoke to her quickly, in a low voice and in French.

'Marie, please, you have to help me. This man Gerard, if that is his name, he is very dangerous. Please, please Marie, trust me. I am the good guy here.'

Marie's eyes widened with disbelief. Ross sensed this and tried to pacify her. He continued in French and Marie was even more surprised. 'Please Marie, this man has been sent to kill me. He does not yet know that I am on to him so I have the element of surprise.' She remained speechless. 'Marie, please, are you listening to me?'

'What do you want of me?' asked a very reluctant and hesitant Marie. Ross replied in English this time.

'I sure hope you have your Taser gun. Let me have it. *Now*, before he comes up. No police until I have a chance to explain things to you.'

'Who are you? *What* are you?'

'Trust me, *please* and find me some strong insulating tape to tie him up.'

She said nothing and did nothing. She was motionless but uneasy.

'Marie, please. My life is at stake.' She opened her handbag and handed him the stun gun. Ross kissed her on the forehead. He then went down the stairs, quickly and quietly. He armed the gun to maximum effect and waited outside the men's toilet, 3 yards away from the door. A few moments later the door opened and the last thing Gerard saw was Ross firing the stun gun at him. The metallic probes hit the left side of his ribcage delivering the electric current. He slumped to the floor just outside the door shaking with muscular spasms. Five seconds later he was out cold. At that point Marie appeared with the insulation tape. She retrieved the stun gun and Ross tied his hands and feet and placed a strip over his mouth. He checked the unconscious man's pockets. There was a mobile phone, an old Nokia model and a few hundred Euro notes. He then grabbed Gerard's small sports bag, placed both money and phone inside the bag and turned to face Marie.

'You don't have to do this if you don't want to but I would appreciate it if you do not call the police right away. I need to get my things from upstairs and I will go.'

'Where you go now?'

'I don't know. I need time to think.'

'You remember where my flat is? Good. Upstairs I will give you my key, you go there, I come soon.' Ross was thinking about it. 'Now time you trust me,' she added. 'What of your *friend?*'

'How long will he be out? Unconscious I mean?'

'I don't know,' she said. 'I don't read instruction.'

'All right. Help me put him inside the toilet. We shall lock the door and you can place a piece of paper on the handle saying that it is… err, out of order or something. Not working. Then I will pick up my things from the room and I shall wait for you at your apartment.'

Thirty-five minutes later Ross let Marie into her flat, a modest single bedroom apartment. He only had time for a quick look into Gerard's sports bag. However, he had seen enough to know that he was definitely compromised.

'We cannot stay here long time,' she said.

'What happened?'

'I called Andy to take my place. I said to him I am not feeling good. *Je ne me sens pas bien.* I say also that you check out this morning but no refund from pay for two nights. He was happy.'

'You said nothing about the man in the toilet?'

Marie smiled. At last her beautiful smile was back. 'You say you wanted time, so I give you time. *Bien?*'

'Good girl.'

'Now, Monsieur Taylor. You say to me what is happening and who you are. Your friend will wake up. He saw me and he know my name. Correct?'

'Correct. Marie I will tell you everything in good time, but I need to know how to get to an airport. Do you have a car?'

'No, but there is train station near here. I can telephone to see what time trains go.'

'Yes please do that. Find out where the next train goes to and when.'

While Marie was on the phone, Ross sat at the little kitchen table and looked again inside Gerard's bag. There was a loaded hand pistol in there which he recognized as a

175

Glock G27. A French passport under Gerard's name. A passport that was issued just two weeks earlier. There was a print out from an email that was sent from an internet Yahoo account to a Google internet account. The sender's name was Richard White and the recipient's name Gerard Adams. The names were probably fictitious but it was the actual email addresses that drew his attention. *rw_vc6@yahoo.co.uk* and *ga_vc6@gmail.com*. He was sure that the 'vc6'part of the address referred to Vauxhall Cross the MI6 Head Quarters. These were front, untraceable, email addresses used for covert operations, the emails themselves most probably sent from internet café computers. The initials were most likely real, but not the names. Now he was getting somewhere. He then took a closer look at the print-out. It was transmitted very early that morning. He quickly read it again:

Hi G, confirming earlier telcon. Carry on with story as is. Believe that info extracted from hairdresser accurate but proceed with caution. Black helmet a must. Meeting at parking bay on the Quai du Port, directly opposite Rue de la Mairie at 1015 hrs this morning. Confiscate his travel docs and incapacitate him. Do NOT delete him. I repeat, do not delete him or harm him. The boss wants to talk to him. We think his assumed name is Richard Rat or Alex Rats. We shall send team to pick him up. Below is a recent photo of Ross. However he could look different. Proceed with caution. All other info as per telcon. Bro.

Ross assumed that Michel was compromised and that he was probably dead. How else could they have known about Nick Porter? They must have tortured him or used chemicals on him or both. At least good old Michel had given him time. They do not seem to know his assumed identity. This was a big plus as he could still use his new passport. If they knew about Michel they most likely knew about Paulina too. He feared for her life. He felt helpless.

'Richard, there is train leaving in forty minutes for Montpellier. It stop at Narbonne for change. *Voyage* 85 minutes.' Marie suddenly noticed the Glock on the table. *'Mon Dieu!* A gun Richard?'

'It is not mine. It was in his bag. The man is an assassin, *agresseur*. Montpellier? Good connections from there?'

'What you do with it?' Marie's eyes were still fixed on the gun.

'I'll get rid of it as soon as I get out. How far is the station?'

She went close to him, very close and looked into his eyes. 'I want to come with you,' she said. 'Please take me with you.'

Ross was at a loss, momentarily. 'Marie, it is too dangerous. You don't know anything about me.'

'You say I save your life. I have nothing here. *Rien.* If people are looking to find you, you are better together, as a couple, no? *Un couple marié* ' Her eyes were pleading.

'You have a valid passport? French?'

'Yes.' Marie's eyes lit up.

Without giving it a second thought, Ross agreed. He felt he could trust her. After all it was him who chose the hotel where she was working. No way could she be connected with any intelligent services. He decided to tell her everything. The truth, the *real* truth. For some odd, inexplicable, reason Daphne seemed a distant memory. He was on survival mode now. He was at odds with himself but that is how he felt. Here they were. Two people who met for the very first time a mere 15, 16 hours ago, ready to embark on a dangerous journey into the unknown. Marie prepared a small hand luggage with some clothes and other necessities and called a taxi.

***

Back in the sanctuary of Alexandra's hotel room in Myrina, Efi was recollecting her thoughts. She had been to the police station and had given the police her mobile phone number and was awaiting the call to go and formally identify her father's body once he was brought back to the hospital morgue. Although the police accepted the fact that Mitsos was murdered, he was still the prime suspect for Zoe's murder, his guilt based purely and solely on the evidence gathered from within and around the crime scene.

Alexandra poured Metaxa Brandy in two glasses and offered one to Efi. They were both silent, both in deep thought. Efi downed her drink in one and broke the silence.

'Yes, I wanted to prove my father's innocence. But not like this.' She sobbed once more.

'I don't think anyone believed that your father killed my sister.' Alexandra was showing compassion and solidarity. Efi's mobile phone suddenly rang. The calling number was unknown to her. She answered it.

'*Iphigenia Nicolaou, parakalo.*' Efi listened for a moment or two and then spoke in English. 'Thank you. Where did you get my number from and how is this any of your business?' She listened again. 'All right, we can both meet with you in 30 minutes at the hotel cafeteria. I take it you know where that is. Fine.'

'Who was that?' asked Alexandra.

'George Webb, the British Embassy man. He wanted to commiserate me for Mitsos. He wants to talk to both of us, regarding Zoe and Mitsos.'

'I can understand his interest in Zoe as she is a British national, but your father?'

Efi took a long breath and shook her head. She poured herself another brandy and went out to the room's balcony. She lit up a cigarette. 'I don't know. He will most probably avoid telling us the obvious, that Anderson killed both Zoe and Mitsos. He has an agenda. We'll meet him downstairs in half an hour.'

'I'll pop in the shower then. Can't get used to the humidity.'

'That is all right Alex. Take your time. I will be downstairs.' Efi finished her drink, stubbed her cigarette in an ashtray that was on the balcony table and headed for the door.

Twenty-five minutes later, Alexandra joined Efi at her table at the hotel's garden cafeteria. She looked fresh and beautiful, wearing a pair of shorts and a lose T-shirt.

'Not here yet?' she asked.

'Unlike for a Brit to be late. Would you like a coffee or something else?'

'To be honest, I feel a little hungry,' replied Alexandra.

'No problem. Let us get Webb out of the way and we can go to a fish tavern down the road.' At that point a tall slim man, around sixty with a neatly trimmed greying moustache approached their table.

'Ladies, I am George Webb and I apologize for being a few minutes late.'

Both women stood up, introduced themselves and shook hands. He offered both women his condolences. He was good looking and very polite. The two women ordered iced coffee. Webb asked for tea.

'Yes, I was delayed because of various urgent phone calls from the Embassy. However please let me say, again, how sorry I am for your losses. This is a difficult state of affairs but I am sure you both appreciate the necessity of our meeting.'

'Mr. Webb, who actually authorized you, or rather, *who* requested that the British Embassy be involved in this? I am the only next of kin and I did no such thing. Who then?' Alexandra went straight to the point. Webb was taken by surprise by the directness of the question.

'Well my dear, that I… I will have to confirm that when I next speak to the Embassy in Athens.'

'You mean you don't know? Who asked you to be here?' Alexandra was not going to let go.

'The Ambassador himself has asked me to be here, so obviously someone did request either the Embassy directly or the Home Office back in London. It is not unusual for the overseas diplomatic personnel to offer assistance when…'

'That is not very relevant right now.' It was Efi who wanted to push on. 'What do you have to tell us Mr. Webb?'

'Mrs. Nicolaou, with all due respect, you do appreciate that our, that is the Embassy's primary concern has to be with the victim, Zoe Coburn and her missing fiancé, George Anderson. Both being British nationals I mean.'

'You mean the double killer,' Alexandra was hardening her stance. Webb was unruffled.

'Miss Coburn, I can only imagine what you must be going through, but you must not let what surely must be a huge psychological blow cloud your thinking.'

'Don't you patronize me…' Alexandra did not finish the sentence, as she fought to control her obvious anger.

'What do you think *did* happen Mr. Webb?' asked Efi.

'My dear it is not what I think. We are looking at the evidence and gathering information with the assistance of the local police. They want this solved the sooner as they think that this unfortunate incident may affect the tourist season.'

'I will ask again. What do *you* think happened?' Efi managed a smile, a smile of defiance and assurance. She was not going to give up.

'Well, let us see... ah the drinks are here. Please allow me to pay for these.' Webb gestured to the young waitress who kept looking at Efi.

'You can pay when you are back in your own country,' said Efi as she handed the waitress some money. 'We look after our visitors and our guests Mr. Webb. It is called *Elliniki philoxenia,* Greek hospitality. We don't go around butchering our tourists.' Webb seemed unsure and felt uneasy for a moment or two.

'We are still waiting for your version of the story.' It was Alexandra who spoke.

'All right. We, that is, the police as well as ourselves, believe that... this is rather difficult for me you understand and the investigation is still on-going. I wish to neither offend you nor hurt your feelings but the facts; they all seem to point to one thing...'

'Please get to the point.' Efi was becoming irritated. Exasperation was setting in. At that point Alexandra started to laugh. She looked at the amazement on Webb's face and she laughed more. She then looked at Efi who started to laugh along with her.

'I am sorry, I don't understand. What is so funny here?' Webb was genuinely puzzled. Alexandra resumed her serious look and bowed her head towards Webb's face. Her eyes were on fire. She was hissing like a venomous serpent, whispering to him in a firm and uncompromising way.

'Look you pathetic little so and so, we know what your game is here and if you want to stay in one piece I suggest you fuck the hell back down the hole out of which you crawled from.'

'I beg your pardon! How dare you speak to me like this? Grief or no grief where are your manners woman?' Webb was looking at Efi for support.

'What will your own report say Mr. Webb?' Efi was not asking. She was demanding. She was also being sarcastic. 'That my father killed Zoe and then committed suicide?'

'Mr. Nicolaou, your father, we believe killed Miss Coburn. The evidence is overwhelming, fingerprints on the knife, cigarette stubs on the floor, the boat, the basket with the fish outside the caravan.'

'How very convenient,' said Alexandra. She was more composed now. Webb ignored her and carried on.

'We believe that as Mr. Nicolaou tried to get away he run into Anderson who may have killed the fisherman in a frenzy of revenge when he realized what happened. He panicked and he fled. We are still trying to locate him.'

Alexandra was about to explode but Efi raised her hand in order to deter her. Alexandra simply got up and left for her room.

'Wild little thing isn't she? I can understand her pain but I am only trying to help her.'

'Yes, of course you are,' said Efi. 'Tell me Mr. Webb, what is the motive here?'

'Motive? Well, this is why I wanted to see you. To find out if your father had shown aggressive sexual behaviour before. Zoe Coburn I understand is, was, a very attractive woman, just like her sister.'

'So you are telling me that the attack was sexually motivated? That my father was a pervert, a dirty old man?' Efi remained relatively calmed.

'I am sorry Mrs. Nicolaou, I used no such words. May be the late Miss Coburn provoked him or even seduced him and things got out of hand.'

Efi suddenly stood up and slapped Webb hard across the face. 'She was his godchild. Do you understand what I am saying? My father was Zoe's godfather; he christened her. In our country that is sacred, she was like a sister to me. Do you understand what I am saying? *Do you*? Leave the island, for your own safety, you little muppet.'

Webb composed himself and looked at the people looking at him, seating at nearby tables. 'Are you threatening me?' he asked.

'Yes I am,' said a defiant Efi as she left for Alexandra's room.

Chapter 14

By the time the train was pulling into Montpellier station in the South of France, Ross told Marie, who he really was, what he was, what he is, what his beliefs are and how the events of the last few days had changed his retired life. He also told her where he may end up and gave her the choice to leave if she wanted to. Ross took a huge gamble in disclosing every little detail about his previous life. He felt that he had to. He had to do it for his sanity if not for anything else.

Marie listened, taking mental notes as Ross talked and talked. She was amazed to hear what she had heard, yet she sponged every little detail. She was genuinely intrigued. Ross also mentioned Daphne and what she meant to him. He told her he has blue eyes and his hair is pure white. He felt a cleansing within his body and soul, a cleansing he never experienced before. His whole life had been a lie, a life full of deception and black ops, all for the good of the Realm. A heavy load was off his conscience. For the first time in his adult life he was truthful. Marie compared him to James Bond. She told him that as long as they were together she did not mind the cold or the isolation and that she welcomed the challenge.

He smiled and kissed her on the forehead. Marie kissed him back, a full French kiss. She had lots of questions, lots of whys, but she held back. She noticed how his voice softened, how his tone became nostalgic when he talked about Daphne. She let it go. She knew she will have time to go over things again. They disembarked from the train and got a taxi for the airport.

An hour after they arrived at the airport they boarded a flight for Paris where they would spend the night before catching a morning flight to Athens. However, Ross had time to make two calls from an airport public phone booth before they boarded. He called Daphne's boy, Nick Porter in Switzerland and asked him to use some excuse at work, drop everything for a week and get a flight to Athens, Greece the next day where they would meet.

He drove the point home that Nick should tell absolutely no one, not even his mother as to where he was going or who he was meeting and that he would explain everything to him in Athens. Ross asked Nick to check in to a specific hotel in Central Athens and gave him instructions on how to contact him. He told him that it was time, time for action. The second call was to Jacques Petit, who was conscripted by his old deceased Surete friend and Hub collaborator Claude Duval. A meeting had been arranged. They would spend the night at a safe house in Paris. Air tickets to Athens would be issued, two untraceable French-number mobile phones and two new French passports for Ross and Marie would be made available. They would be brought new clothing for their trip the next morning. It was going to be a long night. Jacques was the Deputy Director, number two in command, of the Direction Centrale du Renseignement Intérieur, the French MI5 equivalent. A bloody good contact to have thought Ross. *Little Jack* was certainly not *petit*, he was huge!

Ross had another meeting to attend the next day in Athens. A meeting not yet arranged. One of the permanent office staff at the British Embassy in Athens was the nephew of an old and trusted friend. Gavin Addice. The legendary *Gladys* of the MoD did his best to protect his nephew from the usual vultures of the intelligent services. Nobody, except the hairdresser knew about the connection, not even Ross until Michel gave him the contact as well as the password and other details that would secure a meeting with Trevor North. He would know of the happenings and the ongoing scenarios on Limnos Island. He may even have answers as to why Ross was being hounded all of a sudden.

***

The Air France airbus touched down at Eleftherios Venizelos, the Athens International Airport just after 2.00 p.m. Ross and Marie took a taxi to the Athenaeum Intercontinental Hotel at Syngrou Avenue near the center of Athens. Jacques Petit had made the reservation. They were husband and wife. French nationals Rober and Marie Martell, in Athens to celebrate their wedding anniversary. There was a Bollinger champagne, Belgian chocolates and red roses waiting for them in their hotel suite on the 6th floor. The room had a stunning view of the Acropolis. Ross was staring at the Parthenon through the window. He hadn't been to Athens for a good 30 years.

'It's so very, *magnifique*, so beautiful,' she said.

'Not as beautiful as you.' Ross took her in his arms and held her for a few moments before he spoke again. 'Mrs *Martell*, I am beginning to have, erm, how shall I put it, deep feelings for you and frankly, I am scared. *Je t'adore.*'

'*Merci.* If you scared, how I feel you think?' She looked at him and smiled. 'Tell me, what do I call you Mr. *Martell*? You change name every three hours.'

'Bob, call me Bob,' he said.

'I prefer *Rober*, it is more French.' She kissed him and he kissed her back. They looked into each other's eyes and it was not long before they were making passionate love on the large double bed. Ross felt a man reborn. Marie was fulfilled as she hadn't been for a very long time. They fell asleep in each other's arms.

Chapter 15

The gentle theme music to Edith Piaf's classic song *Non, Je Ne Regrette Rien* awoke Ross, as he momentarily struggled to orientate himself and realize where he was. He felt Marie's warm naked body in his arms as his eyes tried adjust to the dark environment of the hotel suite. He allowed himself a smile, obviously satisfied with himself, but quickly turned his attention to the repeated ringing tone of Piaf's classic coming from one of the two mobile phones given to them by Jacques Petit. He gently untangled himself from Marie's body, turned a light on and looked for the phone in his bag. Marie mumbled something, turned over and went to sleep again. Ross accepted the call.

'Hello.'

'Monsieur Martel. This is Jacques. Just ensuring that you arrived safely,' said Petit.

'Thank you my friend, just dozed off for a while.'

'Pardon. Just to let you know that should you need to contact me *as Mr Rober Martel*, please disregard the old phone numbers you have for me and use the one I will give you.'

Ross listened, noted the new numbers and thanked Petit who wished them both, good luck.

'Who that was? What time now?' Marie was now awake.

'Hello beautiful, *amour de ma vie*. It was the French policeman who helped us and it is… erm,' Ross looked at the mobile phone and then his wrist watch on the side table. 'Eight forty, local time I guess. We've been sleeping for a good two hours.'

'Open curtain please.' Marie got up and engulfed her immaculate body in one of the hotel's robes. 'Oh la la!' she exclaimed as Ross drew the curtains open and a stunning view of the beautifully lit Acropolis caught her sight.

'I have to admit, even I am impressed,' said Ross with a smile. 'How about I take us up there, or thereabouts for a good traditional Greek dinner?'

'They have restaurants on the Acropolis?'

Ross smiled again. 'No, not *on* the Acropolis but beneath the hill there is an area known as the *Plaka,* or at least I sure hope it is still there, which is dotted with picturesque and cozy tavernas. We can drink *retsina* too.'

'Ressina?'

'Retsina. It is a pine-resin tasting local wine. You will love it.'

Marie shrugged her shoulders and said rather sarcastically, 'And I think all the time I have to start drinking vodka now...'

Ross laughed. 'Vodka? Why vodka? Oh, I get it... Vodka is good, but only if you like vodka. Come on, let us get ready. We deserve to enjoy ourselves.'

'I like very much to go out. But it will not be very late? By time we reach restaurant?'

Ross embraced her and kissed her gently on the lips. 'This is Greece,' he said, 'Athens by night. Greeks eat late and the city comes alive close to midnight. Don't worry.'

'Port-La-Nouvelle becomes, how you say, *mort,* it dies by midnight.'

'Well let us get on with it and enjoy the night the. Tomorrow is going to be a hectic day. Shall I go first in the shower or will you?'

'Un moment s'il vous plait. I quickly go to toilet and then… we can both go inside shower, no?' Marie giggled as she went to the bathroom.

The thought of Greece, Greek food and Greek drinks could only have made him think of Daphne at that moment. In fact he was thinking of Daphne ever since he boarded the plane for Athens. He had confused feelings, but he liked Marie, so much. Oh, how she absolutely rejuvenated him. But now he had to focus on the task ahead. The days ahead. His life now will never be the same. But first he will make a night of it. Chill out as they say. The phone ringtone came to his mind again as he found himself murmuring the Piaf song… *Non, Je Ne Regrette Rien…* Did he have any regrets? Only time will tell.

****

James Marlow Scargill tossed away his mobile phone with the unlisted and untraceable number. He had just finished a call, speaking in French to an intelligence officer in Paris. He picked up the receiver of the secure landline phone that sat on his desk, deep into a sterile basement room of the SIS Head Quarters at Vauxhall Cross.

'Ray, come in.'

A few moments later an angry looking Ray Wise walked into the room.

'At last, we have found Gerry,' he said.

'Alive?' Scargill showed no emotion.

'Yes thank God. He was tied and gagged in the toilet of some brothel of a bed and breakfast joint at that French shithole of a place. He was zapped with a taser gun. Zapped! You believe that?'

The head of the MI6 still showed no emotion. 'I am happy for you that your illegitimate half-brother is well, but what info of substance do you have, if any?'

'One of the whores that worked there is missing. She's either dead or more likely Ross used her as a decoy or cover to flee the area. I have her name written down somewhere.'

'Give the name to Dobson and tell him to look into her past. I will alert counter intelligence in Paris to look out for them.' Ray was about to leave the room when the Director of SIS spoke again. 'Ray, ask Gerrard to come home. Be here tomorrow. I may need you to take a trip together. Also find out if we have a trusted arsonist or an explosive expert on our off-the-record roster.'

'Explosions? As in bombs?' Wise looked interested.

'Yes. We need to turn a few traitors into fireworks.'

'Now you are talking. Don't have to look far. Gerry had explosives training with the SAS,' said Wise as he left the room.

Scargill opened one of the draws on his desk and took an elastic band which he, nervously, twisted and turned between his fingers.

'We are too close to fuck up now. Too close,' he whispered to himself. The elastic band suddenly snapped between his fingers. He cursed. He picked up the secure phone again, pressed one of the memory buttons and waited.

'I hope I am not inconveniencing you or intruding in any way at this late hour madam.' Scargill dished that out with a trace of sarcasm.

'You know that our kind never sleeps JMS. Feeling lonely? What's on your mind?' The words from Eleanor Bishop, the Director General of MI5 carried their own dose of sarcasm.

'It is a lonely job Elle. Feeling lonely, being lonely is part of the job. You know that.'

'So you called mother for a bit of comfort, have you?' Elle laughed out loud.

'I know I am relatively young for my position but you are not exactly a relic and you should stop thinking like one. Besides, you are not old enough to be my mother.'

'All right cut the bullshit. What is it you want Scargill?'

'Ross.' Scargill's response was swift and cold. Elle laughed.

'Robert Ross? Don't tell me he's turned into a ghost now?' There was no reply from JMS. 'You've lost him? He slipped through your net?'

'Why are you protecting him? We are supposed to be on the same side, are we not?' Scargill cleared his throat and lowered his voice. 'He will compromise the Prime Minister. You as the head of Home Security should be losing a lot of sleep over this. Are you?'

'As far as my department is concerned, Ross is of no threat to the State or the government and should the PM have taken the trouble to ask my department for a report, as he was obliged to do, I would have told him the same. No we are not protecting Ross and we are not hounding him either. Why should we?' Elle paused for a second or two before she continued. 'Unless Jim you have damaging information about him which you are not widely sharing with Her Majesty's Intelligence Services and Home Security.'

'You know how he acted in the past. You have the files on him.'

'Yes we do have files on him, as we have files on you. He's an open book. And mentioning the word *book* yes, I am aware of the rumours that he is about to publish a book exposing all the clandestine black ops of our intelligence networks over the last forty years or so. Rumours, Jim, just rumours and we all know how these rumours came about.' In the absence of a response from JMS, Bishop carried on. 'Bring me hard evidence, a manuscript, anything and I will pick him up for questioning under the Official Secrets Act. And believe me, I will find him.'

'We have to take preventive measures. If he goes public, the damage he will cause to the government and to the intelligence services will be irreversible. Prevention is the solution.'

'Oh I see. Like a pre-emptive strike you mean.' Elle was now being sarcastic.

'Your set up, is it involved with the deletion of one Christos Leonardou known as *the ferret* and a lost package?' There was a silence for a few seconds. Scargill said nothing more. He waited.

'I am impressed, I must say. You don't miss much do you?' Elle's voice softened somewhat. 'You seem to have more moles in MI5 than we do in MI6.'

'Scratch my back and I will scratch yours. We are both British and working for the same government, are we not?' Scargill felt that he had the upper hand now.

'I am certainly British, and proud of it. Sometimes I do have my doubts about you though.'

It was Scargill's turn to laugh now. He regained his composure quickly. 'Elle, we need to meet to discuss a common strategy. It would be very beneficial to the both of us. You can do with some positive publicity within the government and I can do with a helping hand here and there. I know they are grooming someone, a kind of, how shall I put it, an introvert and ambiguous personality to replace you early next year. What do you say?'

'Balderdash, I say.'

'I can line you up for a *damehood*. Dame Eleanor Bishop. It does have a nice ring to it, does it not? Come on, let's arrange a meeting.'

'You are the last man on the planet I want to meet.' Elle sounded uncompromising.

'Elle, I have Leonardou's package.'

An eerie silence greeted Scargill's last comment. He persisted.

'It is very detailed and well documented. No gaps. The evidence is clear as daylight. Elle, it is yours. No strings attached. Come on, we need each other.'

'You fucking son of a bitch. This is blackmail,' snapped Elle. She was breathing heavily.

'A lot of people did die at Lockerbie. Innocent people.'

'Let me know the place and time.'

'That's my girl, I am sure that...' Before Scargill finished his sentence, Bishop ended the call. He allowed himself a smile as he replaced the receiver. He leaned back in his comfy designer desk chair and rested his feet on his desk. He closed his eyes, his thoughts fast-forwarding to the near future, a few years ahead. Now he was able to realistically dream of No. 10.

***

Ifighenia Nicolaou and Alexandra Coburn were having their evening meal at one of the many fish tavernas that surround the old Myrina port on the island of Limnos.

'I must say I find the red mullet quite agreeable,' said Alexandra. 'Not to mention the mussels cooked in sea-water.'

'Eat slowly because there is more to come. Lobster and grilled prawns.' Efi raised her wine wineglass. 'To Zoe and Mitsos. May they rest in peace.'

Alexandra raised her glass too. 'I will drink to revenge,' she said.

'To payback,' was Efi's response.

Alexandra's cellphone rang. She answered it.

'No, that is all right. I am still awake. It is only 9.30 p.m.' Alexandra listened for the next minute or two, nodding her head and acknowledging what she was being told. 'Thank you Gus. I appreciate the information. My regards to Langley and no I don't miss it. Limnos is beautiful in the summer but I am not on holiday. I have unfinished business here. Shop and personal. They go hand in hand. Will do.'

'Anything of interest?' Efi was anticipating some good news. A breakthrough perhaps.

'It is almost certain that George Anderson worked, works, for the British Secret Services. Not clear which department and in what capacity yet. He was planted at the therapy sessions in order to befriend my sister.'

'Does that make sense? I mean why would the SIS want to murder Zoe, if Anderson was, indeed, the murderer?' Efi was perplexed and so was Alex.

'I don't know, yet but there's more. Anderson was on active duty in Paris at the end of August 1997.'

'Paris? You've lost me there Alex.'

'Efi, that was the time Princess Diana died in that car crash.'

'Holy shit! You are not saying that…'

'I am not saying anything,' replied Alex. 'I am merely stating the facts as given to me.'

'I need a fucking cigarette. This is deep.' Efi swallowed the rest of her wine and promptly lit a Gitanes cigarette. She drew a long drag, puffed it out nervously and carried on. 'Let us suppose that Anderson killed Zoe and my father too. What is the connection between Zoe, Mitsos and Diana – if any?'

A waiter approached their table and served a lobster and a dish of grilled prawns.

'Suddenly, I am not hungry anymore.' Alex finished the white wine in her glass. 'I would not mind some more wine though,' she added.

Efi summoned the waiter and asked for another bottle of wine. When it arrived Alexandra politely asked the waiter not to pour it into their glasses.

'Let us take it back to the hotel,' she said. 'We have a lot to analyze.'

Efi paid the bill and politely dismissed the mild remonstration from the waiter regarding the untouched lobster and prawn dishes.

As the two women were walking the short distance back to Alexandra's hotel, a man coming out of the street's shadows approached them.

'Good evening ladies,' he said.

The surprised women turned round. It was Efi who spoke first.

'Your audacity is beyond imagination. What the fuck do you want now?'

George Webb smiled and opened his wallet which he placed in front of Alexandra's eyes.

'Is this for real?' Alex removed a card from his wallet and inspected it closer. She was impressed by the security clearance code of the high-ranking officer of the Clandestine Service Department of the Central Intelligence Agency.

'You are welcome to call Gus in Langley to verify it if you wish.'

'I will,' said a stunned Alex.

'Jesus Christ!' It was Efi's turn. 'He's one of us?'

'We have a lot to talk about ladies.' Webb had a trace of remorse in the tone of his voice. 'I apologize for my conduct in our earlier meeting. Developments dictate that I expose my cover to you.'

'Sorry about the slap in the face. What developments exactly?' said Efi.

'I fully deserved it my dear. The slap I mean. Shall we enjoy the wine you are holding?'

'What developments?' Efi persisted.

Webb lowered his voice. 'Things may not be what they seem. We are missing the bigger picture here. We'll only know what the final picture is after we place the very last jig saw piece on the puzzle. Whatever is happening is happening for a reason. Seemingly unrelated events are interrelated, links in a long chain of events.' For a few seconds none of them said anything.

'There is a lot to talk about,' said a serious sounding Alex.

Three people, none of them American born but all three working for the Central Intelligence Agency, gingerly made their way to the Castle Beach Hotel. They would be sharing information, exchanging information, analyzing information and making suppositions deep into the night. There were questions that needed to be answered, much sooner rather than later.

Chapter 16

'All right all right, I am coming.' Daphne opened her apartment front door. Stanley the building's porter was standing there. He nodded.

'Sorry to bother you Mrs. Daphne, I sure hope I am not inconveniencing you. Your door phone not working?'

'Stanley? What is it? Did you ring?' she asked.

'Yes but it seems dead. Can I have a look at it?'

Daphne nodded and he went in.

'Ah, the receiver isn't sitting properly. There you are.'

'What is it Stanley?'

'Well there is this man downstairs, well, there's two of them who say they're from the government…'

'The government? The British government?'

'Yes ma'am,' said an apologetic Stanley. 'The guy who seems to be the guvnor has shown me identification from some government department. Looks real enough to me.

'Sir Robert is not here, he is abroad. Tell them to come back next week and take their name.' Daphne was about to close the door when Stanley spoke again.

'Begging your pardon Mrs. Daphne, it is you they want to see. The bloke asked of you by name. Mrs. Daphne Porter.'

'Me? Who is he?' Daphne sounded surprised.

'His name is Wise. Raymond Wise and he's here on behalf of a Mrs. Bishop.'

Daphne's eyes suddenly widened. 'Bishop you said? Show them up.'

'I can stay outside the door until they go if that makes you feel any better Mrs. Daphne.'

She smiled at him. 'No, no it is all right. Ask them to come up. Thank you, Stanley. I, I appreciate what you say.'

****

It was almost midday and the summer sun was feverishly beating down on the island of Limnos in the north-eastern Aegean Sea. But the morning *meltemi* wind was still going strong and carried with it a fresh northern coolness, making conditions a little more bearable for Alexandra Coburn, who was not used to these temperatures. Together with Efi and her husband Stelios, the island's Coroner, they had earlier visited Keros beach where her twin sister was brutally murdered. It was hard and difficult to comprehend the violence that took place in such a beautiful and serene environment. Before they returned to Myrina they stopped at the nearby village of Calliope. Alex was sitting at the village *kafenion,* the coffee house sipping on a gluey frappe coffee. She was the only woman customer of the coffee house and a few old men were taking a discrete interest in her, whispering and gossiping on the recent events that unsettled their little community. Efi and Stelios went to see the village priest. The two women decided to bury Mitsos and Zoe at the small cemetery in the village of Calliope. The village was in close proximity to Keros Beach and Kotsinas fishing harbor where Mitsos had his summer tavern. There were some formalities that had to be addressed before the burial could take place and Efi, with her husband, were sorting things out.

'Miss, good day.' Alex turned round and saw one of the coffee house customers standing on top of her.

'Good morning, I mean *kalimera,*' said a rather wary Alex.

'No, I speak little English,' said the old man. 'All here, we are very sad, sorry for your sister and the doctor's father, Mitsos. Very sorry.'

'Thank you,' said a surprised Alex.

'We here will speak to the Mukhtari and the priest…'

'Sorry the muht, what?'

'Mukhtar, he is, he is…'

'Calliope community leader. My wife is his sister.' shouted another customer. 'I live in Australia for some years, I know how to speak the English,' he carried on from an adjacent table. 'He must say ok with priest, together, to accept for burial for people who don't live here or have family here. Calliope village law.'

'Oh, I see. I cannot thank you enough.' Alex smiled at them and before anyone else joined in the conversation, Alex caught sight of Efi and Stelios heading towards her and she got up to greet them.

'Tomorrow 10.00 am,' said Stelios. 'Don't worry, I will make all the arrangements.' Alexandra hugged him and kissed him on the cheek.

'Thank you, thank you so much. Can we get back to the hotel now please? I am drained.'

'Of course,' said Efi. 'We are all distraught and shaken. We could do with some peace of mind. We'll be there in just over half an hour.'

They said their goodbyes to the locals and boarded the Range Rover owned by Stelios. Alexandra sat in the back and half-closed her eyes. She was not sleeping though. In her mind she recalled all that was discussed the previous night between the two women and the surprise package, as she labelled him, one George Webb, senior CIA field operative for Eastern Europe, the Middle East and West Africa. George explained that his cover for many years was that of a director in the international conglomerate that was the T&S Group, active in the Middle East and West Africa. He was also the liaison, the go-between bridging the British Ministry of Defence and the arms sales via the British-based T&S Group to foreign governments approved by the MoD. While Robert Ross through the Hub and in consultation with the British Prime Minister, did his best to promote British arms sales and technology in the Middle East and elsewhere, especially in the aftermath of the six day war in 1967, George Webb was in fact working for the Americans under his MoD cover and discretely sabotaged British arms deals by pushing for American arms sales and therefore American dependency of the state involved. Webb and the CIA were instrumental in the demise of the Saudi king's confidant Sheikh Khalid Bin Ibrahim Al-Assaf, in Jeddah in 1983. The agency also sanctioned the killing of Hub member Patrick Brennan, thus removing the British competition in the sale of arms to the Kingdom.

Webb joined the CIA when in his twenties in 1978. A graduate of political sciences and international relations, he became disenchanted with James Callaghan's leadership of the country in the late seventies. He befriended Carl Santori, a Commercial Liaison Officer at the USA Embassy in London. They met playing squash. It was not long after that they took a holiday trip to the USA. It was early September in 1978 and the anti-Callaghan majority in the U.K. expected the then PM to call early elections with Margaret Thatcher waiting in the wings. Callaghan backed out from holding autumn general elections and Thatcher accused him of running scared. That did it for Webb. He was convinced by Carl to join the CIA, believing that this way he could actually serve his country better. So there he was, in an unbelievably expedient position and he took full advantage.

Webb also recounted the story of how he compromised the Trident Shipping Agency Manager in Nigeria, Lars Bergman by paying him off to participate in the 'disappearance' of the MV Iphigenia, a ship indirectly owned by Efi's father through a Liberian off-shore company. The fisherman had named the ship after his daughter Iphigenia. Efi was a short name. At long last the truth behind the vanishing of the cargo vessel Iphigenia was revealed. Webb had said that just like Iphigenia in Greek mythology, the MV Iphigenia was also sacrificed for what they believed at the time to be for the greater good. Efi had been listening with great interest as Webb told the story. What really happened was that the ship, loaded with 15,000 tons of bulk American corn destined for Lagos Nigeria was, in fact, carrying a much more valuable cargo, unknown to the ship's owners and most of the crew. Packed in two secure and insulated steel-reinforced concrete cases well hidden in one of the ship's cargo holds there was a quantity of twenty-five pounds of enriched uranium and ten pounds of plutonium 239. Enough material to manufacture an atomic bomb! The USA State Department was covertly sending a gift to the Nigerian military government with a promise to assist them develop nuclear power stations in the future and solve the unending problem of electricity cuts in the country. In return the USA will be the only supplier of arms and technology to the military regime and American oil companies will have first option and priority in lifting Nigerian crude oil, especially the high quality crude known as 'Bonny Light.' A move made necessary by the overthrow of the pro-western Shah in Iran by Ayatollah's Islamic Revolution and the exile and banishment of all things American in Iran. The USA had to find new regular sources of crude oil from elsewhere and Nigeria was the answer.

The CIA on the other hand had information that the military government in Nigeria would fall and give way to a civilian government 'within months.' So when the CIA clandestine operatives became aware of the special cargo, they could not risk it falling into the hands of, may be, a not so American-friendly civilian regime. The Israeli intelligence services – namely Mossad, through the American Jewish Lobby as Webb had later explained, were very instrumental in influencing the US Government and in effect the CIA black ops departments, to redirect the special cargo to other shores. While the vessel was loading at the grain elevators in New Orleans with the special cargo already on board, the CIA had arranged for the ship's chief engineer and another 6 able seamen to be taken ill with a mysterious virus. They deliberately infected them.

Through Trident Shipping and Lars Bergman, who represented the ships agents and the ship's crew managers, the CIA had arranged to replace seven of the 20-strong crew with agents and a few mercenaries. Webb himself visited Trident in Apapa-Lagos and handed one hundred thousand USA dollars, personally, to Lars Bergman who retired soon after. Twenty hours prior to the ship's arrival in Lagos Nigeria and about 320 nautical miles west from the port of destination, the armed rogue crew took over the ship and dismantled the ship's communication apparatus. The only functional communication equipment on board was the CIA issued radios. As Webb pointed out, this was 1983 and well before the age of the international mobile phone.

They forced the rest of the crew, at gunpoint, to repaint the ship a different color and rename the ship *Inverness.*

They replaced Iphigenia's Liberian flag with that of Panama and gave the ship a new call sign. New logbooks and manuals and charts with the ships new name and fictitious owning company were put in place. They threw some debris, paint and fuel oil overboard in deep waters off Abidjan to suggest a sinking. The ship charted a new course, much further south. Port of destination was now the Port of Saldanha in South Africa. The special cargo would eventually end up in Israel through the apartheid government of South Africa. There was a reason for it.

A few years earlier Israel's Defense Minister Shimon Peres signed a secret security pact with his South African counterpart, P W Botha. In no time South Africa was the largest importer of Israel's defense industry. The military relationship between the two countries strengthened considerably to a point where the USA government was embarrassed. Israel even offered South Africa nuclear-capable Jericho missiles. When the US President was informed of the events he did not know whether to be happy or sad. Arlington County and the Pentagon were definitely happy. The MV Iphigenia became a pawn in the geopolitical and military international chessboard. The crew was never seen nor heard of since.

However, as Webb pointed out, the real Iphigenia is alive and kicking and he's happy she's on the same team as he is. Webb had apologized to Efi again and confided to her that George Anderson was in fact a psychotic assassin assigned to the British SIS. He also said that he was One hundred percent sure that it was Anderson who murdered Zoe under orders. The reason for the brutal murder bordered on a suspicion that Zoe's late father and ex Hub agent Ian Coburn alias Fabian Cabus, a few days before he was pushed under a train, may have passed on to Zoe a microfilm containing highly damaging information regarding the British Government and British Intelligence Services. Zoe was ten or eleven years old at the time and that was the time when she had her tonsils taken out and it was thought that whilst under full anesthesia the microfilm may have been surgically implanted on some part of her body. It was not. Not then. A Ministry of Defence analyst, Gavin Addice, also known as *Gladys* had it all the time and a technologically upgraded copy of the microfilm was in fact inserted in Zoe's right breast during her cosmetic surgery after the underground bomb blast almost killed her a year ago. Addice saw to that by coming to an arrangement with the surgeon. He was going to contact Zoe later and explain everything. What the information meant and how she may use it. He didn't. It is now assumed that Anderson retrieved the microfilm and it is now in the hands of the British Intelligence Services, although not clear which department actually has it.

Alexandra suddenly opened her eyes as the information sunk in, again.

'We're halfway there,' said a smiling Efi. 'Another twenty minutes or so.'

'I miss my bed,' said Alex with a yawn.

'That will teach you drinking wine till the early hours of the morning.' It was Stelios who spoke. 'My loving wife showed up as I was getting out of bed! Really! Can you imagine the gossip?'

'Stop moaning Stelios. Next time we'll take you with us, but you go all the way. No excuses.' Stelios of course knew nothing of Efi's or Alexandra's clandestine immersions. Alex leaned back and closed her eyes once more. She was in deep thought again. Her life was flashing by her. She remembered how she recruited Efi. Alex and Zoe first met Efi in early 1989 about a month after the funeral of Ian Coburn, alias Fabian Cabus, the father of the twins. The funeral took place in Antwerp where the twins were growing up under the care of Ian's aunt. Mitsos could not be present for his friend's funeral. He took Efi there a month later for the memorial service. Efi was twelve at the time and they spent a full week with the twins who were two years younger. Robert Ross or Uncle Bob as the twins affectionately knew him was also there, offering whatever comfort he could to all concerned. And now to have the intelligence services on both sides of the Atlantic to insinuate, to suggest that Ross had gone bad, that he turned was really hard to stomach for both the women. He was in danger and both women realized that they had to protect him at all costs.

As they grew up, Efi kept in touch with Alex while Zoe was roaming the globe with the World Health Organization. In February of 2003 after being engaged for a year, Alex got married to an American who was a logistics manager and advisor to the US military and she moved to Fairfax in Virginia where he lived. Both Zoe and Efi attended the wedding. Ross was also there, one of his rare trips abroad after retirement. He had to be there. He was instrumental in bringing Alex and the American together. He had his reasons. Two months later, in the middle of the USA-British led war against Saddam's Iraq, a government official announced to Alexandra that her husband was killed in Iraq. Alex demanded from the government and from the military to tell her what he was doing in Iraq and under what circumstances he lost his life. After a lot of perseverance and thorough investigation of the circumstances of her husband's death, it was finally but confidentially disclosed to Alex that he worked for the CIA under cover in Iraq during the war against Saddam. One thing led to another and Alex enlisted out of respect for the man she loved.

Efi meanwhile was studying medicine at King's College in London and Alex was there for her graduation in the early summer of 2004. That was well before the time when Zoe was almost mutilated by the King's Cross tube bomb on the Piccadilly Line. They were appalled by what was happening in the world. Alex had told Efi that her deceased husband's father, whom she never met, was also killed by terrorism. He was a passenger on the Pan Am flight that exploded over Lockerbie and how by a twist of fate, years later, she had received information from an unknown source that the explosive device on the plane was *allowed* to remain on board, after it was detected thus ensuring the flight's catastrophic fate. The culprits who allowed this to happen were the British Home Intelligence Services and more specific the head of Counter Terrorism at the time, one Eleanor Bishop. They had an agenda. What made her take note of this monstrous allegation was the fact that the source *proved* that this information originated by non-other than Alexandra's own father and that this was the reason he was killed. Efi knew how close her own father had been to Ian Coburn, alias Fabian Cabus. She told Alex that she felt helpless, incompetent to help put things right. That was the signal for Alex to step in and recruit her with the Agency. She would remain a sleeping agent and used if and when required. Her only contact with Langley would be Alexandra Coburn who was a rising star within the Intelligence and Analysis Department of the Agency. The DI as it is known.

'Hey, sleeping beauty, we are here.' Efi gently stoked Alexandra's blonde hair to wake her up.

'Gosh, I was tired,' she said.

'Don't you want something to eat?' It was Stelios who spoke.

'I prefer another hour's sleep if you don't mind.'

'No problem, let us all get together tonight then,' said a smiling Stelios.

'I will come and see you in 2, 3 hours after I finish from the hospital.' added Efi. 'And let me know if you need some clothes as you have been travelling light.'

'Any decent shops in Myrina?'

'Some but don't expect designer clothing. Light summer clothes, yes. On the other hand we don't differ that much, body-wise, you are welcome to come home and pick whatever you want.'

'Thanks Efi. I really appreciate that.' Alex nodded her approval, got out of the car and headed for her hotel room.

****

'Thank you Mrs. Porter. You have been very helpful.' Ray Wise was standing just outside the front door of the apartment in Manchester Square expressing, rather loudly, his gratitude to Daphne. His half-brother Gerard Ambroise was standing next to him holding a large brief case. 'And thanks for the tea too' he added. No response was heard from Daphne. He nodded his head and then he closed the door.

They entered the lift and Wise pressed the button for the ground floor using his pen. He felt his jacket pocket and retrieved a syringe and a small ampule containing a light yellow liquid. He filled the syringe and waited. It was the same syringe he had used on Daphne Porter a few minutes earlier.

'Everything all right then, gents?' Stanley went towards them as the lift doors opened on the ground floor.

'Yes thank you,' said Wise as his eyes scanned the reception area. It was deserted.

'We sign visitors in and out and I would require your signatures in the book if you don't mind.' Stanley flipped his log book open and pointed to the spot where he wanted them to sign.

With a swift move Wise injected the needle in Stanley's neck. Four seconds later he was on the floor, dead. The goon belonging to the Director of the British Secret Intelligence Services took Stan's log book and left the building with Gerard. Any autopsy on Stanley would show the cause of death to be the result of heart failure. The syringe fluid was untraceable. Minutes later a huge explosion shattered the tranquil surroundings of Manchester Square in Central London. Menacing flames with dense black smoke were now coming out of the blown out windows of the flat on the third floor. Sir Robert's apartment no longer existed.

A few blocks away driving in a southward direction, Gerard Ambroise was smiling, grinning with joy and satisfaction. It was not long before the grinning turned into a psychotic loud laughter. Wise, sitting next to him was shaking his head.

'Keep your eyes on the road and try to look normal, if that is possible,' said Wise.

Gerard laughed louder. 'I'll do my best bro, I'll do my best. Let the old wanker try and zap me again, if he has the balls.'

'Just drive...'

Chapter 17

Ross and Marie finished their breakfast and ventured out in the little streets surrounding their hotel. He was holding a small shopping bag containing a couple of newspapers which he took from their hotel suite. They avoided the main street that was Syngrou Avenue which was on the side of the hotel. This is a very busy and long street adjoining the city of Athens with the coast at Faliro, Piraeus and southern sea resorts. Too many security cameras. Marie was still excited about the previous night, their traditional Greek meal at a traditional little tavern in Plaka on the foothills of the Acropolis. She just loved Greek music and the way the locals danced sirtaki. She had drunk ouzo and retsina and Ross had to almost carry her into the hotel room. Halfway through the night she woke him up and made passionate love to him. He was a man reborn. No doubt about it.

Ross stopped at a pavement kiosk and bought a public telephone credit card for 20 euro. He used it the moment he spotted a public telephone booth that was working. He dialed the British Embassy and asked to speak to Trevor North, the contact given to him by Michel the hairdresser. He was asked to wait. Then a different person came on the line and asked him for his name and the reason he wanted to speak to North. Ross knew how Embassy staff worked and he expected this. He gave the name of 'Michael Dresser' and his business was information about exporting

DIY goods from England to Greece. After a while another man was talking to Ross.

'Good morning Mr. Dresser. I am Trevor North. How can I help you?'

'Good morning to you Mr. North. I am a director with Partoline Ltd and I require some advice on exporting our products to Greece.' Ross used the words as advised by Michel. There was a pause before North responded.

'I would be happy to meet you. Do you have a preferred meeting place, near the embassy? I can be free in about an hour.'

Ross looked at his watch. It was 10.10 in the morning. He then checked a piece of paper he was holding. 'There is a cafeteria opposite the Houses of Parliament in Constitution Square. The name is 'Zanetos.' I will be there at eleven thirty precisely reading a copy of the Financial Times.'

'Good,' said North. 'I am about five foot eight, slim with short blonde hair. White shirt, no jacket.'

Ross replaced the receiver and dialed another number. A direct number to a specific department at the Russian Embassy in Athens. Three minutes later he summoned Marie. They sat at a nearby bench where he gave her some instructions. They then took two separate taxis and headed for Constitution Square, *Syntagma,* as it is known locally. Marie arrived first and she took a seat in the second row of tables at the cafeteria. She ordered French coffee and insisted that she paid there and then. She left her purse on the table. Ross arrived a few minutes later, having first visited the Grand Bretagne Hotel on the other side of the square where he left a message in an envelope at the front desk. He sat at a table next to Marie's right. He ordered an orange juice and pretended to read one of the newspapers he had with him. It was a colorful Greek football newspaper. His eyes were inconspicuously scanning the area mainly to his right where the stairs led to the street in front of the Greek Parliament building. The British Embassy was not far from the Parliament building and that was the direction North would take, normally. He glanced at his watch. 10.55 a.m. The central Athens square was busy with people walking about as usual, crisscrossing the large square. Most of them held a small bottle of cold water, taking a sip every now and then. The heat was almost unbearable. He did his best not to look towards Marie who pretended to speak on her mobile phone. Five minutes later Ross noticed two well-built men in their thirties descending the staircase from street level into the square. The fact that they wore jackets on a hot summer's morning placed Ross on alert. They could be carrying guns he thought. The two men casually walked past the spot where he was seating and then sat at a table to his left, about 10 meters away. He heard them order iced coffee in Greek but they had a foreign accent.

Ten minutes later another man in a suit was walking towards Ross. He casually looked at him but did not stop. Ross was still reading his newspaper. However the corner of his eye did catch the brief exchange of a glance between him and the two men sitting to his left. That was enough. Amateurs, he thought. A few moments later the two men placed some money on the table, got up and approached Ross. One of them spoke but just before he did he ever so slightly pulled his jacket back ensuring Ross saw a gun in a holster.

'Sir, we are British Embassy security staff. We are to escort you safely to the Embassy.'

'Pourquoi? qui êtes-vous?' Ross was asking them why and who they were, in French. He spoke loud enough to ensure Marie had heard him. Before anyone could respond

Marie got up and sprayed both men in the face with a strong pepper spray. The men instinctively covered their eyes with their hands as they yelled. They were temporarily blinded and Marie slipped her purse in the jacket pocket of one of the men. She then shouted in broken English.

'Help, they steal my purse, they steal my money.'

As other customers and staff rushed to her aid, with a swift move Ross buried his knee in the groin of one of the men and punched the other in the stomach. Both fell to the floor. Four or five people incapacitated them and Marie pointed to the one with her purse in his pocket.

'Him, in his pocket,' she shouted. The cafeteria waiter searched him and retrieved her purse. Upon noticing the gun he immediately yelled that somebody should summon the police and as more and more people congregated to the scene, Ross and Marie slipped away. Trevor North had been obviously compromised.

****

Nick Porter sat at the back of a yellow cab which was heading for the Grand Bretagne Hotel at the center of Athens, adjacent to Constitution Square. His Swiss Air flight had touched down at Eleftherios Venizelos international airport an hour earlier. He was in tears. George Clayton, Sir Robert's doctor friend left urgent messages on his mobile phone to contact him immediately. He must have tried to phone him during his flight from Geneva to Athens. Nick did call from his Swiss-number mobile phone the moment he disembarked. Clayton had asked him where he was and if he had any news from Ross. He told him he was in a meeting and his phone was switched off and no, he had not heard from Sir Robert. He asked Clayton what was wrong. And then it hit him. Hard.

Clayton said that his mother, Daphne, was killed in what seemed like an unfortunate gas accident which blew the flat to bits. He could not reach Sir Robert who was abroad, somewhere. After the initial shock, Nick tried to compose himself and said what he thought was a normal thing to say. That he would be in London in the morning. He did not see his mother on a regular basis but he did love her. He was almost in shock. Before he left the airport building for the taxi rank, he located a bar and quickly downed a couple of whisky shots. He had to come to his mother's home country to find out that she was dead. He thought of getting the next flight to London. However he blindly trusted Sir Robert and wondered if his secrecy regarding their meeting in Athens had any direct or indirect links to his mother's death. He also wondered if Sir Robert knew of Daphne's death. He would find out soon.

***

Alexandra Coburn sat in the little coffee house drinking Greek coffee and sipping brandy. The same place she sat the day before. This time it was packed. She was wearing a long black dress which Efi gave her. She had no make-up on and donned a pair of dark sunglasses. She had just buried her sister along with Efi's father at the little village of Calliope on the eastern part of the island of Limnos. It was tradition in Greece that after the burial, family and friends get together in a common place such as a coffee house and go through a social process known as *parigoria,* comfort in other words. This entailed the drinking of local coffee with brandy, eating pieces of bread, local cheese and olives and the telling of good-natured stories about the deceased. People also offered their condolences to the bereaved. Stelios and Efi were finalizing some church documentation regarding the burial service that took place earlier. George Webb was sitting next to Alex.

'Alexandra, before Stelios and Efi return from the church, I would like us to have a few words alone please.' Alex looked at him but said nothing. Webb carried on. 'There is a lot of work to be done here. We have to piece the jigsaw together. I also need to tell you, confide something to you. Something that has worried me ever since I arrived on the island. Not pretty but we've got to discuss it. Just you and me.'

'The cafeteria next to the hotel where I am staying in Myrina. At nine tonight.' Upon finishing her sentence Alex got up and greeted Efi and Stelios with a hug and kissed them both on the cheek.

'All is done,' said Stelios. 'I will take care of the graves and what have you in due course.'

'What was all the talk about Zoe being allowed or not allowed to be buried here?' It was Webb who asked.

'The main obstacle was that the priest here can only bury Greek Orthodox Christians and Zoe being foreign, her religion came into questioning,' said Stelios.

'However we did prove that my father christened Zoe when she was a baby and everyone took it for granted that if Mitsos was an Orthodox Christian so must have been Zoe,' added Efi.

'And what does that make me?' Alex directed her rhetorical question to Efi.

'We have to ask *your* godfather, when we find him.'

'And who might that be?' It was Webb asking.

Alexandra took her sunglasses off and looked at Webb. 'Sir Robert Ross,' she said. It seemed as if an electric current run through Webb's spine. He was lost for words. Efi quickly seized the moment and took Alexandra's hand before she spoke.

'When I was old enough, I remember my father telling me of the double christening in Antwerp and how Mr. Ross said to your father Alex, how fulfilled he must feel with the twins being his whole life's A to Z.' She paused for a moment. 'A to Z, as in Alexandra and Zoe.'

Alex shed a few tears and hugged Efi.

'It is odd that old Mitsos did not reveal to Zoe who he was.' Webb was not really asking anyone. He was murmuring to himself. 'That he was her Godfather I mean. Must have had his reasons I suppose.'

'Drop it George.' Alex was not asking. She was demanding. Webb lifted his hands up and apologized.

Chapter 18

Nick Porter was sunk in an armchair in his luxurious room at the Grand Bretagne Hotel in the center of Athens for the better part of an hour, thinking, trying to make sense of what was happening. He was still in a mild state of shock. He could not believe that his mother was no longer alive, the victim of a gas explosion accident, if indeed it was an accident. He was also thinking about his pending meeting. For the third time he read the handwritten message which Ross left him in a sealed envelope at the front desk of the hotel.

Nick I hope you have made it in time. Thanks a million for coming. Six minutes' walk away from your hotel there is a street called Amerikis Street. Ask the hotel concierge for directions. Find it. At number 35 there is a piano-bar named The Red Gallery. It opens at 7.30. Please be there tonight at 8.00. Go to the basement, sit at a table near the piano and order a drink. I'll join you 10-15 minutes later. Be inconspicuous and do not use your cell phone. R-REN21

Not use the cell phone. He already did. He called Clayton. Nick doubted whether Ross knew about Daphne. At least the old legend made sure that Nick accepted the message as authentic, coming from Ross himself, by the reference he made to REN21 – the Renewable Energy Policy Network for the twenty-first century. Nick took part in the conference in Bonn in June 2004 from which REN21 was launched. He looked at his watch. An hour before his rendezvous with his mentor. He headed for the shower.

At 7.58 Nick Porter entered the basement bar on Amerikis Street. He looked very handsome and chic dressed in a light beige summer suit. He was six feet tall with an athletic body and rich, strong black hair, just like his mother. He paused as he checked the premises. The ambiance was good. The lighting soft, the décor had class. Black and red the predominant colors. Black furniture with red curtains on all the walls and a red carpet. The room was cool and pleasant. It was well ventilated. There was a large bar with ten stools and around twenty low level tables. There were red ashtrays and burning red aromatic candles on each table. Around the tables there were low level black sofas with red cushions instead of chairs. There was a handsome woman seating at one of the tables in the far corner opposite the black piano sipping a long drink. Their eyes met momentarily. She had striking green eyes which complimented her dark complexion. The 'lady' of the house he thought. There were no other customers.

'*Kalispera.*' A smiling waitress had approached him. Her attire left little to the imagination.

'Good evening,' said Nick. 'English please.'

'Good evening. I am Katerina.' Her English accent was quite good.

'Katerina. Nice Greek name.'

'It can also be a Russian name, no? Do you have a reservation Sir?'

Nick was taken by surprise. 'Erm… no, are you fully booked?' He grimaced as he gazed at the empty tables.

'We shall be very busy later on, yes. We have just opened. If you want to stay till after eleven o'clock, then I

218

would suggest you take a seat at the bar, otherwise you can use one of the tables.' She smiled at him.

'Eleven? No, no. Maybe an hour, an hour and a half at the most.' He smiled back. 'I'll seat near the piano. I am expecting company any moment now.' Nick took a seat on the low sofa.

'Do you need a menu sir?'

'No, not now but I'll have a Scotch please while I wait. Do you have any malt whiskies?'

'Which one would you like?

'You have Talisker?' Nick was asking in hope.

'Ten or eighteen year old?'

He was impressed. 'Ten year old, no ice. Make that a double please.'

At that point a man dressed in a black tuxedo sat at the piano, nodded his head in the direction of the woman seating across the room, then looked at Nick Porter and started to play. A few seconds later Nick froze. This cannot be a coincidence he thought. Vasily Solovyov-Sedoi's Midnight in Moscow tune filled the room. He loved that tune which of course reminded him of Sir Robert. Katerina served him his drink accompanied by some pistachio nuts, fresh sliced cucumber and carrots. He held the crystal tumbler close to his nose for a moment or two before he took a rather long sip. He needed that. He leaned back and half-closed his eyes. Images of his mother flooded his mind. He had not seen her for a good 2, 3 years. He recalled the last time he visited Manchester Square and his mother cooked one of her traditional Greek dishes for him and Robert. She was happy. His mind then raced back to his student days at Oxford and the countless meetings and discussions he had with Sir Robert who visited him often. They would talk for hours, about anything and everything. Background CD music from Kenny Ball's instrumental version of 'Midnight in Moscow' would keep them company...

'*Dobryy vecher*. Nick my boy! *Eto bylo dolgo* '

He suddenly opened his eyes to see the figure of a man dressed casually standing in front of him with his arms open. He stood up and mildly shook his head, focusing his eyes on the face of the man with the brown hair and brown eyes.

'Sir Robert? Is that you? My God. *Kak priyatno videt' vas snova*. You, you look ...different.' Both men exchanged greetings in Russian. Nick embraced Ross, both men hugging each other for more than a few seconds.

'You look fine my boy. Oh, am I happy to see you.' The two men sat down. Nick could not hold himself any longer. The emotions were too much. He realized Ross did not know about Daphne. He broke down, sobbed and buried his head in his mentor's embrace.

'She's dead, mother is dead, she's dead.'

'What? WHAT? How?' Ross felt as if a knife tore his stomach to pieces. He felt like vomiting. He became speechless, biting his lower lip hard, trying not to cry, trying not to scream. Tears filled his eyes, blurring his vision. He got rid of his brown contact lenses and put his glasses on.

'Fuck this charade,' he said. 'I am going back to my own hair colour tomorrow.' A minute later The Rolls took over his body, mind and soul. He stood up, gestured to the sobbing Nick to wait and went across the room to where Marie was seating looking extremely anxious by now. He whispered something to her and then instructed Katerina, the waitress to call a taxi for her. Marie was going back to the hotel alone. It was going to be a long night. A very long night.

220

***

Alexandra Coburn walked into the cafeteria next to the hotel where she was staying to find George Webb drinking a beer. She confided to Efi that she was to meet Webb, alone – as per his request. Webb upon seeing her got up and offered a seat at his table. Alexandra gave him a prolonged hug before she sat down.

'That was nice. Thank you my dear.' Webb was somewhat surprised. 'I trust you had a good afternoon's rest my dear.' He summoned a waitress. 'What would you like?'

'Can I have a proper English tea, with fresh milk please?' She shrugged her shoulders and smiled, her blue eyes flashing. She had little or no make-up at all but still looked quite stunning in her long black summer dress – courtesy of Efi's wardrobe.

'You may indeed,' responded Webb. 'Even though I was hoping that we could have shared a bottle of that nice Limnos wine we had the other night.'

'The night is still young,' said Alex with a cheeky wink of the eye. Webb was not quite sure how to interpret that.

'Erm… Absolutely,' he said. He cleared his throat. 'Let's talk shop. Alexandra, what I am about to tell you is classified. The agency has valid reasons to believe that there is a Russian mole, or moles within the higher echelons of the British Intelligence Services.'

'I would have been surprised if they hadn't.' Alex delivered the words with an as a matter of fact tone which took Webb by surprise. 'Do you seriously think that our own agency is free from infiltrators?' Before Webb could respond she carried on. 'Anyhow, what does this have to do with us and how does it affect our case here?'

'We have valid reasons to believe that your sister's murder is connected to this mole and that this mole may or may not have ties with one of our own.' George braced himself for the response which was delivered like a volley of machinegun fire.

'Stuff your *valid reasons* George! Do you have something tangible? Solid proof?' Alex was not letting go. 'If my sister was killed in order to protect a Russian spy or double agent that may or may not have infiltrated the SIS I want names – *names* George and undisputable evidence with concrete verified proof, you understand?'

'You are taking this too personal...'

'Fucking sure I am! Why is Efi excluded from this conversation...' suddenly Alexandra came to an abrupt stop as a sense of realization set in. Webb said nothing. 'Oh no, no, no NO! Surely she's not a suspect.'

'I, I personally, suggested nothing of the kind.' Webb was quick in his response. 'However, others do not exclude the possibility that she is collaborating with the other side.'

'Others? What others? What other side? I have been working with the firm for quite a few years now and you know what? Half the people there are psychotic, paranoid. The other half is full of idiots, just like you. More often than not the truth is right in front of your face and not hidden in dark labyrinths of deceit and mystery. If it is too straightforward people don't accept it.' Alexandra stopped talking as her tea was being served. She waited for a while before she hastily got up.

'You are drawing attention my dear. Let's be civilized. At least finish your tea.' Webb offered to pour the beverage.

'Mr Webb, you have until tomorrow morning to come up with facts and names substantiating all you have said. Do that and I am with you all the way. Fail and you are on your own. I am going to call my boss now. Is that all right with you?'

'I know who your shepherd is. I can call him too.'

'Fuck you.'

Webb shook his head.

'Please! One moment, please Alexandra. Just hear me out.' Webb was almost begging. She paused. 'Does the name Mikel Bengochea mean anything to you?'

Alexandra, reluctantly, sat down again and poured some tea in her cup. 'Yes it does,' she said. 'What about him?'

'He's the young Spanish lecturer at London University who helped your sister two years ago when her apartment was burgled.'

'Yes. He died shortly after he was hit by a car. Well?'

'He was planted there by your godfather. Robert Ross.' Webb had Alexandra's full attention now. 'As far as we know he may have been placed there to either protect Zoe and/or to gain her confidence for reasons yet unknown.'

'And as far as I know the only time they ever met and talked was on the day of the break-in into her apartment. So?'

'Bengochea was from Bilbao, not what we would call One hundred percent Spanish. He was a Basque – Euskal Herria.'

'So?' Alex was getting impatient.

'His mother is one Arantxa Abasolo, a close and trusted collaborator of Robert Ross. An old member of the so-called Hub network.'

'Okay, so Sir Robert assigned someone to look after my sister. Again, what evidence do you have that there is, there was, any foul play?'

'My dear, bear with me and you'll see the bigger picture. The Abasolo woman, Mikel's mother, was taken out by a covert section of our agency ten days ago. She was sixty…'

'Taken *out?*'

'Assassinated.'

Alexandra moved a little closer to him. She pushed her tea out of the way as she leaned on the table. 'All right George. You have my full attention. What else?'

'Abasolo was DGI *and* KGB – well, was KGB, now it is the FSB.'

'DGI? As in Dirección General de Inteligencia, Cuba? Holy shit! What about Mikel, the son?'

He nodded. 'We are not sure about Mikel but the question you should be asking me is why she was taken out by our lot?'

'Can't wait to hear your version…' Alex was being a little sarcastic. Webb ignored it.

'She was about to pass information to the Russians that had to do with the British SIS. Sensitive and damaging information that could have forced the British Prime Minister to resign.'

'Not a bad idea. Blyth is a conniving warmonger, much worse than the idiot we have in power.'

'Careful Alex. That remark can cost you your job.' Webb was not joking.

'But why not hand all the intelligence you say we had to the Brits and let them deal with it. After all it was their neck under the axe.'

'Frankly, we do not know who to trust within the British SIS. I know this is difficult to comprehend, but it is true. There are so many factions, each with their own agenda.' Webb did not mince his words.

'A bit like our lot then.'

'Not really. As I have told you last night I am still assigned to the MoD. Believe me. We do not trust the SIS, not fully. There seems to be a kind of competition between each department as if each head puts his or her personal agenda ahead of the interests of the country. I understand that the Royals are uncomfortable with this situation. Anyhow, enough said.'

'Is that it? You have not told me who the Russian moles are yet. That was the main purpose of this meeting was it not?'

'We don't know but if our intelligence is correct, it would make the Cambridge Five look like kindergarten kids. What we suspect is that Ross almost certainly knows. That is why he's hunted and had to go underground. I personally believe that there is a tug-of-war between MI5 and MI6 as to who gets to him first. I suppose both branches are after the same information but for different reasons.'

Alex fixed her eyes on him. 'Interesting,' she said. 'But who is actually hounding my godfather, the good guys or the bad guys?'

'That is the million dollar question my dear. What I can tell you is that we also believe that Ross may be in direct contact with Efi. They may be working together. I need you to verify this for me, without making waves.'

'By the same token, what makes you sure that Sir Robert is not in direct contact with me too?'

'He's not. I am willing to take the gamble. I trust my instincts.' Webb sounded sure of himself.

Alexandra suddenly stood up. She leaned her head towards Webb's ear and whispered.

'All right George. Tonight as well as last night you said a lot of things. It can all be true or it can all be bullshit. Could be half-truths and half-lies. Either way I'll expect you for breakfast in the morning at nine and convince me that is not all bullshit because if you fail to convince me, I will destroy you. I am not a fan of the misinformation games. I will be calling Langley tonight and I can't stay here forever.' She smiled at him then kissed him on the forehead and left. Webb could not help feeling impressed by the dynamic young agent. He watched her as she gracefully walked out of the cafeteria and into her hotel next door. What he did not see, was the very brief eye contact she had with a bearded handsome young man seating a few tables away enjoying a beer. He had an auburn long stubble and shoulder long hair. He promptly finished his beer and casually walked out into the busy street. As soon as Alexandra entered her hotel she inserted a local mobile phone credit card in her cell phone and called Efi.

'Empros…'

'It's Alex. We need to talk. Now.'

***

Timothy Blyth, the British Prime Minister, awaited the arrival of 'C' who was none other than James Marlow Scargill, the head of MI6. He was in the sterile room deep below street level at Downing Street. He was lost in thought and looked like a broken man. He urgently demanded the meeting earlier in the afternoon, the moment he found out about Daphne Porter's *accidental* death. There was another subject he wanted to discuss with Scargill. The implications, if any, regarding the death of an elderly Basque woman in Bilbao. He had the feeling that on this subject he may be a step ahead of his own intelligence services.

There was a soft security buzz and the door suddenly opened. An apologetic Scargill entered the room.

'I am very sorry Prime Minister. I was delayed by an American visitor who secured a last minute appointment to see me, through the US Secretary of State no less.'

As soon as the door was shut again, Blyth gestured to him to take a seat and went straight to the point.

'One thing at a time. Who was behind the death of Daphne Porter and what is the reason for her… erm how do you people classify these exercises? Oh yes, her *deletion*?'

'What makes you think that it was not a gas explosion accident?'

'Accident? And the building's porter, on the ground floor, shit himself at the sound of the explosion and died of a heart attack, I suppose.' Blyth's facial expression and general disposition suddenly changed for the worse and Scargill immediately corrected himself. 'Very sorry Tim, I take that back.'

'Careful now. That is the second time you apologized within 20 seconds. Well?'

'Mrs. Porter was working for Eleanor Bishop, MI5.'

'What? Are you sure? Why?'

'She was planted there, from the start, to keep an eye on Ross. To retrieve information from Ross, to monitor his movements, his calls. She did gain his trust. I am sure he has feelings for her.'

'But why kill her? What was the purpose? How does her silence serve the country?' Blyth was persisting. Scargill's frosty response was delivered with no strings attached.

'Sometimes I am really at a loss when you ask questions like that. It is just the two of us now, talking face-to-face.'

'Just answer the question.'

It was done for *your* sake. To protect *you*.' Blyth seemed uncomfortably perplexed. Scargill carried on.

'Why do you think she was planted there? What do you think Bishop wanted to achieve? Your downfall by getting her hands on palpable information that you, Prime Minister, returned the favour to your American benefactors by completely and blindly siding with them, on the 'go it alone policy' against Saddam. This was totally against public opinion and left us with a bitterly divided Parliament. The European Union leaders also distanced themselves from the British position. You dragged the country to war with unforeseen consequences – the results of which we started to witness here, in London, two summers ago. Let me remind you that you were seen as the US President's poodle. Need I go on?'

'We do not give in to terrorism. You know that.' Blyth was barely audible.

'Nothing to do with the issue. You have been in the game longer than I have. You know the rules. You placed Britain's political, geopolitical, economic and trade allegiance with the States ahead of that of our natural partners—the European Union. You have succumbed to American pressure, measures, objectives and policies which will have an eroding effect on our democracy, our sovereignty and our independence if you carry on like this. Not to mention the economy. We are not a fucking US satellite for God's sake.'

'You are exaggerating everything and you are the last person to give me lessons on democracy. You don't believe in democracy, you said so yourself.'

'Tim, Tim my dear friend. Bishop knows you have been generously supported by the Americans. She knows of your, how shall I put it, your implication, your involvement of the US backed T&S Group. They made you part of it. That is why they have you in their pocket. Bishop wanted proof so she could serve your head on a plate.'

'Fucking politics. Filthy business. Worse than running a drugs cartel.' Blyth whispered the words.

'I am not a politician. Well, maybe not yet. I am a fucking spy!' Scargill took a deep breath and looked at the Prime Minister with some sympathy. 'Tim, I will explain all there is to explain in a minute but right now I wish to speak to you as a friend – and believe me, you haven't too many friends left. I think you should consider resigning, stepping down – sooner rather than later. Find an excuse before irreparable damage is done, both, to you personally and to the country. There seems to be no panacea in sight. Please!'

'I have already taken the decision to step down a few days ago. In fact the very day after our last meeting in this outlandish room. Arrangements have already been made to hand the party leadership to the Chancellor of the Exchequer, tomorrow.'

Scargill seemed surprised. 'Tomorrow? Then what?' he asked. 'Elections?'

'No, no, no. No elections. Then, in a few days, I will move out of No. 10 and the Chancellor will become Prime Minister until the end of term. If we go to elections now, the party will be annihilated.'

'Why the Chancellor? Not that I dislike Gordon Braddick but I would have thought there are others, better suited.'

Blyth sighed deeply and threw his arms in the air. 'It falls in line with a silly promise that was made over a few drinks years ago. He also knows about my indirect connection with the T & S Group and all the arms deals that were done in the eighties. In short, he has me by the balls too. Anyway, the media will be informed in the morning.'

Scargill was pleased in a way. 'I think it is the right decision Tim. I am happy for you. You and I know that you should have done it sooner. For the good of the country. You could have told me about Braddick a lot earlier. You know what we do to blackmailers.'

Blyth listened but said nothing. Both men stared at each other in silence for a few moments. It was Blyth who spoke first. 'Talking of Ross and the book you say he's about to publish, *Whitehall After Dark* was it? I am informed that another book will be out before the end of the year regarding the weird or strange death of a certain scientist we both knew. The author is a Member of Parliament for God's sake! How the fuck can I sleep at nights? Enough. I am out.'

'One man's conspiracy theory that the scientist did not commit suicide but was murdered. Nothing more, nothing less. He can't prove anything,' said a reassuring Scargill 'Politicians from both sides of the House, already look upon him as if he is the village idiot. What happened to decency? Protecting our own? Protecting each other and the profession?'

'Discrediting people is part of your job. But you and I know, don't we Jim? We both *really* know.' Blyth hid his face in his hands. He was indeed a broken man.

'Tim, what is done is done. Let us finish with this.'

'Yes let's.' Blyth stood up and walked nervously around the room.

'After this, as Director of MI6 I should not tell you anything regarding Daphne Porter and Abasolo, the Basque woman. Yes, I know that you have been informed about her. My department is in the know. We are not totally incompetent. However, as a friend and probably someone who will almost certainly be asked to resign by your successor, I will fill you in and then erase the board. Who knows? I may need you to scratch my back in the future. Deal?'

'I'm listening.'

For the next 10 minutes, Scargill embarked on a monologue, stating facts, dates and events on how the USA Government had managed to manipulate circumstances and fabricate events in order to gain popular support to implement their strategic plans to invade Iraq and therefore resurrect specific sectors of the American economy in the process. However, in order to avoid global outcry and condemnation the Americans needed a trusted ally to go the distance with them. This would also ensure a soft landing at the United Nations where the 'legality' of the military operations would be ferociously questioned, especially by the UN Security Council. Britain would oblige. Some of the US companies that would benefit from the intervention in Iraq were directly connected to Timothy Blyth's early benefactors. The revelations were not alien to Blyth for he knew most of this from first-hand experience and direct, voluntary, involvement. The Americans were cashing in on their investment. Blyth was therefore blindly supporting the US initiative despite very strong objections from the public at large and across the British political spectrum. The disapproval from within his own governing party was immense. This had raised eyebrows and the intelligence services started to investigate the preposterous possibility that their own PM may have been 'compromised' by friendly and allied foreign intelligence services or that he was simply being blackmailed for some reason. It was not long before the SIS established that Timothy Blyth was being groomed for the PM's job with generous support and assistance, political and economic, from organizations in the USA – the CIA as well as the Pentagon included. They also used their main device in

Europe, Africa and the Middle East. The T&S Group. A group funded by faceless American investors who were simply implementing US foreign strategy, geopolitical and economic, through the inconspicuous trade policies and actions of the Group.

This process had begun in 1994, with Blyth being installed leader of his party. Later that same year, the US started sending troops to the Gulf – the first stage of their long-term plan. Robert Ross and the Hub also became aware of this and reacted. It was not handled well, it became messy and later that led to the decommissioning of the ghost government agency that was the Hub. Ross kept records. This is the information that Elle Bishop wants. Ross filed everything in a dossier, records of meetings, dates, documents even recorded conversations that a possible future British Prime Minister could be politically influenced by a foreign government – friendly or not. For Ross, this was his healthy retirement insurance, should things turn sour – and they did. A couple of years later when Blyth was elected to power, the Hub was promptly decommissioned by direct No. 10 intervention. Scargill assisted the new Prime Minister with the Hub's disbanding and his reward was his later appointment as head of MI6. Meanwhile Ross, for reasons of his own, decided not to do anything about the damaging information he gathered. He therefore entrusted his dossier to his real mistress which was none other than Hub collaborator Arantxa Abasolo in Bilbao. She was a young divorcee with a baby child when Ross took her under his wing. He trusted her 100% and he became her lover for a period. MI6 had their own mole within the Hub – one Charlie Chow and that is how they knew of the dossier's existence. Chow is still active and MI6 is using him to get to Ross. The CIA dared not contact the British SIS on the subject of the dossier because it was of their own doing and they were not going to parade their dirty laundry. The fact that an unofficial black ops department of the agency burnt Abasolo's house to cinders, with her in it, suggests that they did not retrieve the damaging dossier. The same black ops department were also taking out other known members of the Hub, just in case...

Scargill informed Blyth that he will probably hand in his own resignation, soon, before he is asked to resign. He felt that his position would become untenable with a new Premier. To Blyth's surprise, Scargill confided to him that he is thinking of going into politics.

***

George Webb looked at his watch. It was about twenty minutes since Alexandra kissed him on the forehead and left. Ten minutes after that Efi showed up unexpectedly. She hugged him and he asked her if she wanted a drink. She politely refused, pointing to a bag with clothes she was holding. She was going to take them up to Alex and then call it a night. They agreed to meet for lunch the following day. Webb said goodnight and sat down again. He thought it was too early to call it a night himself so he ordered a gin and tonic. He leaned back in his seat and thought of Alexandra for a while. He thought of her with lust and feelings that were alien to him for such a long time. He could not help but notice that she was not wearing a bra and as she leaned towards him when she greeted him, he caught a glimpse of her breasts. He found her extremely desirable and although he was twice her age he would have made his move under different circumstances. However, he could not betray the love of his life, his companion, the man who gave him so much pleasure and happiness over

233

the last 30 years. He wondered what he was doing at this time. Still early evening in London. He ordered another drink and promptly dismissed Alexandra from his mind. He retrieved his cell phone from his pocket and called Carl Santori, his lover. They spoke for about ten minutes. He promised he would be back home soon. He felt better. Oh how he missed Carl and how he wished he could be with him tonight. He finished his drink and contemplated having another. He thought not. He felt a little woozy. He left some money on the table and took the dimly lit coastal road back to his bungalow hotel, less than fifteen minutes' walk away. He felt the need to walk and breathe in the evening sea air. Half way down the road with the sea on his left and a small park to his right, he was approached by an athletic young man wearing black pants and a baggy white summer shirt. He was holding a small leather shoulder bag.

'*Kalispera.*'

Webb looked at the young man who smiled at him. The moonlight shone on his long auburn hair. He looked like an angel.

'Erm, good evening my Greek is not so good...'

'Do not worry,' replied the young man. 'I speak English. My name is Antonio. I am from Torino. Italia.'

'Hello Antonio from Torino. I am George from London. What can I do for you?'

Antonio hesitated for a moment before he spoke. 'You seem like a decent man, a gentleman. I was seating close to you where you had your drink just now.'

'And?'

The young man lowered his eyes and spoke softly. 'I thought you may be lonely and in need of some company...'

Webb's eyes scanned the surrounding area. There was nobody about. He did not hesitate. He gently stroked Antonio's hair. 'What do you have in mind?' he asked.

Antonio opened his handbag and produced a sachet containing a condom. Webb felt movement in his loins.

'Where?' He asked. 'I don't think my hotel is a good idea.'

'I have a hotel room but it is on the other side of Myrina. They don't ask questions there. But we'll need taxi. Here if you like, there is nobody around. The park, at this time, is deserted,' said Antonio. 'Look, there is a gazebo, how you call it, a small pavilion out of street view just over there. No lights, only moonshine.'

Webb glanced behind him and spotted the pavilion behind a few trees. It was in the middle of the park about 50 yards away. He placed his hand in his inner jacket pocket and felt for his gun, a small Beretta. Security, just in case he thought. He then placed his palm on Antonio's bearded face and caressed it.

'You have a lovely smile and an inviting mouth.' Webb gently pushed his thumb inside Antonio's mouth.

Antonio sucked it for a few seconds and then gently ushered him towards the gazebo. He asked Webb to seat on the bench while he kneeled on the floor in front of him. He unzipped him and smiled.

'I am going to give you the best oral sex you ever had in your life.'

In a flash, Antonio produced a syringe from his hand bag with which he swiftly injected Webb's genitals. The CIA agent quivered as the young man placed his hand over his victim's mouth until he stopped shaking. Five seconds later the CIA agent was dead. The killer retrieved the syringe and placed the dead man in a seating position on the bench. He then inserted a used envelope in the inside jacket pocket of his victim and left the park in an opposite direction from which they entered it. He made his way back to the front of Alexandra's hotel. From street level he looked up at the window of a specific room on the third floor. The light was on. He took a small canister out of his bag, shook it, and promptly but discreetly sprayed the white wall of a bar across the street from the hotel with the letter X. He then took a taxi back to his own hotel. In his room, he undyed his hair and beard back to their normal color which was black. He tied his hair into a ponytail and donned the robes of a monk. He would take the very early morning ferry to Kavala and then the bus to Ouranoupoli on his way back to the monastery. The assassin Georgy Gorelov, operating under cover as a monk in the St. Panteleimon Monastery on the Holy Mountain, successfully executed his mission. His boss, one James Marlow Scargill, will be pleased.

***

Back at her hotel room, Marie waited deep into the night for Ross to arrive. When he did enter the room, well after midnight, she could not help but detect the strong smell of alcohol emanating from his breath. The stench of cigar smoke covered his clothing. She rushed toward him and hugged him. She did not say anything and she did not ask him anything. She sensed that he needed time. He would talk to her when he felt ready. For a second or two she stared at his blue eyes, the first time she laid eyes on him without his coloured contact lenses. She smiled and he kissed her on the forehead.

'I need to get out of these cloths,' he said. 'In fact I need a shower and tomorrow maybe I can also revert to my real hair colour. I'm fed up with this charade.'

Fifteen minutes later Ross came out of the bathroom wearing the hotel's bathrobe. Marie was still awake. She offered to dry his hair. Once done they were both in bed. Ross started to talk. He talked for a good half-an-hour. He shared the pain he felt for Daphne. He told Marie that he needed to be strong, for Nick's sake. He explained that Nick was more than a son. They had a special relationship that was built on trust. A relationship that was built on the strong foundations of the ideals they both shared and believed in. They both had a strong sense of justice. They despised the lies that their government and Her Majesty's allies were brainwashing public opinion with. They were sick to death by the way the controlled media, on both sides of the Atlantic, was influencing events through fabricated reports and unfounded stories. They were sick to death by the way their government was demonizing specific countries and praising others, all in the name of profit and geopolitical gain. People did not seem to matter anymore. They were just numbers. Sir Robert Ross and Nick Porter were one on such matters, in harmony with each other's thoughts and beliefs.

Marie listened and then she told him that when she took the decision to leave Port La Nouvelle, to leave her old meaningless life, that yes, she did take a gamble on a man she only met hours before, when she followed him into the unknown. Yes, she had doubts but with every hour in his presence, the doubts and the risk factor evaporated. She would follow him to the end of the world and would die with him if need be.

Chapter 19

Lykavittos Hill, or *Lycabettus* as is also known among the many tourists that visit it, is a steep limestone hill rising to almost one thousand feet above sea level in the middle of Athens. There is easy access to the top via a funicular railway. At the top there is a small plateau housing the St George chapel and an open air cafeteria. It was mid-morning but pretty warm, so Nick Porter was seating under an umbrella at a table near the edge. He was admiring the breathtaking view. At this height, the cacophony of everyday life on the busy streets of Athens below was totally missing from the serene environment of the cafeteria. He was enjoying a morning coffee and a toasted sandwich. In his mind he was analyzing the events and conversations with his mentor the night before at the Red Gallery. Once the tears had dried, they had a few drinks and then more drinks and spoke at length. Ross explained in detail what was happening to him and where he was heading. He described the importance of the bigger picture. His spoke of his chance meeting with Marie and their journey from to Port La Nouvelle, to Greece via Paris. He recounted his encounter with the British Embassy people at Syntagma Square. They chatted a lot over drinks and decided on what steps to take next. They had to make three phone calls, using an unlisted phone number in a private room at the Red Gallery. Nick was impressed by the set-up of the joint, which was recommended to Ross by a friend in the Russian Embassy in Athens. The club was, of course, secretly funded by the Russian Government. The first call was to George Clayton in order to make arrangements for Daphne's funeral in a few days. The second call to a lady in Limnos Island. The final call was to a trusted friend at Vauxhall Cross, the MI6 Headquarters using a series of sterile and pre-agreed test numbers in order to locate the right person. A trusted friend with whom he had no direct contact for over twenty years. A friend who he himself sat in the very club Ross was seating at now, twenty-seven years ago. Nick had made the first and third calls while Ross made the second call. The Red Gallery was a front for the FSB, the Russian Federal Security Service, which is the modernized version of the old Soviet KGB. Ross and Nick plus another person will be revisiting the Red Gallery in the evening – a good thirty minutes before the bar opens for the public.

***

The sudden demise of George Webb was made known very early in the morning. He was discovered slumped on a bench in the park by early morning joggers. The British Embassy in Athens was informed via the EYP, the National Intelligence Service of Greece. They were told that the police in Limnos were in possession of some very sensitive documents which they retrieved from the deceased. The British Embassy gave specific instructions that the body was not to be tampered with in any way and that no autopsy was to be carried out until a British led team arrived on the island. They also insisted that all documentation and personal belongings found on the dead British national should be kept at a safe place and handed over to the Embassy people. At this stage there was no suspicion of foul play and the local police were initially contributing the death to a heart attack. An elderly man who had a few drinks the night before and who felt unwell on his way back to his hotel. Perhaps he paused at the park to catch his breath.

Alexandra and Efi identified the deceased and spent the mid-morning at the main police station in Myrina on the island of Limnos where they gave statements to the police regarding their last face to face meetings with Webb. They were also asked to confirm their whereabouts the night before. That was easy to do as Efi was in Alexandra's hotel room for a good three hours immediately after both women were seen, cordially, talking to Webb at the cafeteria the night before. The two women twice ordered drinks to be taken to their room and the hotel staff confirmed this. Alexandra asked the police if they had any other need for her as she planned to leave the island later in the day. They said she could go but asked her to leave a contact number in case there were new developments regarding her sister's death.

***

James Marlow Scargill boarded the first coach of the Piccadilly Line train at Osterley Station in South-west London. He was dressed very casually, sporting a Pirelli jockey cap and dark Ray-Ban pilot sunglasses. He was carrying a copy of the Daily Mirror newspaper. It was early morning and the train was packed with commuters heading for their work in Central London. He checked the time and at the next station which was Boston Manor he walked out of the train and casually made his way to the other end of the platform. Two minutes later another train arrived and he entered the last coach. He stood near the middle carriage door and was reading his paper. A few stops later, at Hammersmith Station, quite a few people got off the train. His eyes discreetly scanned the platform. He saw what he wanted to see. A woman in her late fifties, smartly dressed, with the classic 'cauliflower' hairstyle as he often described it. She was holding a shopping bag and boarded the last carriage of the Piccadilly Line train heading for Cockfosters. Their eyes met momentarily. At the next station Scargill got out and boarded the next carriage where he managed to find an empty seat. A few stops later at Hyde Park Corner, the smartly dressed woman did exactly the same thing. There was an empty seat next to Scargill and she sat herself down. Scargill carried on reading his newspaper while the woman was checking the contents of the shopping bag she was holding. They did not look at each other and they did not speak. Thirty-five minutes later the train was pulling into Arnos Grove Station, a station Scargill had visited only a few days before. At the station the last passenger in that carriage got off, leaving Scargill and the woman as the only passengers. As soon as the train was on its way to the next station, the woman spoke.

'You watch too many spy films JMS.'

'Better safe than sorry Elle. Let us get off at the next station and get on a southbound train. We can talk then.'

Eleanor Bishop, the head of MI5 Home Security, smiled. 'You do know there are cameras on these trains now days, don't you?'

'Yes, but they cannot record what we are about to agree on. Let us finish this and then we can go to the oyster bar at Selfridges and have something to eat like normal people…'

'Normal? Did you say normal? All right young man, we can be normal for a while I suppose.' She laughed out loud before she composed herself once more. 'And agree we shall, otherwise we are not getting off the train.'

'Absolutely,' said Scargill. 'We'll do ourselves a favour and serve our country at the same time. After all, we are on the same side, are we not?'

'I don't know. Are we on the same side? I received an overseas phone call at the crack of dawn today. I suppose your department has nothing to do with the execution of George Webb, has it?'

'What?' Scargill looked and sounded surprised.

'Come on Jimmy, let us cut the bullshit and talk like adults. I suppose you can do that...'

'All right Elle. I will give you some information on Webb that should make you concerned. I will also throw in some free info on your psychotic assassin Anderson. The sooner he goes the better for all of us I can assure you.'

'Can't wait to listen to your stories. It is going to be a defining day, I am sure.'

An hour and a half later they were seating at the Oyster Bar at Selfridges in Oxford Street. A few seats away Ray Wise and Jason Bell, goons and bodyguards for Scargill and Bishop kept a discreet eye on the unlikely couple. This was an *official* social meeting between senior personnel of two intelligence services and the goons had to be present. The serious talking had been done. All that was going to be discussed from here on is how they can't wait for September when native oysters will be available and how the weather managed to spoil the day at Wimbledon, again!

***

That same night the head of the MI6 was sat at his desk in his underground private sterile room at Vauxhall Cross, reflecting on the day's events. His fingers were twisting and turning an elastic band. He was looking at everything and nothing. His mind was racing ahead, to events yet to

242

happen. He was close. Very close. No fuck ups now and no backing out. He had to be calm. He had to be in control. No way was the elastic band going to snap between his fingers, this time.

He was happy with himself. He had reached a *gentlemen's agreement* with Eleanor Bishop. An agreement that was purely based on blackmail. Scargill was to bury the evidence which proved that Bishop, in her capacity as head of the counter terrorism back in 1988, knew that the Pan Am plane that fell on Lockerbie was carrying a bomb and yet she let it go in order to implicate the Libyans and therefore force pro-British political and commercial agreements with Gaddafi. In return Scargill was to resign and run for Parliament. Bishop was to assist him rise to the top in any way she could. He was eyeing the Prime Minister's job within the next few years. Bishop herself was to make way for a new head of MI5 and she promised to cooperate and actually make the right statements in a pending enquiry regarding the war in Iraq. She would support the idea that the invasion of Iraq was wrong as there was no real evidence that Saddam was manufacturing weapons of mass destruction and that as a result of the USA-British intervention in Iraq, al-Qaida was able to establish a foothold in Iraq with all the consequences that followed.

In a sense she would be crucifying her old adversary Timothy Blyth and she was happy with that. A win-win situation. Scargill allowed himself a smile. He also promised her that once on his way to the top civil job, he would give her a few names of suspected Russian spies living as US citizens and Canadian citizens. She was not to disclose her source and she could use this information to repair British-US relations after she testifies that there was no sound reason for going to war with Iraq. A win-win situation again.

His mind raced back to when it all started. Back in 1983. He opened his wallet and retrieved an old football match ticket, amazingly still in good condition. He looked at it and smiled. *League Division 2, Chelsea vs Cambridge United Saturday 10th September 1983. Kick off 3.00 p.m.* He remembers nothing about the actual football match, but clearly remembers who sat next to him on that day, a day that was to define his future life. He looked at the seat allocation on the ticket. *Row RR seat 100.* The row letters *RR* still encircled with red ink and the seat number *100* underlined with red ink. Old KGB coding for one Robert Ross with a clearance of 100 – top clearance in other words. What Ross was to say to him, it was law!

There was a knock on the door.

'Yes?'

Scargill's trusted goon, Raymond Wise, walked in the room.

'It's done boss. Anderson is part of that new building that is going up in the City. No loose ends.'

'No loose ends then. Thanks Ray. Take a seat.' A wary Raymond sat down. Scargill had never offered him a seat in his private office before. 'As you know the PM announced his resignation today. In a few days I will hand in my own resignation. I want to be a step ahead and quit rather than wait to be told to quit.'

'I'm very sorry to hear that, sir.'

'I am not asking you to resign, but whoever it is that will take over from me, he will almost certainly replace you. He or she will replace you after they extract whatever little stories they think you might have to tell them.'

'You know me, I will tell them nothing…' Raymond's protestations were cut short by Scargill raising his right hand in the air.

'I know that Ray. You do know that I trust you with my life. I want to inform you first hand that I plan to go into politics, run for Parliament in fact and challenge the leadership in our party. We can't let any Commies run the country now, can we?' Before Ray could respond, his boss carried on. 'Take a couple of years off and you are welcome to join me once elected. How does that sound?'

'You know me, I am okay with whatever you say. Thanks to you, I've got some savings to see me through. No worries Sir.'

'Good man,' said Scargill. 'There are two things I want you to do. The first one is rather urgent. Remember our fat friend?

'The Chinaman? How can I forget him? He eats like a pig.'

'Turns out the filthy yellow elephant is a Chinese agent, spying on Her Majesty's Government.'

'No! The filthy swine. I never liked him Sir. I never like anyone who eats that much.'

'Send him to hell. Use the heart attack method. If it's messy we could get investigated. Do it tomorrow if you can. He lives on the third floor on top of his restaurant in Bayswater. Ray no mess. A clean deletion.'

'Got you, sir. And the other?'

Scargill sighed. He looked at his goon with some genuine sympathy. 'On Sunday morning, take your brother and drive to Liverpool. Be in the parking area of the usual hotel we use up there at exactly 1300. A man named Scott Brown will contact you with my instructions. Do not use a government car. Take your own car. Brown will have your registration number. You will only be there for two hours at the most.'

'Is it some kind of a hit? Do I need to take *tools* with me?'

'No, don't worry. All you will have to do is to deliver some very sensitive documents, Brown will give you, at an address in Liverpool, so do have a city road map with you. And Ray, not a word to anyone about this. Not even to your brother. Just take him along for protection, just in case. When you are done come back here, the same night and let me know how it went. No phone calls. You, here in person. Is that clear?

'Crystal clear as they say. You will be here next Sunday night?' Raymond had a puzzled expression on his face. Scargill nodded.

'Yes, in this very room. Sunday is just another day for us. After all this time with me, you should know that by now and Ray, until Sunday take the rest of the week off.'

'But it is only Tuesday, sir.'

'Finish with fatso tomorrow and then go on leave. No problem. I will also take a couple of days off from tomorrow. I fancy going to Greece. Next communication here, face to face Sunday night and remember the name, Scott Brown.'

'Consider it done. Thanks boss.'

'Here's six hundred quid Ray. Job well done. Go and do what you do. Have a drink.' Ray smiled and took the money. He paused at the door and looked at Scargill.

'I love you, boss. I would die for, you know that. Goodnight.'

Once Ray left, Scargill repeatedly cursed at himself and hit his fist hard on his desk in anger. He almost fractured his fingers. He did not care about Ray's imbecile brother, but Ray has been very loyal and extremely faithful to him.

But he knew too much. There was no other way. No panacea in sight. He was sending them to their graves. Scott Brown was a ruthless paid assassin. No loose ends.

Chapter 20

The refined looking middle-aged Nigerian gentleman walked through the arrivals exit door at Dublin International Airport. He was smartly dressed in a navy blue suit. He was holding a small briefcase in one hand and his cabin luggage in the other. A businessman attending the local trade show perhaps. He did not pause to look around. He was not looking for a taxi. He walked across to the short term car park where an athletic looking redhead lady was waiting for him. They embraced and kissed each other on the cheek. She ushered him into her car and they drove off.

**

Alexandra Coburn made a few male heads turn as she walked out of Eleftherios Venizelos Airport in Athens. She wore skin tight blue jeans with a matching short-sleeved denim shirt which complimented her long blonde wavy hair. Her dark sunglasses added to her obvious sex appeal. She could have graced any top catwalk in the world. But a fashion model she was not. She was a double agent. Formally working for the CIA but she pledged her allegiance firmly with the FSB, The Federal Security Service of the Russian Federation, the offspring of the Russian Federal Counterintelligence Service, which itself evolved from the original KGB. Her godfather, Sir Robert

Ross had a definite influence on her political and moral beliefs. He recruited her at a young age. Alexandra was the more intelligent twin of the two. She wanted to change the world and she was doing something about it. She paused and stationed her Hartmann mobile traveler on the floor, next to her as she looked around. An attractive dark skinned woman was holding up a placard with the name *'Alex C.'* on it. Alexandra approached her and she could not help but notice her stunning green eyes.

'Green eyes confirmed,' she said. 'You must be Marie. I am Alex.' They shook hands.

'High Alex. I have to tell you my English not very good. Come, I have taxi waiting.'

'Your English is fine and if you get stuck, *Je parle français.*'

'*Très bien...*' The fact that Alex spoke French made Marie feel more at ease.

'I must say Uncle Bob's taste is improving with age. He told me on the phone last night that I can trust you One hundred percent. A man who has always maintained that you must never trust anyone One hundred percent – not even yourself! Beautiful *and* trustworthy. He must really love you.'

Marie momentarily blushed but quickly composed herself. '*Coup de foudre!*'

'Come on, we can talk in the taxi.'

***

Deep into the night, the wine was flowing freely at one of the corner tables inside The Red Gallery bar in Athens. Nick Porter, Alexandra Coburn and Sir Robert Ross, sporting his natural hair colour, were engaged in conversation as the piano player played their favourite tunes. The place was packed, the lights low, in fact only wind-protected candle light was available, giving the place ambience. The three of them, including Marie, had earlier dined at one of the many tavernas in Plaka. Marie then returned to the hotel as the rest of the party had a lot to talk about. Marie was of course invited to join them, but she politely declined. Ross noticed the chemistry that was building up between Alexandra and Nick. From the outset they felt comfortable in each other's company. Perfect, he thought.

'I wanted to ask you a question Uncle Bob. Face to face. I was tempted to do so, many times. I think I will do it now.' Alexandra was looking at Ross, expecting a reaction. A few seconds later Ross spoke.

'Why now?'

'Because I feel that now, I have the balls to do it.'

'You want to know who killed your father, right?'

Alexandra's beautiful eyes were suddenly filled with tears.

'I suspect – no, I know as to who it was. It is the why I want to know. Why? Why? WHY?' She started to cry. Nick was at a loss. He tried to comfort her.

'I know exactly how you feel, Alex. I just lost my mother. She was my only relative.' Alexandra completely ignored Nick as she turned to Ross again.

'Why?'

Ross tried to cuddle her; he tried to hold her hand. She pulled back and quickly retrieved a BU9 Nano Beretta handgun from her bag and shoved it onto Ross's rib cage.

'Holy shit? What the fuck are you doing?' It was Nick who spoke as he pulled back.

'Stay out of this Nick,' said Ross.

'Why?' Alexandra was persisting as she pressed the gun deeper into Ross.

'He was going to expose me Alex. There was no alternative.' His eyes were filled with tears. 'I loved him but he was not one of us. He could never be one of us. He was a true patriot, he really did serve Queen and Country. I'm so, so sorry. I really am.'

'Fuck, fuck, fuck.' Nick's eyes almost popped out. 'You, you killed Ian?'

'Yes. I was decent enough to do it myself. It haunts me every minute of my miserable life. I have been waiting for this moment for almost twenty years. I am glad you asked Alex. I could not sleep at nights.'

'Did you try to convert him?' It was Alex who spoke as she put the gun away.

'For days I tried. I could see that he was fighting with his conscience, but he would not succumb. I asked for time but when I told him that I would be going to Spain, I knew that he was going ahead with it. I knew he was going to hand all the information he had to Gladys, to Gavin Addice. Another good man who paid the price of patriotism with his life. He would have exposed me. Friendship counts for nothing in these circumstances. Nothing.'

'So you did not go to Spain but followed him.' Alexandra was composed again. Nick offered her his handkerchief and she wiped her eyes, her mascara smudged across her face, causing the two men to momentarily smile. 'Did he see you? Did he know it was you?'

'No he did not,' said Ross. 'I am not that insensitive.'

'I'll go to the bathroom and fix my face,' she said.

'Alex my precious, not that this makes it right, but did you know that your father was dying from cancer? That he only had two, maybe three months at the most, to live? That he gave up on his chemotherapy? That he was in pain?'

'Yes I did and that is the only reason you are still alive.'

'Oh my God!! This is way above my league. I'm a fish out of water here.' Nick put his arms in the air.

'Well if you want to be a fish, at least ensure you are a piranha or a great white shark because if you are a goldfish, you have no place here.' Alexandra delivered that with plenty of frost. She then headed for the ladies room. A half-stunned Nick, summoned a waitress and ordered a Talisker.

'She knew all along. She's not stupid. She's the greatest operative I have ever known. She's more intelligent than you or I will ever be Nick.'

'She's some woman.'

'Yes she is and if you are thinking of flirting her, dating her, a word of advice son. Never lie to her and never, never, never patronize her.'

'When are you leaving?'

'After I meet Scargill, tomorrow here in Athens.'

'Marie will be all right? Living in Russia I mean?'

'I think so. She had no life back in France. Hey, my boy. Nothing will replace your mother's memory, but you knew this was how it was going to end.'

'It is best that she did not know,' said Nick. 'I am not sure she would have approved. My dad was a Royal Navy man after all.'

The waitress returned with Nick's malt whisky, which he downed in one. 'Much better,' he said.

Alexandra returned to the table, looking prettier than ever.

'Was that a real Beretta? Never seen one like that before.' Alex ignored the question.

'I am all right,' she said. 'I understand that you had to do what you had to do but this does not mean that I forgive you.' She then turned to Nick. 'You are quite handsome

Nick. And gentle. But, you have to toughen up. Oh, and yes I can be the cuddly loving wife and be brilliant in bed, no problem, but when need be I can also be the most venomous snake. *Vy ponimayete?'*

'Oh yes. I understand perfectly. I am shocked, I am a little drunk, I am in grief, even a bit confused, but *ya ponimayu.'*

She beamed a smile at him, her blue eyes flashing in the dark environment. He seized the opportunity.

'I think I am falling for you Alex. I am sorry but that is how I feel. *Ya lyublyu tebya.'*

'You are not the first and you'll not be the last. You are all right Nick. A bit intoxicated but I see where you are coming from.' Alexandra leaned towards Nick and she kissed him on the lips. She ensured he felt her tongue too. He blushed.

'The gun. What was it?' It was Ross again.

'It is a new nano beretta, US made but not in production yet. May be in a couple of years it will be in the shops...'

'Oh well. I am done with guns. They'll put me out to graze soon. How is Efi by the way? Haven't seen her since, oh since, I guess since a long time ago?'

'She's good. She doesn't know everything but then again I think she chooses not to know everything. She's happy in Limnos and she's always ready to perform if asked.'

Ross shook his head. 'Poor Mitsos. It must have cost her. JMS has told Nick the other day on the phone that Anderson, the psychotic assassin, was working for Bishop, MI5 Home Security. I have my doubts about that and a lot will be clearer tomorrow when I meet Scargill.'

'Good luck with that. I hope his ambition and his bigotry do not blur his vision or his logic. Moscow has invested heavily in him.'

'Sasha Azarov. That was his real name before he was adopted in England as a baby. He's the only real Russian in our group. An active Russian spy at No. 10!'

'Unreal,' said Nick. 'This is much better than fiction.'

Ross turned to Nick. 'And you my boy, you will be groomed to become his successor, starting with the Department for Environment. Basic policy. Always have a back-up. A plan B.'

'The CIA would give the earth and the stars for such information…'

'Careful now young lady. We are too close to fuck up.'

'*Sasha* means protector of humanity does it not?' It was Nick who spoke.

'Correct,' said Ross. 'Which humanity he will protect, only God knows.'

'Bob. Bob.' Alexandra almost whispered the words.

'What is it my dear?'

'Don't you think it is time for you to lose that ridiculous hearing aid in your left ear? You are not deaf. That is a recording device, Chinese made, state-of-the-art technology.'

'You never cease to amaze me. I wish it was you being lined up for No. 10 instead of Scargill. May be in…' Alex cut him short.

'Well, you have kissed that possibility goodbye the moment you asked me to join the CIA. We'll work on Nick here if Scargill lets us down.'

'I am not sure I qualify,' said Nick.

'Not your decision my darling. It is someone in the Red Square who decides, on our advice.' Alexandra winked at Nick who was simply mesmerised by her beautiful eyes.

Ross laid back deep into the sofa and momentarily closed his eyes. The pianist in the bar started to play Moscow Nights. He was happy. He knew that in his godchild he had found his perfect and most able successor. Alexandra Coburn was no ordinary woman. There is a God after all he mused.

CHAPTER 21

The following morning Ross visited the Russian Embassy in the northern suburbs of Athens. Marie was with him. They were going *home.* His contact there was the Head of the Section for Science and Technology Alexey Vasiliev. He would make all the arrangements and provide the necessary travel documents for their quick getaway the next day and their new life in mother Russia. This was of course all part of the plan. Once they were both safe, Scargill would announce to the world that Ross was spying for Russia and that is why the British Intelligence Services were after him. That they forced him to flee the country. The stage was set for Ross to be crucified as a traitor and for Scargill to gain serious political points. He would gain extra points and sympathetic support by using the Ross 'defection' as a reason to resign his post and discretely point a finger in the direction of Home Security and the former Prime Minister for their reluctance to stop Ross.

Although the day was not as warm as the previous one and clouds were menacingly gathering over the Athenian sky, Sasha Azarov under his adopted name of James Marlow Scargill had dark sunglasses on and was generally dressed very lightly. He wore a large white jockey cap on his head with the Greek flag at the front and the name Hellas written beneath the flag. He wore blue tracksuit bottoms, sandals and a white T-shirt with the Parthenon embossed on it. There was a camera hanging from his neck and he was holding a street map of Athens along with a small bottle of water. Just like the thousands of tourists roaming Athens and he, just like a proper tourist, took the funicular train up the Lykavittos Hill. His meeting place with Ross. When he reached the top he turned left away from the chapel and headed to a corner table at the cafeteria where Ross was already waiting for him. Waiting for a lot of answers. He had his Fedora hat on and his multifocal sunglasses. On the table there was a book entitled 'Helen of Troy.' Scargill, still standing next to the table pointed to the book and asked.

'So, who were the bad guys in the end? The Greeks or the Trojans?'

'They were all Greeks, so they were either all bad or all good.' Ross gestured to the Director of the British Intelligence Services to seat.

'Time has been kind to you Bob.' JMS picked up the book and quickly leafed through it before he placed it down again.

'Nice T-shirt. How is everything Sasha?' A waiter approached and Scargill ordered whatever Ross was drinking in perfect Greek.

'It has been twenty-four years since that meeting at Stamford Bridge. Much water has flowed under the bridge.' It was Scargill who spoke. The two had not met in person for over two decades but they did have a few contacts over the phone using tested and encrypted sterile lines.

'Indeed and I see that you did well for yourself.'

'I had divine help…' Scargill was being sarcastic.

'Daphne. Why?' Ross tried hard to keep his emotions at bay. His lower lip started to tremble.

'No other way. I'm sure you faced the same dilemma with Ian Coburn.' Scargill was cold and unmoved.

'You are such a bastard you little shit….'

'I'm your own product Bob. Get hold of your emotions. *No loose ends*. You drummed that phrase into my brain all those years ago.' Scargill took a deep breath and carried on. 'Daphne Porter, as preposterous as it may sound, was unofficially working for the MI5. She met with Bishop personally up to seven times in the last 6 months and these are the meetings we know of and meetings which we recorded. God knows how many more there were.'

Ross was momentarily lost for words. He took a sip of wine before he spoke. 'Where?'

'The ones we do know of, took place at the Selfridges Food Store. Casual shoppers bumping into each other but not really discussing the price of fish. Notes were passed from one to another. We have it on record from the store's CCTV cameras.'

'Fucking unbelievable…'

'I am sorry Bob. What we do is filth but it is the filth that *we* chose. I am really sorry.' Scargill sounded genuinely sympathetic.

'No fucking loose ends…'

'To krasi sas kyrie.' The waiter placed a glass of white wine in front of JMS. 'Kati allo tha thelate?' He asked if they wanted anything else. Scargill shook his head negatively and once the water left he turned to Ross once more.

'Bishop of course denied that she was after you. She was after the information Leonardou gathered along with Ian, incriminating her for the Lockerbie disaster. The information ended up with the late Addice.'

'Abaloso? Who was behind that?'

'Nothing to do with us. That was the CIA black ops and I am sure Alexandra can confirm it one way or another. They were looking for your dossier on Blyth and Iraq and before you ask I had nothing to do with Zoe's mutilation. I did not sanction her killing.'

'But you must have got the microchip that Gladys implanted in her body, otherwise how could you have compromised Bishop?'

'Anderson was unofficially on Bishop's payroll. He did the dirty work for MI5. He was recommended to Bishop by a security officer with ties to the WAG.'

'The Way Ahead Group? The Royals?' Ross was stunned.

'No. Not the Royals directly. By someone with ties to WAG. Low level. So when my own intelligence revealed who Anderson actually was, I recruited him by offering a lot more money and supposed protection and he became one of my moles in Bishop's set up. When he retrieved the microchip from the poor girl he gave it to me and told Bishop who sanctioned the killing that he found nothing. After that I immediately deleted him.'

Ross was staring at the horizon to the west beyond the Acropolis into the blue sea of Saronicos Bay and the shadowy mountain lines under the clouds on the islands of Aegena and Salamis beyond the Port of Piraeus. But he was all ears. Every word had sunk in.

'Deleted him. As you've done away with Gavin Addice and his hairdresser along with that young woman, Paulina, Michel's niece.'

'We've done Addice a favour. He was dying from lung cancer. By the way, Addice suspected that it was you who tipped off the Soviets back in 1983 about their pending air space violation by a civilian airline. Yet he gave you the benefit of the doubt. He really liked you.'

Ross said nothing.

'Michel, yes because he knew your new identity and we had to find you, keep close tabs on you, keep you safe.

Your survival and *defection* to Russia is essential to the master plan. Michel belonged to Addice. He was his boyfriend. Paulina on the other hand works for me. Not MI6 but me. She shares our ideals and political philosophy. How do you think we found out about Michel? She's not Michel's real niece. She befriended him and then simply addressed him as Uncle Michel. We knew Addice had close links with the hairdresser and we planted Paulina there to find out if the connection was just sexual or shop too. Paulina is fine and she sends you her love. She will spend next Christmas in Moscow and she would be happy to come and see you. Off the record of course.'

'You know what Sasha?'

'Stop calling me Sasha please…'

'You know what JMS? I am glad I am retiring. Espionage games are getting far too complicating for me. I am tired with the lies, the deceit.'

'Well, the real games are just beginning for me. This is probably the very last time we meet or have contact of any sort. Russia's Foreign Intelligence Service and the FSB will be proud of you. All the info you had given them over the years it all checked out.'

'I spoke to Sergey in Moscow from the Embassy this morning. We agreed to let Britain do the talking regarding my *defection*. Moscow will say make just about enough noise to sort of semi-confirm the British allegations so you can be credited with ousting me.'

'I will hand in my resignation next week. Gordon Braddick is an idiot. I don't like him and he doesn't like me.'

'Timothy Blyth is an even bigger idiot,' said Ross.

'But very essential to our plan. Without him, this would not have been possible.' Scargill paused for a moment. 'Bob, one person we shall spare is Jacques Petit of the

French DCRI. When he finds out you defected to Russia and that you were working for the Soviets in years gone by, surely he's not going to blow his trumpet saying that he helped you and Marie get out of France with false passports.'

'Very good point which you'll use to your advantage. Tell him, off the record, that we all make mistakes and he wasn't to know I was a spy and that his secret is safe with you. This way you'll have the next head of the French intelligence services in your pocket. Bingo!'

'I'll send you a postcard from No. 10 in a few years' time.'

'Before you do that, who or what was Ian Cross, who happened to drown in the Thames the night Addice left the living world?'

'He was one of Bishop's jewels! He was also my mole in MI5 but became greedy and arrogant. He exposed Gladys and was also responsible for the fake kidnapping of Zoe Coburn in Iraq – on Bishop's orders. She was obsessed with the microchip.'

'What of Charlie Chow?'

'Charlie may be a lot of thinks but he is British through and through. He is very loyal to me as he is, or was, loyal to you. He keeps tabs on what's happening in China so he's a good source. He may become useful in the future. He lives!'

'He will lose a few pounds in weight when he finds out that I am a red!' Ross had a little chuckle.

'Knowing him he might actually gain some weight,' said Scargill. 'He, along with you, will be the sole survivors of the notorious Hub.'

'Talking of *notorious*, does IOPS really exist? Is it still active?'

'Did the Hub ever exist?' The two men smiled.

'Final question. Who was behind the murder of Patrick Brennan and the Saudi Sheikh in Jeddah back in 83? Surely not the Israelis.' Scargill's response was immediate.

'Your man in the T&S Group was taken out by direct orders from David Webb, Ministry of Defence.'

'The late double agent David Webb,' added Ross.

'Correct. Nasty case. Our Georgy is special but he is really religious believe it or not. Wasting his talent on the Holy Mount in Chalkidiki. He planted documentation on Webb indicating that he was also working for the CIA. Let the two countries clear that one out!'

'When that shit hits the fan, it should be fun... what?'

'And Bob, before you ask, in case you are wondering, nobody touched your Cubans. As far as I know it was an unfortunate car accident. Anything else?'

'The T&S Group. Is it still active and is it still a tool for the Americans?'

'The T&S Group's primary role was to implement American foreign policy without the US government becoming officially involved. They recruited people such as Webb, just like you recruited Brennan and obviously grooming others such as Timothy Blyth to carry out policies that were in the interests of the USA national security as well as to boost the USA economy. In return the company would get lucrative construction and oil contracts. We have seen this happening on a big scale in post Saddam Iraq. However, they have slowed down in recent years because they have seen what was happening to some of their prodigies such as Blyth. A few whistle-blowers have blown off their cover too.'

'I understand that it was only a couple of years ago that some investigative reporters in Ireland, connected to the ICIJ, the International Consortium of Investigative Journalists have uncovered some of the early work of the

T&S Group and did shed some light on the slaughter in Jeddah back in 1983.'

'I see you are up to date despite your retirement old boy,' said Scargill. 'I guess that is why Blyth is so despised. He was, still is I think, an off the record shareholder in the Group and his rise to power has to do with the funding and influence he received through this Group.' Scargill took off his sunglasses and stared at Ross. 'Anything else Bob?'

'You have not touched your wine,' said Ross.

'I only drink red wine. Red. That's the only colour for me.'

Ross extended his hand and the two men shook hands. 'Go, I'll get the bill,' said Ross.

Chapter 22 –
Epilogue

It was almost midday and the black limousine with the tinted windows sandwiched between two police cars pulled up in the lay-by at the front of the main entrance at a hotel in central Dublin where the ex-British Premier, Timothy Blyth, was to present his book on his years in office. In his book he was mainly trying to justify Britain's involvement and participation in the Iraq war. The newly elected British Prime Minister, James Marlow Scargill personally, but off the record, warned Blyth as an old friend, that he should stay away from Ireland. Blyth did not have many admirers or supporters there. He decided to go. He wrote a book giving his version of events, his explanations, his arguments and how he did what he did for the greater good of the United Kingdom and the free western world in general. He wanted justification. He was looking for vindication. He wanted a best seller!

It was a cold but windless clear sunny day in Dublin and the protestors were out in force, shouting abuse at the '*warmonger, mendacious Blyth.*' They obviously disagreed with most of the narrative in his book. There were many placards on display, none of them complimentary. Three minders emerged from the car and momentarily stood on the pavement assessing the situation. Police officers ensured that the two hundred or so protestors were kept well away from the hotel's entrance. One of the minders gestured at the ex-Prime Minister and he stepped out of the car. He did not wave at the crowd. Two minders stood either side of him while the third followed close behind. It was a short walk to the hotel entrance, a mere 12 metres. As he hurried towards the entrance the back of his head suddenly exploded, splashing blood around him as small pieces of brain tissue landed on his minders who fell on top of him trying to protect him from a possible second shot. It was all in vain. Blyth was dead before he hit the ground. Within seconds, pandemonium broke out as deafening police sirens bellowed and police officers were pushing the stunned crowd away. Wheels screeched on the streets as police were cordoning off the area. Antiterrorist personnel were called in and a few minutes later a police helicopter was scanning the rooftops in nearby buildings.

Moments after the fatal shot was fired, four hundred and seventy meters across the street to the left a curtain was pulled across the window of a third floor apartment. Inside that room a woman with a dark headscarf resembling a hijab, wearing black pants and a light brown anorak was quickly and expertly dismantling the British made L115A3 AWM long-range sniper rifle. She packed it in its case, then lifted part of the carpet off the floor and removed two small floorboards. She placed the case in the pre-prepared hiding place and replaced the boards and carpet. She picked up the bullet shell from the floor and flushed it down the toilet. She then used a chemical to disinfect the area and her clothing. She removed the headscarf to reveal a full crop of ginger hair. She took her anorak off and together with her headscarf she placed them in a plastic shopping bag and then placed the bag in a wardrobe. She straightened her black cardigan, took a deep breath and inconspicuously run down the stairs. At street level, she walked into the next door fast food burger shop and went straight to the seating area in the basement where a man was waiting for her with two full meals at the ready. She removed her leather gloves and handed them to her companion. The place was half full. Some of the customers had gone up to street level to see what all the commotion was about. She nodded at the man and he smiled at her. She quickly ate about a third of her burger and then she placed a broken toothpick which was in her pocket in the middle of the burger. She then went upstairs at the service area and kicked up a fuss about the toothpick in her food. She had her alibi. Just in case.

***

That same evening, in a second floor apartment in the town of Drogheda, just over 35 miles north of Dublin, Siobhan Brennan, daughter of the murdered Patrick Brennan and Justin Oladapo, an ex-radio boy at the Trident Shipping Agency in Apapa-Lagos, Nigeria, were watching the news on television. James Marlow Scargill, the British Prime Minister had said that whoever was behind the cowardly assassination of ex-Premier Timothy Blyth will be brought to justice. Britain and the free world he said will never tolerate any kind of terrorism and that terrorism will be defeated by all means available.

By an unimaginable twist of fate Justin and Siobhan were brought together a few years earlier when the two met in Poland. Justin had lost his job at the shipping agency in Nigeria and he decided to do something with his life. He persuaded an uncle of his to send him abroad to study. His uncle had Nigerian friends in Wroclaw in Poland so young

Justin went there and stayed there. Twenty years later he ended up teaching the art of jungle warfare and target shooting at a private academy in the area.

Siobhan attended the academy in 2004. She was an active security officer with a large security firm in Ireland and she was sent to the academy in Poland for a ten month crash course to upgrade her skills and position within the company. She also became a sharpshooter and an explosives expert. Her employers, the Ireland based security company had high hopes for her. Justin fell for her and one day he took the courage to approach her. To his surprise, as well as to his delight, she was receptive. She asked Justin if he was a Christian. He said yes. She then told him that she was a Catholic and Justin responded by saying that if she's a Catholic, he's a Catholic too.

They started dating and during that time they talked about their lives and Siobhan mentioned that her dad was murdered in Saudi Arabia while working for the T&S Group. Justin told her that his very first job was with a T&S Group Company in Lagos and how he lost promotion and eventually his job because of the disappearance of a ship that was assigned to him as a trial run, a test case to prove his capabilities. The murder of her dad remained unsolved and so did the vanishing of Justin's ship, the M/V Iphigenia. Their quest for the truth took epic proportions and they both embarked on a dark and dangerous trek through the labyrinth of time to get to the bottom of the two cases.

Over the next few years they befriended a couple of Irish journalists within the International Consortium of Investigative Journalists, the ICIJ, who unearthed a wealth of information, which they deemed too dangerous to publish at the time. Justin and the redhead Siobhan continued to dig until they more or less put the jigsaw together. They had help and financial support from an unlikely source. A source who also wanted revenge for different reasons. A source that had a master plan, a source with a score to settle.

Justin and Siobhan lived as a couple but never got married. First they wanted their revenge. They both wanted justice, their own kind of justice. They were the judge, jury and executioner. They said to themselves that people's lives matter and their own lives were almost destroyed by greed, international politics and war games, as if war was just an innocent table game. A table game it is not. Real people die. Real people's lives are destroyed. They were going to do something about it. Timothy Blyth was the first obvious target. He succumbed to the Americans because of his greed and lust for power and followed them blindly and set fire to the Middle East through the Iraq invasion and all the mayhem, the chaos which followed. For Justin and Siobhan, Blyth was responsible for the unprecedented blind violence, the deaths, the countless refugees and the subsequent change of Europe's demography. Terror became almost commonplace. Europe, North Africa and the Middle East were never going to be the same. The domino effect was in full swing and unstoppable. Add to that the gains, the huge economic profits that had come to American companies on the back of all of these actions, profits that were created through the death and pain of ordinary people. Someone had to pay. Profit and greed above innocent human lives is not acceptable. And all this made possible, be it up to a point, by the pawn that answers to the name of Timothy Blyth. For sure he was the first on the list. There were two more names on that list. The current British Prime Minister James Marlow Scargill and Baroness Eleanor Bishop. Payback time.

***

Nizhny Novgorod, Russia, a Month Later

At an open air cafeteria veranda on the banks of the River Volga, Robert Ross and his wife Marie were soaking the mid-morning winter sun, dressed in a *telogreika* type of heavy winter jacket and the *ushanka* type of hat with the ear-flaps down and wrapped around their cheeks. They were of course made of imitation fur. Ross was drinking black coffee and straight vodka while Marie was enjoying a glass of red wine trying her best to keep it relatively warm, cupping the glass with her gloved hands. The view across the meandering river was breath-taking and the temperature just below zero. A mild day by Russian standards. Nizhny Novgorod, located east of Moscow, has been their permanent home for a while. During the Soviet years the town was heavily industrialized and involved in scientific projects, but in the last few years it had turned to tourism with some success. The Gorky Automobile Plan was still there producing light cars and trucks like the famous GAZelle brand and the old Soviet Volga cars. Scientific research is still rife. They both settled in well. They were given a free modest two bedroom house and were enjoying their lives on the pension granted to them by the Russian authorities. It was as if they were on an extended holiday. They were genuinely happy, just living their days in an easy going manner. Ross was smoking a Cuban cigar. He had cut a deal with the Russians that he would have regular supplies of authentic Cuban cigars and the Russians did not disappoint him. As he puffed on his Partagas cigar, he was thinking. Thinking what the hell is happening back in England. He shook his head in disbelief.

'Nothing is never what it seems,' he said. '*Rien.*'

'We are real,' said Marie. She smiled at him and he kissed her.

'We are real all right. What's not real is what has been happening back in the UK. Three top politicians assassinated within a month? It is unheard of. An ex-Prime Minister, shot in Dublin, the current Prime Minister shot on his way to his party conference and a baroness blown up in her car. That is definitely not real no matter how you look at it. Our liaison in the Kremlin has had a fit.'

'A what?'

'A seizure, *saisie.*'

'You are not *responsable chéri.*'

'No I am not but I wish I knew what the devil is going on. I suppose plan B will go into effect now. Nick Porter will be lined up. Always have a back-up, a plan B. I'll contact Dmitry and find out what is happening.'

'Let it go *chéri.* You've done your bit. What is done is done.'

'*Logique feminine!* I guess you are right my beauty. Let's enjoy our retirement.'

Ross downed his vodka shot in one and put his arm around a smiling Marie.

'Let them all kill each other. No worries as long as this does not affect whatever years we've got left.'

'*Absolument,*' said Marie with a sparkle in her eye. She placed her wine glass on the table and her hand slipped gently between her lover's legs and got a tight grip on his genitals. 'How about one of your quickies? Now, here?' She winked at him.

'Are you crazy woman? You'll not be able to find anything down there. Not with this bloody cold…'

She embraced him and gave him a full French kiss. 'I love you *Rober.*'

'I love you too my dear, more than you think. Fuck politics. I'm retired.'

***

Whitehall, Central London, England

Under the shadow of Big Ben in a busy pub in Whitehall, two people were having a discrete conversation. They were sat at a table on the first floor of the pub where the main restaurant was. They were each drinking a pint of English ale and eating traditional steak and ale pies, the pub's speciality food. They were a couple. The man was the Right Honourable Member of Parliament Nicolas Oliver Porter and the woman was the American Embassy Minister Counsellor for Political Affairs in London, Alexandra Coburn. The couple were engaged to be married. Alexandra's official title was of course a front. In reality she was the CIA Station Master in London, one of the highest positions for a CIA employee outside the US.

'Nick, we've been over this before. You just have to trust my judgement on this one. You'll be offered the job of Secretary for the Environment in the interim government until the next elections. Take it.'

'It is not the position I am worried about. It is going for the leadership of the party. I think it is too soon. I only have 4 months until the party leadership election and another 4 months to the General Elections. I don't think the party base will support me to fight the next General Elections.'

Alexandra leaned towards Nick and kissed him. 'That is why I am here Nick. I am your fairy godmother. You will have help to your rise to the top from the Russians as well as the Americans. We'll brainwash the British voters.

It is now or never.' She lifted her glass and toasted her fiancé.

'It would be very interesting to know what Robert Ross will think, or how he'll react, if he knew the truth. I mean the real truth.' It was Nick who spoke.

'For him and the Russians it will be the truth. They will think that they have a Russian spy at No.10 when in reality if we want to be accurate, we'll have an American spy at No. 10. It is best for the Brits. The yanks will look after them. Cheers my man.'

Nick lifted his glass and toasted Alex. 'I never thought we could pull it off. All the years we've been secretly in contact, I had my doubts…'

'It is payback time my darling. Because of Ross and their so-called master plan my sister and father are dead, murdered and so is your mother. They will get what they deserve. We'll have our man at the helm of the country and feed the Russians whatever chicken feed we decide to feed them. The CIA is fully behind you. Trust me. You WILL be elected Prime Minister. The Russians will be happy thinking that you belong to them…'

'But we'll be happier,' added Nick. 'What of Justin and Siobhan?'

'As of three days ago they are US citizens living happily in Baltimore. Might as well have them close at hand. Just in case.'

Alexandra Coburn finished her beer and promptly ordered another pint. Yes, she *was* a double agent but she knew where her true allegiance really lies. She felt fulfilled. She removed the protagonists from the scene and she, along with her fiancé are now taking centre stage. However, neither she nor her fiancé noticed the small listening device that was attached beneath their table. In the world of politics, nothing is what it seems.

The End